NO-ONE EVER HAS SEX ON A TUESDAY

Tracy Bloom started writing when her cruel, heartless husband ripped her away from her dream job shopping for rollercoasters for the UK's leading theme parks, to live in America with a brand-new baby and no mates. Determined to see it as an opportunity, she turned to her love of words and comedy and started to write *No-One Ever Has Sex on a Tuesday*. It went on to be successfully published internationally and topped the Amazon bestseller list in 2013 as well as being awarded the Best Author Published Read at the Festival of Romance 2013. So now Tracy is chuffed to bits to have a new dream job, making people laugh and sometimes cry through her writing. Back in good old England now with the husband who is forgiven and two children who create mayhem around her, as she cracks on with creating other stories about people who screw up their lives in a hilarious fashion.

NO-ONE EVER HAS SEX ON A TUESDAY

TRACY BLOOM

arrow books

Published by Arrow Books 2014

13

Copyright © Tracy Bloom 2011

First published in Great Britain in 2013
This edition first published in 2014 by
Arrow Books
Random House, 20 Vauxhall Bridge Road,
London SW1V 2SA

www.randomhouse.co.uk

Addresses for companies within The Random House Group Limited can be
found at: www.randomhouse.co.uk/offices.htm

The Random House Group Limited Reg. No. 954009

A CIP catalogue record for this book
is available from the British Library

ISBN 9780099594758

Penguin Random House is committed to a sustainable future for
our business, our readers and our planet. This book is made from
Forest Stewardship Council® certified paper.

For Bruce

As always my biggest and best cheerleader.
I wouldn't be here without you.

Chapter 1

There are those who get to choose the father of their child and those who don't. Those who spend years sifting through the giant haystack that is the male population and those who get unexpectedly ambushed.

Katy never thought that she would be one of those who got ambushed. She certainly never thought that at thirty-six she would be pregnant, unmarried and with a boyfriend eight years younger than herself. A boyfriend who was now sitting beside her dressed in his football kit, as they drove off for their first antenatal class. She felt sick. She put this down to pre-class nerves and the fact that Ben had come straight from school, where he was a PE teacher, smelling unpleasantly of gym shoes, teenage-boy sweat and mashed potato. As she stared across at him she comforted herself with the knowledge that at least she could rely on him to offer up some well-thought-out words of wisdom to help calm her fears.

'So this guy at work says that all you do in these classes is talk about tits and fannies for two hours. How good is that?'

Katy continued to stare at Ben for a moment then sighed and put the car into gear.

'Please don't say that,' she said wearily as they drove off.

'Say what?' asked Ben as he fiddled with every knob, switch and dial he could reach on Katy's dashboard.

'Fannies,' said Katy, slapping his fingers.

'It's better than a lot of other words for it,' said Ben. 'I mean, I could say . . .'

'No, no more words,' interrupted Katy. 'You know my gran wouldn't like it.'

'Why? Is she coming with us?' said Ben, pulling open the glove box and peering inside.

'Her name was Fanny, I've told you that before,' said Katy, starting to lose patience.

Ben turned to stare at Katy in complete admiration.

'You have never ever told me that. That's exactly the sort of information that makes my life worthwhile and certainly not something I'd forget.'

'Really,' said Katy. She hesitated, wondering if she wanted to continue the conversation before realising that what she was about to say would probably make Ben's day. 'So I've never told you her surname either then?' she asked him.

Ben paused for a moment, deep in thought, until he erupted enthusiastically.

'Vagina. Must have been vagina,' he said, bouncing up and down. 'Please tell me it was vagina and I will die a happy man.'

'Mycock, actually,' said Katy, more than a little triumphantly.

Ben stared at her again in shock, his mouth hanging open.

'You are kidding me,' he said finally. 'Her parents called her Fanny with a surname like Mycock. Were they insane?'

'No, stupid. Mycock was her married name. She wasn't *born* a Mycock.'

'She was called Fanny and married Mr Mycock?'

'Yes.'

3

Ben was quiet for some time before he declared solemnly, 'Your gran was a comedy genius.'

They didn't speak for the rest of the journey as Ben was fully occupied with texting or calling his friends to share the funniest name story of all time. He was still on the phone as she started to muster up the effort to get out of the car. She eased her swollen belly in the vague direction she wanted her body to go in, hoping the rest would follow. Looking down at the carefully chosen acre of magenta poly-cotton flowing in all directions over her lumps and bumps, she hoped she looked like a woman in control of her pregnancy. But the memory of the lack of control that had landed her here in the first place led to the all too familiar sensation of a fist grasping tightly around her heart. She looked over her shoulder, seeking Ben for some reassurance, and caught sight of his knees, which were decorated in school-pitch mud.

'Your knees,' she exclaimed, pointing at the offending items.

'I'm not proposing now,' said Ben in mock anger.

She shook her head in despair, took a deep breath and set off towards the hospital entrance. She thought she'd pretty much nailed life until this. All the big boxes had been ticked. University, career, homeowner. Admittedly the marriage box had remained conspicuously empty, but that was exactly the way she wanted it. A truly traumatic experience with her first love as a teenager had left her heart never quite able to recover its full emotional capacity. Since then the slightest flutter of love had alerted her to heartbreak fast approaching, allowing her to lock down the situation quickly with a clean and swift break-up. She knew this approach had served her well over the years as she watched her friends suffer the humiliation of being dumped from a great height, over and over again.

She had lost count of how many times her friends had declared that they had met *the one*. It saddened her to know that approximately two weeks later the friend would be on her doorstep, sobbing out a tragic but pre-dictable tale of *the one* obviously not realising she was *the one*, by getting caught with another *one*. Katy would patiently pour the wine whilst they poured out their hearts, until inevitably the night would end in drunken dancing and singing round her dining room table to boy band music. Then there would be an emotional love-in where they told her she was the best friend in the world.

Finally in the early hours one of them would throw up over the balcony.

It amazed her that they couldn't learn that if they put their heart out there for someone, they would be cast aside as carelessly as last season's away kit as soon as the next piece of skirt passed by. These days, though, nights spent consoling the lovesick seemed to have dried up. One by one, they had finally all found men who appeared to want a relationship for longer than five minutes, and had enjoyed the weddings they had always dreamed of.

She had, in her opinion, suffered two years of near mental torture as the cream invites lined up frighteningly quickly on her living room shelf. Her heart sank every time she picked up yet another painstakingly selected envelope, which no doubt had been chosen to match the bride's knicker elastic, and tipped out the invitation, handmade by the future bride herself. She would close her eyes in despair as she read the words *Miss Katy Chapman and Partner*. Why oh why was it the law to go to weddings as a couple? Was there some terrible fear that single people at weddings were bound to run off with the bride or groom given half the chance? Perhaps it was one of the wedding vows: *Thou shalt always have attached friends to prevent any possibility of straying*. It made her dread the so-called happy events, forced as she was to find some random chap she had once had a drunken snog with, who in exchange for free food and alcohol could endure the steady stream of well-meaning relatives saying, 'So will it be you next?'

Eventually she had decided enough was enough and that she should make a stand for all strong, independent women and stop pandering to the stereotype that happiness was attached to a man. When she was next invited to a wedding she made the genius decision to take Daniel from the advertising agency where she worked. The look on the face of Laura's great-aunt, who was making polite conversation during the wedding breakfast, was a joy to behold. Daniel sweetly told her that yes, it could be him next, as he'd been seeing his boyfriend Rob for over six months now and neither of them was having sex with anyone else, unless you counted the night he'd had sex with Stanley, his ex. However, he didn't think that counted, as he'd been very drunk at the time and Stanley had been dressed as a navy officer, because it was at a fancy dress party – and who could resist a man in uniform?

From that moment on Daniel had become her new best wedding partner.

*

Katy jumped when Ben caught hold of her hand as she walked through the doors of the hospital.

'So what do you reckon then?' he asked, spitting on his other hand and leaning over to try and wipe the mud off his knee as he trotted beside her.

'Sorry, I was miles away. What did you say?' asked Katy.

'I said, what do you reckon the other people in the class will be like?'

'Oh, they will all have read every book, know exactly what they are doing and ask really intelligent questions.' Katy could feel the panic rising again. She was painfully aware that up until now she had put her pregnancy firmly in the 'deal with it later' file. It was clear that 'later' had most definitely arrived.

'Mmmm,' said Ben, absorbing what Katy had said. 'So you think we'll be the troublemakers sitting in the back row while the swots hang on the teacher's every word at the front?'

'Probably,' sighed Katy.

Ben glanced over to her.

'The back row always has more fun,' he said, grinning.

She couldn't help but grin back.

'You're right,' she replied, feeling better. Ben knew

exactly how to stop her taking life too seriously. That was what had first attracted her to him when they met last summer on one of the worst nights of her entire life.

Chapter 2

Katy knew that the night was a disaster waiting to happen the moment she caught sight of herself in the grimy mirrors of the Pink Coconut toilets. Surrounded by the nubile bodies and fresh faces of the under-twenty-five-year-old clubbing set, she realised she looked utterly ridiculous dressed in a schoolgirl costume.

How on earth had it come to this? Despondently, she eyed her smeared fake freckles and tatty pigtails tied up with fuchsia pink ribbon. She'd accepted the drop in standards that was necessary to remain a part of the singles social scene after her friends got married, but it was totally unacceptable to have to plunge to these depths. Initially she had been horrified when one by one her friends began muttering the most depressing words any female can say when being asked on a girls' night out.

'I'll have to ask David.'

Or even worse . . .

'Only if Steve doesn't mind.'

Or absolutely the worst of all . . .

'Only if Edward can come too.'

She had quite literally wanted to shake them, with their pathetically apologetic faces. But rather than witness her friends' descent into domestic hell, she had left them to it, seeing them only on special occasions when they exchanged awkward conversation as they drifted further and further apart.

Somewhat depressed at this change in her social life, and finding herself with extra time on her hands, she had thrown herself into her career and scrabbled around for new, unattached buddies. Eventually, and with considerable effort, she forced herself to learn to appreciate the company of some gym bunnies she had somehow fallen in with during a social event at her local Fitness Forever.

She was surprised to discover she could tolerate their perfect spray-tanned bodies, their fresh as a daisy make-up after ninety minutes of Step and Thrust, and even their incessant giggling every time one of the buff personal trainers came within ten yards of them. She suspected they only adopted her once they learnt she was an account director in advertising, assuming that she might one day invite them to audition for a shampoo commercial. Still, after a few Bombay Sapphires she could find them quite entertaining, and certainly a step up from the utter degradation of being at home on a Saturday night.

That was, however, until things finally went too far. The gym bunnies had almost wet their gym knickers with excitement when their favourite nightclub had decided to do a school disco night. Katy had been dismayed but reluctantly agreed to go as it wasn't beyond the realms of possibility she might meet someone interesting, even if he did look like Billy Bunter.

On the summer night in question they arrived at her riverside flat, just outside the centre of Leeds, in a cloud of designer perfume, a cacophony of high-pitched, excruciatingly girly laughter and a noisy clatter of six-inch-high stilettos. Katy winced as they all trooped in, knowing full well she should have called with an excuse – like the neighbour's cat was dead.

Within moments there were suspenders, stockings, make-up, fake hair, fake eyelashes, straighteners, curlers, push-up bras, plunge bras, create-cleavage-visible-from-space-bras – you name it – strewn all over Katy's flat. She looked at her beautiful vintage 1920s coffee table, bought during a weekend away in Brighton with a guy who might have been called Jonny, and wondered whether it would ever recover from one of the girls sitting astride it and giving it six of the best with her headmistress's cane.

After the obligatory group photo, which Katy insisted on taking to ensure there was no record of her participation in this very grim pantomime, they set off with Katy skulking at the back, praying none of her neighbours would choose that moment to go out.

The gym bunnies of course went crazy for the attention they got in every bar they visited, not seeming to notice that the quality of the attention was of a particularly poor standard. Unless, of course, acne-ridden, overly cocky teenage boys or middle-aged men pretending they were still overly cocky teenage boys was your thing.

By eleven o'clock they were in the club and in the middle of a heaving mass of bodies on the dance floor. It was dawning on Katy that maybe she was getting too old for this when Christy, the most pert and bouncy of the gym bunnies, on hearing the opening chords of 'Going Underground' by The Jam, proclaimed that it was utter shit and who the bloody hell were The Jam anyway? How could she be out with someone who had never heard of The Jam? Katy stopped, swayed slightly, then turned around and stormed off to the bar, aghast that she had got herself into this situation. Old enough to know better, dressed as a stupid schoolgirl with so-called friends who were virtually half her age and, to top it all, had said bad things about the God that is Paul Weller.

As she made her way through the crowd cursing to herself, she didn't see the bloke backing away from the bar with three pints in plastic glasses balanced pre-cariously in his hands until she was virtually on top of him. She grabbed his arm to steady herself, which caused him to lose his grip on the wobbly glasses, two of which dropped like stones to the floor whilst the third did a quick somersault, soaking Katy's white shirt. She stood there for a moment wondering if her life could get any worse as the cold liquid seeped through her shirt, then her bra to her skin. She dared not look down at the carnage, knowing full well that her shirt was now probably completely transparent, displaying her wares for all to see.

'Why the hell don't you look where you are going?' she screamed at him.

'Easy, Tiger. It could be worse, it could have been bitter,' said the guy.

A wisecrack was the last thing she needed. What she needed was to let rip. And so let rip she did.

'You have just topped off nicely the most depressing night of my life. Not only am I way too old to be dressed as a bloody schoolgirl, I am here with a crowd of Barbie bloody bimbos with not a brain cell to share between them, who don't even know who The Jam are, and think that this song – yes, "Going Underground" – is shit.'

'My night is worse,' he said calmly.

'Look, this isn't a game. My night is utter crap and no-one is going to take that away from me.'

'Oh, but I so can,' he challenged her.

'Bollocks you can,' she retorted. 'Did I mention that a sweat monster from hell asked me how I liked my eggs in the morning?'

'Clearly desperate,' he nodded.

'Wow, thanks, I'm not that old,' she said in dismay.

'I didn't mean you,' he said quickly. 'I meant desperate if he had to use a line like that.'

'Really,' she said sarcastically.

'No, honestly,' he said. 'Anyway, I like older women. They're good for conversation.'

'I wouldn't call this a conversation,' she said angrily. 'This is you chucking beer all over me and then insulting me about my age.' She turned to go.

'No, please don't go,' he said, catching her arm. 'You're right. I'm sorry. It's all coming out wrong. You see, I really am having a bad night. I'm a teacher, so a school disco is my idea of hell. My mates who dragged me here think it's all dead sexy and I am like no, no, no, this is bad. I can't look at a woman in school uniform and think it's sexy.'

Katy turned back to face him, surprised to find herself wondering what he thought of her, dressed the way she was. 'Besides, I don't get it,' he continued. 'Tell me, who wants to be reminded of their school disco days anyway? Crap music, crap dancing, sober, and no way on earth you were ever going to snog who you wanted to because they were way more popular than you.'

'Well, I guess you have a point,' she said eventually. 'But at least you're here with mates, not lipsticks on legs.'

'There is that, I suppose. But all that still isn't the main reason why my night is worse than yours.'

'Go on then, put me out of my misery,' she said,

noticing the look of mischief in his eyes and trying very hard not to like it.

'OK then,' he paused and drew breath. 'I went to the men's and the bloke next to me stared at my you-know-what and said, "Shame about the ginger pubes."'

Katy couldn't help but giggle. Just like a schoolgirl.

'But surely you knew you had ginger pubes before you came out?' To her horror, she could feel a blush starting to emerge.

'Of course, but to have a total stranger point them out to you during what should be sacred time is wrong on so many levels.'

He looked genuinely upset, which caused Katy to burst out laughing. He started laughing too, obviously pleased he had at last won her over.

'I'm Ben, by the way,' he said, offering her his hand, still sticky from spilt lager. 'So now we are united in misery I can either offer to buy you a drink or we can make a run for it, and go really upmarket and grab a kebab?'

Before she knew it she was sitting on a cold stone step outside Gonads' Kebab House spilling chilli sauce on her black stilettos, knowing this was probably the highlight of her evening.

Talking had been surprisingly easy. She was relieved

that he hadn't offered any embarrassing chat-up lines or false flattery. There was no sob story of a wife who didn't understand him or a tricky divorce, which seemed to be par for the course with the older men she had been attracting lately. He didn't even ask her what she did for a living. He just talked utter nonsense about anything and everything, which made a refreshing change to the 'I'm more successful than you' conversations she was used to with the image-obsessed men she met through work. In fact, she realised, for the first time in a long while she was with a man and not worrying about what she said or how she looked.

Before long he finished his kebab, licked his fingers one by one, then, screwing up the greasy paper, announced he had better be off.

'Football tomorrow,' he said. 'You OK to get yourself a taxi?'

'Yeah, fine.'

He turned to go and then at the last minute he looked back.

'Fancy a drink one night?' he asked.

She hesitated. She had enjoyed his banter but she didn't want to give the poor lad false hope.

'OK, but just a drink, that's all.'

'We'd better go out on a Tuesday then,' he said seriously.

'Why?' asked Katy.

'Because no-one ever has sex on a Tuesday.'

They had met for a drink on a Tuesday, then the following Thursday, then the Monday after that, then finally they had had sex on the Saturday.

'You see, Tuesday is such a nothing day. Sunday you have end-of-the-weekend sex. Monday you have bloody-hell-I-need-something-to-cheer-myself-up-because-it-is-still-the-start-of-the-week sex. Wednesday you have maybe post-scoring-nine-goals-at-football or boring-night-on-the-telly sex. Thursday is the new Friday, so you go down the pub and then have oh-dear-aren't-I-wild-and-crazy-I've-had-too-much-to-drink-on-a-school-night sex. Friday you have thank-Christ-another-week-survived-at-work sex. And Saturday. Well, Saturday is it's-bloody-Saturday-I-should-have-sex sex.

'But Tuesday, you see, is tricky. What reason on earth is there to have sex on a Tuesday? You ask everyone. I bet you no-one can remember the last time they had sex on a Tuesday.'

Now, as she slogged her way down endless hospital corridors, following barely legible handwritten signs, she struggled to think of a good reason to have sex on any day of the week. In fact her entire opinion on sex had changed since that fateful morning six months ago when she had woken feeling queasy for the fifth day running. Initially she had put it down to a very bad and much extended reaction to a lively client dinner. However, she was finally forced to admit that this was not her usual hangover sickness. She froze and racked her brains. When had she last had her period? She could vaguely remember the office Christmas party and having to cram tampons in the lovely little glitter bag she had bought specially to go with her hideously expensive little black dress. She rushed to the kitchen to check the calendar, her heart thumping so loudly she thought it might wake Ben, who had stayed over. She flicked back to December and held her breath as she counted the weeks up until now. The first attempt got her to seven. No, that couldn't be right. She checked again and again but the answer was seven every time. Shit, shit, shit. This could not be happening. She was on the pill. You didn't get pregnant on the pill – that was the whole point of it, surely. She couldn't have a baby. She was going out with Ben. He wasn't ready to be a father. He was eight years younger than her. He was born in the Eighties, for God's sake – practically still a child himself.

She sank to the floor – her beautiful Moroccan tile floor in her beautiful designer flat – and buried her head in her hands. The implications flooded uncontrollably through her mind. What about her career? What about her life? What would everyone say? What would her mum say? She knew she would be horrified, since she'd spent Katy's entire adult life telling her not to get trapped like she had. She was convinced that had it not been for marriage and kids she would have been a star in Vegas, despite the fact she was a terrible singer. Now she was making up for lost time in their villa in Spain, spending most nights down the karaoke bars with her cronies.

'Who the hell's is it?' would be her mother's first question. They had long ago stopped discussing Katy's relationships, as they changed so frequently and her mum had lost interest. Well, at least she knew it could only be Ben's, given that they had been 'hanging out', as they both liked to call it, for a good few months now. In fact she had been amazed at how well it was going. They never promised to call, they just did. They introduced each other to their friends but hotly denied any romance, and there was no way they were ever going to ask to meet each other's parents. He took the mickey out of her pretentious world of advertising, and she scoffed at his million weeks of school holiday a year and ability to be home in time to watch *Neighbours*.

'Undemanding, uncomplicated and under-age,' was how she had laughingly described it to a bemused Daniel.

'I have no idea why I didn't think of going for a younger man before,' she added. 'He's too young to take life seriously, so we have a laugh, and he's not old enough to want to settle down, so I'm not constantly planning how to extract myself. It's perfect.'

It was also with much relief that she had given up her nights out with the gym bunnies. They had called and begged but she had made her excuses. So there had been no drunken nights without Ben in a while, no dodgy end-of-night snogs or even dodgier one-night stands.

'Fuck,' shrieked Katy suddenly as she sat bolt upright, dropping the calendar on the floor. 'No, no, no, no, no, no, no,' she chanted as she grabbed at the calendar. 'Please no, if there is a God, please don't do this to me.' She flicked back to December again and there, in scribbled blue biro, two weeks after the office Christmas party, were the last words on earth she had wanted to read: *Dove Valley School Reunion – 8 p.m.*

Katy shuddered as she recalled the events surrounding the discovery of her pregnancy and did her best to stop her mind going into overdrive yet again as they finally reached the door of the room where the antenatal class was being held. Ben reached for her hand.

'Good luck, partner,' he said, giving her a wink.

She smiled at him gratefully. Maybe everything was going to be alright. She took a deep breath and stepped into the room.

As Ben and Katy entered, seven expectant faces turned to stare at the last members to arrive.

'Bloody hell, I don't believe it. No wonder he hasn't been turning up for football practice!' exclaimed Ben, staring at a young lad slouched in a chair.

But Katy hadn't heard him as the sight of someone else in the room had made her gasp for breath and lose the ability to make her legs move. How could he be here? He didn't even live in Leeds. What the hell was going on? She grabbed the back of a chair to steady herself. She felt like she was suddenly in some weird Sunday night

TV drama where no-one is content until everyone's lives have been completely destroyed.

'So the local under-nineteens' team performance goes down the toilet, all because my best striker has got some girl pregnant,' Ben continued, oblivious to Katy's distress. 'What an idiot. Look at him: he should be out practising his penalties, not stuck in here with a load of old pregnant women.'

Katy was too bewildered to take anything in. She could just about sense now that they were walking towards the group, the point of no return. All she wanted was to turn and run as fast as possible, but there was nothing she could do to prevent what was going to happen. At that moment the last man on earth she wanted to see looked up and saw her. A smile sprang instantly to Matthew's mouth as he recognised her, but it disappeared the moment he saw that she was pregnant.

Chapter 3

Approximately eight months earlier

Matthew's day had gone badly. It had taken two tedious hours just to get out of London that morning, followed by a further punishing three hours to make it to Leeds. His mobile had rung constantly with clients wanting blood, sweat and tears, as well as minor miracles. Being a tax advisor didn't mean you could wave a magic wand and miraculously uncover a way of paying no tax at all, he wanted to scream at them. He could understand that all his clients had somebody squeezing their bollocks constantly for bigger profits, but they should get off his case and go and make more money. It was quite simple, really.

Matthew had put his phone on silent in the end, deciding that poor phone reception up the M1 was a plausible excuse for not being at everyone's beck and call. Besides, the luxury of being able to listen to Radio 5 Live on a weekday, allowing his mind a respite from his personal stresses to peruse the possibilities during this football season's transfer window, was too great an opportunity to miss.

He was just pondering the acquisition options for Leeds United when Alison's name began to flash persistently on his phone screen. He found to his dismay that he hesitated before answering, frightened that he might say the wrong thing again. She had been in tears as he left that morning, the anguish of going through yet another course of fertility treatment sending her way over the edge at the slightest comment. He could tell that every drop of her energy was focused on willing it to be this time. Any distraction or diversion he attempted to calm her down was met with utter disdain and a look of withering contempt. She failed to understand how on earth he could talk about anything other than getting pregnant, let alone suggest something as trivial as her travelling with him to Leeds and seeing the match with him on Saturday.

He fleetingly remembered the time when his heart would have leapt at the sight of Alison's name flashing on his phone screen. But that was a different Alison. That Alison had mesmerised him: so cool and calm and sophisticated, and yet still interested in him. That Alison, who had made him feel like the king of the world simply by resting her perfectly manicured hand on his arm. Whose determination to get somewhere in life had slowly re-educated his chaotic take on how to go about the business of living. That Alison, who, ever so gently, had encouraged him to settle into a career rather than jobbing from one company to the next, invest in his own property rather than renting with his mates, go out to dinner rather than down the pub, buy wine from the top shelf not the bottom, read the broadsheets rather than the tabloids, all the kinds of stuff that proper grown-ups did.

As for this Alison . . . She had had her cool, calm sophistication sucked mercilessly out of her to be pumped full to the brim of fear, doubt and a crippling sense of failure. That Alison had not tolerated failure. This Alison had absorbed the knowledge that she was not able to conceive naturally like a sponge, soaking up every negative feeling she could possibly connect to discovering her body was defective. She had become nervy, edgy and obsessive.

Deciding to start fertility treatment had briefly revived the old Alison as she sensed a whiff of regaining control. She attacked the whole thing as she would a full-time job, the relief of being able to do something practical written all over her face. She took reassurance from the fact that no-one could have researched it more than she had, or prepared their body better, or been more careful each time they went through the process. Slowly but surely, however, the relief had faded from her face to be replaced initially with a distinct hue of disbelief followed by a constant black cloud of pain and fear as time and again her body refused to fall in line with what she so desperately wanted.

Matthew braced himself before he touched the pick-up button, ready for another minefield of a conversation.

'Hiya,' he said, trying to sound as bright and breezy as possible, hoping that this would at least start the conversation off with a degree of buoyancy.

'Hi. I called to say I haven't gone into work today,' said Alison.

'I see. You feeling alright?' Matthew asked hesitantly.

'What do you think? I'm a nervous wreck, Matthew. I'm sitting here yet again obsessing about whether I'll soon be thinking about how to decorate the nursery or absolutely devastated because we've failed again. Isn't there any way you can come back tonight?'

'I'm really sorry, Alison. You know I would, but I'm the only one from the consultancy going to the match now, and someone's got to be there to look after the clients. Ian had to pull out because his daughter is singing the lead in the school play. She was the understudy, but the other girl got caught in some big scandal, sleeping with one of her teachers or something, and was banned from appearing. Now poor old Ian has to suffer two hours of sitting next to his ex-wife, listening to out-of-tune kids warbling *The Wizard of Oz*, rather than the joys of corporate hospitality at the Leeds game. He's pretty pissed off, I can tell you.'

There was silence on the other end of the phone.

'Alison, are you still there?'

The silence continued until he heard a sniff and knew she was crying.

'At least Ian has a daughter he can go and see in a school play. I would trade that for a million afternoons in stupid bloody corporate hospitality. Does he have any idea how lucky he is?' she spat out.

'Oh Alison, I'm sure he does. It's just sod's law, isn't it, that it all happens on the same day.'

'Sod's law that he gets a daughter he can't even be bothered to go and see in a school play and we get nothing.'

'Hey, come on, it might work this time.'

'But what if it doesn't? I can't even think about how I will cope. I just don't think I'll be able to pick myself up again and carry on.'

'Alison, it doesn't do you any good to think like that. We will cope because we'll have no choice but to cope. Look, why don't you call Karen and see if she wants to meet you for lunch, take your mind off it for a while?'

He hoped this would get her off the phone. He felt guilty, but he had lost track of how many times they'd had a similar conversation, and it was grinding him down. Yes, he wanted a child too, but he hated what it was doing to them both. Before all of this, it was Alison who had kept their lives on track, always somehow knowing the right thing to do. But that Alison had long gone, and he was now the one desperately trying to hold it together for both of them – and, he suspected, failing dismally.

'Christ, Matthew, you never want to talk about it, do you? Why can't you be grown up enough to just talk to me about it?' she sobbed.

He closed his eyes briefly. It killed him when she said things like that, as it brought out all his insecurities. That he wasn't good enough for her. That he didn't impress her with his desperate attempts to be the kind of guy he thought she wanted him to be, with his career in financial consultancy, his company car and his expense account. That underneath he was still the chancer he'd been when she'd met him.

'I try, Alison, believe me, I try, but you have to get this into perspective somehow. Look, nobody died, did they?'

The moment the words had left his mouth he knew it was possibly the most idiotic thing he had ever said.

'Well, that just says it all, doesn't it? You have absolutely no idea.'

Call Ended blinked up on his screen.

All he could feel was relief. He knew he should call her back, but he would get it wrong all over again. Where was the manual for dealing with a wife who had changed out of all recognition the minute she started struggling to have a child?

The radio cut back in and he listened to the guys ringing in, airing their views on which players should go to which teams. He wished he was as free of worry as they were, with time to rant on national radio that they were the only people who really knew what to do about the trials and tribulations of the state of British football, and if it wasn't for the day job they could have been the best manager the country had ever known.

He was late when he finally got to his meeting at the Leeds office. His colleagues could not resist the usual jibes reserved for anyone based in London.

'Get lost, did you? Forget that England does actually exist outside the M25?' asked Ian.

'Very funny,' said Matthew. 'The fact that I am born and bred Yorkshire and you are a southern wuss masquerading as a tough northern bloke seems to escape your memory.'

'Southern wuss?' exclaimed Ian, getting up and grabbing his discarded tie from the coat stand. 'And there's me busy telling the client you are the shining star coming all the way up from the big smoke to give them some dazzling PowerPoint action.'

'I hope you haven't built me up or anything.' Matthew was starting to feel nervous.

'Not at all. I just told them that your bar charts inspire the same awe in finance directors as art lovers experiencing a Van Gogh for the first time, and your little jokes about hedge fund tax will have them rolling in the aisles.'

'Thanks, I really appreciate that,' replied Matthew gloomily.

'Any time, my friend. Any time. Still up for a few cheeky beers later?' Ian asked. 'I need to drown my sorrows, seeing as I've been denied coming to the match with you tomorrow.'

'Absolutely. You have no idea how much I need it too,' replied Matthew.

Ian was talking nineteen to the dozen but Matthew had switched off momentarily. The beer had done its job and painted the world a sunnier colour. He smiled a little smile, feeling relaxed and almost carefree, an unusual state of affairs these days. He had called Alison when he got to his hotel room, but the conversation had been short and terse. He had promised that he would drive back straight after the match tomorrow, which rather put a dampener on the free booze he could have been drinking.

'Are you listening, mate? Christ, you were miles away. I was just saying that Chris is leaving and you should go for his job. Get yourself back up here.'

'Sorry, I *was* listening really. Yeah, maybe. Not sure Alison could cope with a move at the moment, though. Besides, it might feel a bit weird coming back to where I grew up. I was invited to a school reunion tonight, as it happens, but I thought it would feel a bit strange. It's bound to be full of all the tossers I never talked to anyway, telling everyone how well they're doing.'

'Did you say school reunion? You mean to tell me we've been out all this time with me trying to drag a smile onto your pathetic, downtrodden face when I could have been pouncing on the easy prey of thirty-something women who have been married just long enough to realise that it's not all it's cracked up to be?' Ian leant back in his chair, put his hands behind his head and closed his eyes. 'I can see it now. There'll be hundreds of them gagging for it. All hoping for a snog from their childhood crush, who will transport them from their domestic hell to the fairy-tale life they were promised by Enid Blyton. Of course they'll be gutted because dream boy will have grown an enormous gut by now, clearing the way for a poor, recently divorced, charming young man like me to console the desperate young ladies.'

He opened his eyes again, a serious expression on his face. 'Hopefully they'll have piled on the pounds too, and be a bit depressed about it, making them hugely grateful for some male attention.'

He sprang up from his chair and started to put on his coat. 'So what are we waiting for?'

'You didn't even go to the school,' Matthew protested.

'Aw, bollocks to that. I'll pretend I joined in the fourth year. No-one ever remembers the latecomers. Come on, let's go.'

'No, really, I don't want to go.'

'Why? It'll be a laugh, and you get to dance to Spandau Ballet with some old girlfriends. Or is that the problem? Did you go out with some right mingers you're too embarrassed to let me meet? I bet that's it, isn't it?'

'Actually I only went out with one girl at school. That's the problem really; we didn't exactly finish on good terms,' said Matthew, surprised to find his cheeks starting to feel hot.

'Oh, come on, how long has it been? Nearly twenty years? She'll be married, fat, stretchmarks up to her ears, flashing photos of her little darlings to all and sundry.

She won't give a damn about some long-forgotten school fling.'

Ian dropped to his knees and clutched at Matthew's arm.

'Don't deny me this chance of a shag, mate, I might never forgive you,' he pleaded.

Matthew had to laugh at Ian's sheer optimism. He wasn't exactly God's gift, although he did seem to have the gift of the gab. Sod it, he thought. Who knew when he would next get the chance for a night out? And Ian was right. If Katy was there, it had all happened so long ago that she would either have forgotten about him or at the very least forgiven him for how it ended. Not that he had ever really forgiven himself. His stomach still lurched when he thought about it, which was surprisingly often. For some reason, he was frequently reminded of Katy – silly things like catching a glimpse of Mickey Mouse on the TV. Katy had a slightly irrational hatred of Mickey Mouse. 'Smug bastard who should learn to speak properly,' she had often shared with anyone who was or wasn't interested in her opinion of the diminutive superstar.

'OK then, we'll go. But if it's crap we leave. And don't show me up,' he said finally.

'Fantastic.' Pretending to be in a clinch, groping some poor imaginary woman, Ian broke into the classic Eighties smooch song: 'Move closer, move your body real close until iiiiiiiiiiiiit feels like we're really making love . . . woah . . . woah . . . woah.'

'I really think I am going to regret this,' Matthew muttered under his breath.

Chapter 4

The school was less than a twenty-minute cab ride away. The erratic driving of the taxi driver was making Matthew feel slightly woozy. He hadn't had this much to drink in a while, since Alison had insisted they both cut down to virtually nothing to increase their chances of conceiving.

Ian had sung Matthew his entire repertoire of favourite Eighties songs during the journey, along with a run-down on what he associated with each one. A reoccurring theme appeared to be which girl he was having sex with at the time, and what kind of sex.

'So Caroline was my "Wake Me Up Before You

Go-Go" girl, because she was the dullest bird in bed you have ever known. Now as for the amazing Stephanie – if I tell you our song was "Summer of '69" by Bryan Adams, I bet you can't guess what her speciality was?'

'I think we can all guess, and it's an image I'd rather not have, thank you,' replied Matthew.

'Oh happy days, my friend, happy days,' said Ian with a contented smile on his face.

Fortunately they pulled up at the school gates at that point, putting an end to the magical musical tour of Ian's sex life.

Matthew could just about make out the school sign standing just as it had nearly twenty years before by the iron railings. Now he was here he felt weird. He saw himself as he had been then, sauntering through the gates, Adidas bag high on his shoulder, narrow end of his tie poking out of the top of his shirt, thick end stuffed way out of sight, one half of his shirt already dangling out over the top of his trousers and hair worn fashionably long. His arm was, of course, draped over Katy's shoulders. He had looked, he thought with a pang, kind of cool. It certainly didn't seem possible that the teenager with the cocky swagger could have turned into this man wearing the middle-aged, standard-issue uniform of blue checked shirt and turned-up chinos.

'Right, let the dog see the rabbit.' Ian barged his unwieldy boozy body against the school hall door, making the 'Welcome Back to Dove Valley School' banner flap wildly in his wake.

Matthew had to smile at the sight that greeted them. As if they had gone back in time, Norwegian pop-group A-ha blared out from the disco at the far end of the hall and multicoloured lights spun wildly out of control. The dance floor was, of course, a girls-only domain at this point in the evening. The blokes clustered around the bar, glancing nervously at the women, as if they might be dragged onto the dance floor at any minute. The only things visibly different were the clothes. The scene was awash with little black dresses, sheer tights, perfectly manicured nails and beautifully styled hair, fresh from the hairdressers. No shoulder pads, no neon, no mesh, no chains, no lace, no leather ties and no silk shirts. But by the looks on most people's faces, the sophisticated veneer did not hide a multitude of teenage insecurities that had come back to haunt the partygoers in their old stomping ground.

'Oh my God, is it really you? You look amazing,' Matthew suddenly heard Ian exclaim. 'Even more gorgeous than you did at school. It's Ian, by the way, if you're too shy to say you can't remember my name. Ian Robinson. I only arrived in the fourth year. We did maths together, remember? Lusted after you a bit, actually, from the back of the class. We had that really boring teacher, what was their name?'

'Mr Hopkins,' the bewildered, rather chubby woman wearing an exceptionally low-cut dress muttered.

'That's him. He bored the pants off me. Still, something must have gone in, or else I wouldn't be the high-flying financial consultant that I am today. So are you going to let me buy you a drink as a thank you for your smile brightening up my maths lessons or what? Don't tell me, a Bacardi and Coke, isn't it? With those exotic Latino looks you have to be a rum drinker. Follow me, young lady.'

Ian winked at Matthew and disappeared into the throng around the bar, the chubby woman following him looking surprised but quite pleased.

Left alone, Matthew started to take in the faces hovering around him. Some he recognised immediately, others he had no clue. He realised he hadn't kept in touch with anyone from school, which was probably because he and Katy had been virtually glued together during their last couple of years, so he hadn't spent a lot of time with anyone else.

'My oh my, surprised you've got the cheek to show your face,' said a voice from somewhere on his left.

Matthew turned to see the vaguely familiar grimace of Jules Kettering. She had always treated him with utter contempt, given that in her view Matthew had completely taken over her best friend. He'd always had a suspicion that she might be a lesbian and secretly wanted Katy for herself.

'Jules, how are you? Full of smiles as usual, I see,' he said.

'The sight of you is enough to put a dampener on anyone.'

'Oh, how the years just slip away when you meet old friends.' He smiled sweetly.

'You and I were never friends, and certainly not after what you did to Katy,' challenged Jules.

'Oh, come on, that was years ago,' he said, dismayed.

'It was still shit. I'm surprised she wanted to come tonight, given the possibility of seeing you again.'

'You mean she's here?' gasped Matthew. He felt his

heart do something strange. Sort of contract a bit and then make a play for escape out of his throat.

'Of course. She's not going to let a pig like you ruin the memories of her school years,' spat Jules.

'Charming. So where is she?' he said, looking around wildly.

He couldn't believe that he was about to see her. After all these years. They hadn't spoken since the night she had surprised him at college, a memory that still made him shudder. He'd called, of course, for over two weeks, but she had refused to speak to him. Then he'd received in the post all the compilation tapes he'd ever made for her, stamped on, crushed and mangled. Katy had loved those tapes. They had listened to them over and over in her bedroom and in various lay-bys in the back of his dad's car whilst having a grope. As the plastic shards and the twisted shiny brown ribbon scattered all over the floor, he caught sight of a slightly faded label, *Now That's What I Call Katy and Matthew's Music* scrawled in blue biro. He knew then that there was no going back. He had given her that tape the night before they'd both left to start college – him off to London, and her to Manchester. They had sat in her bedroom listening to it, her in tears most of the time and him trying to cheer her up. Then The Jam had come on and they had jumped up and down to 'Going Underground' for the entire track, laughing hysterically. At the end they'd had an 'only in the movies' moment where they collapsed on the bed, breathing heavily, and stared into each other's eyes. He remembered telling her he loved her and that three years would soon be over and then the world was their oyster. They had carried on talking way into the night, plotting and planning their future. He could still remember her telling him breathlessly that she could already picture the dream home they would buy when they had both graduated and found good jobs back in Leeds. She had in mind a barn conversion, with thick oak beams towering above an enormous, double-height lounge, a kitchen with an Aga that a tribe of dogs could fall asleep next to, and enough bedrooms so all their mates could come and stay, even after they'd had kids. He remembered that he'd been surprised that talk of children hadn't freaked him out, especially when Katy informed him they would have two, a boy named Jacob and a girl called Eloise. But it all seemed so wonderfully inevitable then that there was no cause for panic.

They had managed to see each other every other weekend, taking it in turns to make the train journey.

But doubts had started to creep in. Matthew's new mates were organising things for the weekends when he was with Katy and he felt like he was missing out. Also Freshers Week had started with a bang, quite literally for many of the guys living on his floor in the halls of residence. Released from the confines of parents breathing down their necks it seemed that sex was pretty much on tap. Of course, when they staggered into the kitchen the morning after the night before, they were full of elaborate stories of their conquests, trying to outdo one another on who had gone the furthest.

Matthew, being the only one with a girlfriend, was forced to sit quietly on the periphery as the banter swirled around his head. This wasn't helped by the fact that he and Katy had not had sex that often, maybe three or four times, and it hadn't been the earth-moving experience either of them had expected. In fact it had been downright awkward. He had no idea what he was doing wrong, but it wasn't right. Katy was more likely to moan in pain than ecstasy. They had not talked about it, merely avoided the subject, both of them embarrassed by their lack of experience. He knew deep down that probably all they needed was practice, but he was getting increasingly frustrated, especially when all his new friends appeared to be having the time of their lives.

Then the end of the first term arrived. On the last night there was a fancy dress disco in the college bar, and Matthew and one of the other guys decided to go as a reindeer. Actually there was only a pantomime horse left at the fancy dress shop, so they had added a pair of Christmas antlers and a red nose to complete the look. He drew the short straw and ended up dressed as the back end, which he didn't mind as long as he was well supplied with alcohol.

After a considerable amount of vodka, the makeshift reindeer's back end went. All of a sudden the legs appeared not to want to stay upright any longer and collapsed, dragging the front end down with it. The next thing Matthew knew he was being hauled up by the Virgin Mary, otherwise known as Emma, who lived on the floor below him. Her costume had been met with much hilarity, as she was certainly no virgin, making the most of her release from an all girls' Catholic school and enjoying as fully as possible the company of as many men as she could.

'Matty, come on, get up,' he heard Emma say through what felt like a thick, enveloping fog.

Before he knew it, Emma and another bloke from his floor were dropping him onto his bed.

'I'll just watch him to make sure he doesn't puke before he falls asleep,' she said.

She started off stroking his head then somehow manoeuvred him, still in his costume, so his head rested in her bosom. The next thing he knew she was kissing him and stuffing her hand down the front of his horse's legs.

The drink had stripped away his inhibitions and all thoughts of Katy vanished. He rolled Emma over onto her back on the bed and pulled his fuzzy fetlocks down, just far enough to allow him to fumble out a fairly incapable penis. He aimed up into the hidden depths of the blue sheet Emma had used for her costume, complete with thigh-high split up the side.

And so it came to pass that Christmas that the sight that greeted Katy as she pushed open the door of Matthew's room, having decided to pay him a surprise visit, was the back end of a pantomime horse desperately pumping away at the Virgin Mary.

The look on Katy's face on that fateful day was still imprinted on Matthew's mind, so much so that he half expected her still to be wearing it as he waited nervously next to Jules for her to appear. Eventually she emerged through the doors by the stage, looking as far removed as possible from the broken teenager he remembered fleeing his room all those years ago. She had a strut only achieved through success and maturity. Her designer shirt was clearly more Chelsea than Chelsea Girl, and the faded denim jeans had been replaced by razor-sharp pinstripe trousers, ending in bright red killer heels. She looked totally together, which was somewhat at odds with the sound of 'Like a Virgin' blaring out.

She made her way across the dance floor, head held high, smiling and waving to her bopping ex-classmates. She did not see him until she had almost reached the spot where she had left Jules.

'Look what the cat dragged in,' said Jules.

She looked up. Their eyes met and locked.

How could someone you haven't seen in such a long time look so familiar? He looked at every inch of her face, trying to find something that would make her a stranger, but there was nothing. She was still Katy, his Katy, standing there in the school hall as if time had stood still.

'Hi, it's really good to see you,' he finally managed.

'Ha, I bet you didn't say that the last time you saw her, did you? Too busy relieving Mary of her virginity,' Jules chipped in.

'Thank you, Jules, that's enough,' Katy said.

He smiled gratefully at her but noticed that she looked grim.

'You never gave me a chance. You never let me explain, you wouldn't talk to me – I tried calling you for weeks,' he found himself blurting out. He couldn't believe what he was saying. He sounded like a pathetic teenager. What was he doing? There was no need to make excuses now for something that had happened so long ago, surely.

'Go on then, if you feel you must, if it's been weighing on your mind all this time. Go ahead and explain,' said Katy calmly.

He drew a breath. 'I was drunk.'

'Excellent, well done, Matthew. You've had since 1989 to think of a plausible reason behind what you did to me, and you come out with that. You were drunk. Well, that makes it all alright then, doesn't it?' said Katy, now not quite so calm.

'Wahey, if it isn't love's young dream from the sixth form. Good old Matthew and Katy. Assume you must have stayed together then, by the way the good lady wife is giving you a right mouthful.' It was Robert Etchings, as diplomatic as he'd been at school, always sticking his piggy little nose where it wasn't wanted.

'She's matured well, I must say, Matthew,' he ploughed on. 'Always thought she looked a bit of a scrubber at school. A bit dirty, if you know what I mean. Not that you mind that when you're seventeen though, eh? The dirtier the better, wouldn't you say, Matthew?' Robert seemed unaware of the three dumbstruck faces around him.

Matthew had no idea what to do. His emotions were in a spin over a girl; he was apologising for something really stupid that he'd done without thinking; and he had an overwhelming desire to twat some total idiot he hated at school. It was like he actually was seventeen all over again. Had he done no growing up at all? One step into a school hall and he had gone to pieces.

He looked at Katy, whose anger still seemed to be directed at him, despite the distraction Robert's comments might have caused. What should he do? Eventually he realised he had no choice, and did the only thing his fuzzled state of mind thought appropriate. He twatted the total idiot he hated from school.

'Stop it, Matthew, stop it now,' was the next thing Matthew heard as he gasped for air once he had got Robert pinned to the floor, following an impressive right hook to his chin.

'What the hell do you think you're doing?' Katy shouted, a couple of inches from his face. All he could think was how much he wanted to kiss those bright red lips, just as he felt two sets of arms yank him up and away from a now simpering Robert.

'That's enough now, lad,' said Mr Gelding, who had been Matthew's form teacher at some point. He looked about fifty then and he still looked fifty now.

'You're not at school now, you know,' he said with a twinkle in his eye and smile at the corner of his mouth. No doubt he hadn't liked Robert either.

'I think you'd better take him home, love. Go on, before Robert insists that he's thrown out.' He smiled at Katy and wandered away.

It was then that Matthew realised his hand felt like an elephant had stamped on it.

'Fuck me,' he cried as he doubled up and cradled it. 'For a fat lad, that Robert must have a jawbone made of steel.'

Katy looked him up and down and then nodded, as if

she had just decided something important. She stood up straight and said, 'Right then, let's get you out of here and sort that hand out.'

She reached out and grabbed his injured hand, and squeezed it as hard as she possibly could whilst pulling him across the hall. He was shouting in agony the whole way to the door, but there was no way she was letting go or acknowledging the fact that she was hurting him; in fact the louder he shouted, the harder she seemed to squeeze.

As soon as they got into the relative quiet of the corridor outside the hall she dropped his hand like a stone and turned to face him.

'Do you know what that was for?' she said, glaring at him in a way that made it clear a random guess would not be welcome. He remained quiet, not daring to speak.

'That was for being a complete and utter arsehole, and a shit and every single bad name I could ever think of,' she shouted in his face. Then she gripped both his shoulders and kneed him swiftly in the groin. 'And now we will never speak of it again. Is that clear?' she demanded.

'OK,' he whispered, the pain making his eyes water.

'Now let me have a look at that hand,' she said, thrusting her own hand out. Matthew whimpered slightly and took a step back.

'Are you mad? After what you just did?' he gasped.

'Necessary, Matthew, necessary,' she said. 'Come on, I won't inflict any further damage, I promise, and I am the first-aider for my floor at work. I got the best score in the theory test, if you must know.'

'My, you have come a long way,' he said, relieved to see her smile faintly as he gingerly raised his hand.

She studied it, then pronounced, 'I think it's a pea job. Big bag of peas to reduce the swelling and it will be fine.'

'Marvellous. Know any good pea shops open at midnight?' he asked.

'Well, as long as you think your wife won't mind, I think I have a bag of petits pois that could do the job at my flat, and you can call a cab from there.'

'How'd you know I was married?'

'Gold ring on your left hand is a bit of a give-away, Matthew.'

'Oh yeah. What about you then?' he asked, looking at her left hand.

'No, not married. You see, I had a very bad experience

53

with a man when I was young and became a lesbian; you'll meet Lisa and Rachel when we get back to the flat. We are currently doing a three-way.'

'Shit, no, you are kidding me, right?' said Matthew, his eyes as big as saucers.

'Yeah, you're right, in my dreams a three-way. No, it's just Lisa.'

'I see,' said Matthew, unable to think of an appropriate answer.

She threw her head back and laughed.

'Your face,' she said eventually. 'Actually I'm not a lesbian, and the reason I know that is because I have a boyfriend called Ben who is a PE teacher, as fit as they come, with thighs to die for and eight years younger than me.' *That showed you, you two-timing wanker.*

'Right, maybe I'd better go back to my hotel then. Don't want to get punched by some rugby maniac.'

'No, don't worry. He's away at a stag do, and he wouldn't mind anyway – he's very laid-back.'

'OK then, Miss Chapman; take me to your pea stash.'

Chapter 5

Three hours later the bag of peas was lukewarm but still draped over Matthew's knuckles, albeit very limply. They had pretty much filled each other in on their lives since they'd last seen each other. Much careful editing had occurred to start with, but they got more and more honest as they plunged headlong into their third bottle of wine.

Katy had of course left out the devastation Matthew's drunken shag had left behind, preferring to hammer home her raft of men since then. Matthew, grateful not to dwell on the period after his indiscretion, focused on how he had finally found himself a career and settled down after a few years of jobbing around. He mentioned Alison but found he didn't really want to talk about her too much, particularly given their conversations that day.

Only when they had clearly displayed to each other that they were totally secure and in control of their current lives, and when they were really quite drunk, did it feel safe to reminisce.

They found themselves crying with laughter at some of the things they had got up to. It felt very much like a guilty pleasure, both of them knowing that they shouldn't really be talking about their previously shared intimate life.

'Do you remember that time when your mum and dad went away for the weekend and we thought we had the house to ourselves,' began Katy. 'We were upstairs in your room, music blaring, snogging away, when we suddenly heard someone shout from downstairs.'

'It was my neighbour, wasn't it?' said Matthew, covering his eyes in embarrassment. 'Weren't we half naked so we squeezed under the bed just as she came into the room and turned off the music? Then the nosy old bat started looking through my drawers, do you remember? We were both ready to explode. God knows what she thought she was doing; she was only supposed to be watering the plants.'

'You were convinced that she always looked at you a bit strangely after having scrutinised your boxers at close range,' giggled Katy.

'Yeah, I decided she was a complete perv and stopped Mum hanging them on the washing line.'

'Your undies weren't fit for public display anyway. Weren't you still letting your mum buy them?' said Katy, a wicked gleam in her eye.

'No I was not!' Matthew felt offended until he spotted the evil smirk on her face. 'Stop winding me up,' he said, embarrassed that she had got him on the defensive so easily.

'You know me, there's no way I would give you too much of an easy ride,' she said, looking away quickly.

Yes, he did know her, he thought. That was the totally weird thing. It felt like the last eighteen years had never happened. He was talking to her as if he spoke to her every day. However, what was starting to cut into him was the realisation that actually he hadn't spoken to anyone like this for a while. Just chatting, having a laugh, totally and utterly relaxed, not really worrying about anything. Since he had decided to focus on his career, most of his free time had been taken up with study and he had lost touch with a lot of his mates, who had eventually got bored with him apologetically turning them down for a night out. It hadn't helped that they'd moved north of the river, because Alison preferred it there, making it a long old slog to his old stomping ground in Southwark. And then when they had started to struggle to conceive, Alison's pain had engulfed them both, weighing them down until the ability to enjoy themselves felt like a dim and distant memory.

Being here with Katy somehow took him back to carefree days and awoke part of him that had been dormant for a long time. Boy, did it feel good. A bit like when they brought back *Dr Who* and he wondered how he had coped without it for all those years.

And as for Katy, Christ, she could still talk crap, but it was like fresh air compared to his conversations recently with Alison, which had been drenched in misery.

He would go to the loo and then leave, he decided suddenly, the thought of Alison making him feel guilty. He knew she would not be pleased if she could see him roaring with laughter with an old flame.

'Back in a sec, then I'd better go,' he said.

He staggered to the bathroom for about the fourth

time since he had arrived. He looked across at Katy's oversized bath, lined with a whole host of perfumes, potions and candles in a variety of elaborate glass holders. He couldn't help but picture Katy in there, eyes closed and a smile on her face, relaxed and happy, maybe a hint of breast peeping up over the bubbles. He tried to wipe the image from his mind as he washed his hands and strengthened his resolve to head back to the hotel.

But then some kind of fate struck as the iPod started to play 'Going Underground', their favourite song on the *Now That's What I Call Katy and Matthew's Music* tape. Granted, the Shuffle mode often seemed to have some kind of inner knowledge that could play the right track at the right time, but this was freaky. Matthew half suspected Katy had programmed it whilst he had been out of the room, despite the fact she was sitting exactly as he had left her.

At the sound of the first few bars, Katy leapt in the air.

'Come on, just dance to this and then go,' she cried, already jumping dangerously close to her mock chandelier dangling from the ceiling.

He laughed and let go, trying to savour the feeling of being just a bit crazy. Katy was laughing hysterically as she grabbed his hands and they jumped together, getting themselves into a 'who could go higher?' competition. As the song ended they crashed heavily onto the sofa, their faces for the first time only a few centimetres apart. She had the biggest smile on her face, which made him just want to consume her and her joy in the hope that it would rub off on him.

And so he started to devour this surprise joy. Suck its face off, in fact. They snogged like they were teenagers, mouths wide open, constantly revolving around each other's faces like a well-oiled machine, tongues sliding in and out of each other's mouths, over teeth and lips. And then the hands, unable to stay still, jittered all over each other, first in the hair, then up and down each other's arms, then around the back, and then tentatively up and down each other's legs, each time edging higher and higher, wordlessly playing dare with each other.

For some time that was enough, frantically exploring each other's bodies. Finally Matthew could bear it no longer and began to fumble at the buttons down the front of her shirt, until he was able to push it over her shoulders, revealing a small cupid tattoo. It made him smile and he looked up to see Katy smiling right back at him. They both stared at each other, panting slightly, the magnitude of the moment fizzing between them like an electric current. Then, for the second time that night, Katy made a decision to steer the course of the evening. She launched at him but this time her hands dived straight to the heart of the matter.

'Katy,' he gasped, somewhat shocked that she would do such a thing.

Then he closed his eyes, all thoughts banished from his brain until she stopped suddenly and pulled him down onto the floor beside her, making it clear that mutual pleasure was now required.

At first when he opened his eyes the next morning, he felt like nothing was amiss as he gazed at Katy, hair strewn over the pillow. Then the last eighteen years suddenly flashed before his eyes and he remembered he had not actually lived happily ever after with Katy, but had lived another life entirely. A life that meant he had a wife who was not the woman lying next to him, post-coital in bed.

He leapt out of bed and hunted wildly for his clothes, cursing under his breath. What the fuck had he done? This was a disaster. He was a man with a career and a wife who he was trying to have a baby with. What the hell had happened?

After he had made himself decent, he contemplated whether he should just leave. But he couldn't do it. He had been a shit all those years ago, so the very least he could do was face the music this time.

He gently nudged her shoulder and said her name.

She opened her eyes wide straight away.

'So you thought you would have the decency to say goodbye then,' she said, obviously having woken earlier and heard him making moves to leave.

'Look, Katy, I can't believe I've done this. I really should burn in hell after everything I've put you through in the past. But I have to go. I have a wife. I'm so sorry, I shouldn't have come back here. I was drunk, it shouldn't have happened.'

'Christ, not the "I was drunk" line again. You really need to think of something more original,' Katy retorted.

'I know. I just don't know what to say. I feel terrible.' He looked away, petrified he was going to see the look he remembered on the face of the girl he had betrayed all those years ago.

'Look, Matthew, we're not teenagers any more,' she said, as if reading his mind. 'You really don't deserve this, but don't sweat it. To be honest, watching you feel so guilty somehow gives me a sense of closure on the whole matter. So go home to your wife and forget the whole thing.' She smiled at him as if she really meant it.

He wanted to tell her that he still regretted that day, that he still thought about it more often than he should, but he realised his time was up.

'Well, I guess this really is goodbye then,' he finally managed to say.

He looked down at her still lying on the bed and took in every detail of the way she looked, committing it to memory. He found, to his dismay, that the thought of never seeing her again was terrifying. Lying there she looked so right. It felt good for him to look at her in a bed they had had sex in the night before, not wrong, and not bad. What had he done? He had to get out now, before he looked at her any more and decided he couldn't leave.

'Have a good life,' she smiled.

'And you,' he croaked, then turned and left. He had closed her front door behind him before he allowed himself to breathe and let a small tear slide down his cheek.

Chapter 6

Matthew thought he had done a pretty good job of forgetting since the school reunion. The guilt had almost torn him apart to start with. Not really the sex part – in some ways that felt incidental. What kept him awake at night was the fact that he had taken such joy in another woman's company. The ultimate betrayal. He found himself constantly reliving their meeting, desperately searching for something that would let him off the hook. She must have done something wrong, there must have been something not to like. He just needed something that would banish her from his mind. In the end it was Alison who managed to kidnap his thoughts back again by announcing she was finally pregnant, and miraculously some joy had filtered back into their married life. At that point he had sat himself down and told himself enough was enough. It was a one-night stand that should never have happened and now he must put his all into his wife and their new family on its way.

But here she was. Eight months later. In a hospital. At an antenatal class. Walking towards him. Fat.

'Welcome, welcome,' boomed the lady in charge of the class, interrupting Matthew's highly disturbed thoughts. She rose unsteadily out of her chair, her wobbly bits and greying hair the product of four pregnancies leading to four energetic boys aged from twenty-one to six. Her impressive child-bearing thighs stressed a pair of overwashed black leggings to the limit, whilst pink polka dots romped across her ample bosom, bobbing around like buoys on a stormy sea.

'I'm Joan and you must be Ben and Katy. Don't worry, you've missed nothing really, just the usual toilets and fire exits stuff. Sit down, and now that we're all here, we can do some introductions.'

Ben and Katy took the last two seats, which were directly opposite Matthew. Matthew's stunned glare was pointedly ignored by Katy, who refused to raise her eyes from the floor.

'Right then, shall we continue? Now I know you all feel just a little bit awkward, but please remember we're all here to support each other. I've been running these sessions for many years, and believe me, you'll all be firm friends by the end of it.' Katy stole a glance at Matthew. He stared straight back at her. She looked away instantly.

'So let's start by going round the room and you can each give your name, when the baby is due and tell us what your biggest concern is about childbirth,' said Joan.

Matthew watched, mesmerised, as the man Katy had arrived with leant over and whispered into her ear.

'I think I'll just go and slit my wrists now. Wake me up when they get to the bit about fannies,' said Ben, just loud enough for Matthew to hear.

'Hi, I'm Rachel,' a sweet-looking girl muttered. 'I'm due on the first of September and I'm most worried about knowing how to push and when.' She went bright red, clearly not used to talking in front of strangers.

'Hello, I'm Richard, and I'm most worried about making sure I know exactly what I can best do to help my wife,' he said, smiling at his wife reassuringly and squeezing her hand.

'Fetch me a bucket,' muttered Ben, a little too loudly.

'And what about you?' said Joan gently to a girl in her late teens, clutching the hand of the boy next to her. 'There's absolutely no need to be shy, we're all in this together. Why don't you just start by telling us your name? You don't have to say anything else if you don't want to.'

'Well, Joan, I'm Charlene,' began the girl, moving forward in her chair and adeptly flicking her shaggy, dirty blond hair over her shoulder, causing the numerous bangles on her wrist to jangle noisily. 'And this is my Luke. And he is the father of my child,' she said proudly, raising his hand with hers as if in a victory salute.

'And when—' started Joan.

'We started going out when we were fifteen, when he walked me home from McDonald's after Jez Langton dumped me because I wouldn't give him the toy out of my Happy Meal. I'm his only ever girlfriend, aren't I, Luke?' she said, nudging him. Luke stared at the floor and said nothing.

'Well, that's wonderful. So when are—' Joan started again.

'And we're getting married, aren't we, Luke?' Charlene interrupted again. 'As soon as I told him I was pregnant he went straight out and bought me a ring. I'm not kidding. He's been just brilliant. He is the kindest, most wonderful person you could ever meet, aren't you, Luke?'

Luke nodded at the floor.

'Well, that's just wonderful, Charlene,' said Joan. 'I'm so thrilled that you are both embracing your pregnancy in this way. Now we do like to help our very young mums as much as we can, and it so happens that next week we're all going out for a pizza, so we can all have a proper chat, you know, in a nice, unthreatening environment, about anything that may be on your mind.'

'Which pizza place?' asked Charlene abruptly.

'Well, er, I'm not sure,' replied Joan. 'I guess it'll be Pizza Palace, as that's where we usually go.'

'Sorry, no can do. They don't do deep-pan and Luke only eats deep-pan.'

'I see. Actually, it'll be girls only, so maybe you could come along and leave Luke at home?'

Charlene turned to look at Luke questioningly, who still refused to raise his eyes from the floor.

'We'll discuss it and I'll let you know if Luke doesn't mind,' replied Charlene eventually.

'Right you are then. Now, Luke, is there anything

that you want to add?' asked Joan, turning to the boy sitting next to Charlene.

He slouched further down in his chair and grunted a no.

'Well, that's fine. There'll be plenty of opportunities for you to say whatever you want,' said Joan, beaming at his bowed head. 'So who do we have next?'

Ben was waiting and ready. He looked around the room as if checking to see if his audience was listening.

'Hello. I'm Ben and I'm most worried that the poor kid might be ginger,' he said, grinning from ear to ear.

Matthew's mouth fell open in astonishment. Who was this guy?

Now it was Katy's turn. Matthew could feel himself holding his breath.

'Er, hi, I'm Katy. I'm, er, due in five weeks and I guess I am pretty much petrified of everything.'

Matthew's head started to spin as Katy's words kicked off a chain of thought he had stopped himself from putting into motion from the moment he'd seen her enter into the room. So if she was due in September, that made December nine months ago. When exactly was that damn reunion? he thought desperately. He wasn't exactly sure, until the memory of Katy dragging him across the school hall to the soundtrack of 'Last Christmas' by Wham came flooding back, bringing a wave of nausea to his throat. There wasn't a chance, was there? It couldn't be his. He couldn't have had a one-night stand resulting in a pregnancy, just as his wife managed to conceive after five years of trying. That couldn't happen, surely? Katy would have made sure they were safe. She must have been on the pill. Women didn't get to thirty-six without having a baby and not have birth control fully in hand. And who was the clown sitting next to her? He wouldn't be here if he wasn't the father, would he?

His breathing was going too fast now, too fast not to be noticed.

He looked around nervously and was suddenly aware that everyone was looking at him and Alison was nudging him. Shit, it was his turn. His turn to tell the class what his biggest fear was concerning childbirth. How about your wife finding out she might not be the only one carrying your child?

'Sorry, got to get some air,' he managed to gasp before he got up and virtually ran for the door. Joan chuckling was the last thing he heard as the door swung shut behind him.

'Oh, there's always one who finally gets a reality check once they get to this stage. Give him a minute and he'll be right as rain, you mark my words. Why don't you tell us about both of you?' she said, looking at the woman sitting next to Matthew's empty chair.

'Well, that was my husband Matthew, who isn't normally like that, I promise you. I have no idea what's come over him. Anyway, my name is Alison. We've just moved up from London with Matthew's job because we wanted a house with a garden rather than the flat we were living in. We're really going to need it, you see, because we are actually expecting twins,' she said with rather a smug smile.

A hushed 'Wow' echoed around the room, followed by a spontaneous round of applause. Katy clapped her hands just a little bit slower than everyone else, staring at the closed door Matthew was no doubt hiding behind.

'How could you?' asked Alison, panting slightly as she collapsed in the passenger seat of Matthew's car after the class had finished. 'How could you leave like that and then not come back? I was absolutely mortified.'

'I'm sorry. I just felt really ill all of a sudden.'

'Of course, now they all think you're not up to it.'

'Up to what?' he asked.

'Having babies,' she screeched. 'They all think you haven't the stomach for it, I know they do. I bet they're all talking about us now on their way home. The couple having twins with a husband who can't even bear to sit in an antenatal class and learn about childbirth. That's what they'll be saying. God, I'm so embarrassed.'

Matthew stared silently at the speed dial on his dashboard.

'Are you even listening to me?' she persisted.

'Sorry. What did you say?'

'For God's sake, Matthew, you know how important these classes are and then you let me down like that, in front of everyone.'

'I just . . . I guess I couldn't stay in there any longer.'

'Oh, fantastic,' she said, throwing her hands in the air. 'What are you going to be like when I actually give birth if you can't even stand to be in a class just talking about it? What on earth are you afraid of?'

'Nothing, I promise. It's honestly nothing to do with the whole birth thing. Must have eaten something dodgy at lunchtime, that's all.' Matthew turned to look at her. 'Besides, it's you who needs to know all this stuff really, isn't it? If I'm not there it doesn't really matter, does it?

You know, if, heaven forbid, something crops up and I can't make it for some reason.'

'Matthew, you have had these dates in your BlackBerry for months now. I know, because I put them there. There is nothing that is more important than these classes. What would everyone think if you didn't turn up, especially after your performance tonight?'

'Does it really matter what they think? It's not like we're going to become bosom buddies or anything, is it?'

'Matthew, I'm going to be at home every day with two children. I need to start developing a support network, and I was hoping that there might be some women in this class who I could get friendly with.'

'Oh, come on, Alison. There was no-one in there who you'd have anything in common with,' said Matthew, starting to feel shaky again.

'Oh, I don't know. What about that one you were staring at? I saw you, you couldn't keep your eyes off her,' said Alison accusingly.

'What, the one with the dark hair, you mean?' Matthew was starting to feel sick. 'Oh, it was just that she looked familiar, that's all. I couldn't quite place her, you know how it is.'

'I see,' said Alison. 'Well, I guess you're bound to start

bumping into people you used to know. She works for an advertising agency, if that helps. I have to admit, she was the only one I could see myself being friends with, as she was the only one with anything resembling a brain.'

'But . . . but,' Matthew spluttered, desperately searching for words that might somehow steer this conversation in a safer direction. 'But wasn't she the one with the complete loser of a boyfriend?'

'Oh, he was harmless. You're right, though, they're an odd couple. He seemed a lot younger than her.'

'Well, he seemed like a tosser to me. I'd steer clear if I were you. Nothing worse than coping with horrendous partners.'

'They're probably thinking the same about us, given your behaviour this evening,' she said. 'Her partner was a saint compared to you. He even held my hands when I tried the birthing ball, seeing as you weren't there, so don't forget to thank him for being a surrogate father when you see him next week.'

'A class performance on my part, don't you think?' said Ben to Katy as they stopped at a set of traffic lights on their way home. 'Did you notice how I broke the ice with some light-hearted banter? You can't go wrong with a ginger joke, I always say. I totally held back on the "F" word out of respect for your gran, God rest her soul. And I took all the gory details that Joan could throw at us like a true man, which is more than I can say for that Matthew bloke. What a wuss. I bet his wife isn't half giving him an earful.'

'I know him, actually,' said Katy.

'What, the big girl's blouse?'

'Yeah, we used to go to school together. Small world, eh?' Katy had spent the entire class fighting the urge to get up and walk out. She had, however, worked out that it would be best to admit she knew who Matthew was in case they ever met again.

'So was he this pathetic at school then?' asked Ben.

'Can't remember really.' She hoped he wouldn't detect the quiver in her voice. 'Anyway, I was thinking, Ben,' she said, trying to sound casual. 'I'm not sure we should go to the rest of the classes. I learnt the main bits I wanted to tonight. Let's just read the books, I'm sure we'll be fine.'

'You what? Are you for real?' said Ben, aghast. 'I have suffered all week in the staffroom from Bob and Dennis taking the piss, telling me there is no way I would be

75

able to cope with all the details of the blood and gore. If I go back now and say we're not going again after one class they'll rip me to shreds.'

'Just tell them it's me who doesn't want to go,' she said desperately.

'Yeah, right, like they'll believe that. Anyway, I have to go to the next class. I never thought I'd say this, Katy, but thank you for making me do this,' said Ben earnestly. 'The future of the Leeds North under-nineteen football team now depends on me attending that meeting and convincing Luke to come back and be our striker.'

Chapter 7

At the time, Katy thought sleeping with Matthew had been a positive turning point in her life. Knowing that he wanted her and she could walk away had gone a long way to erasing the years of rejection and hurt that had built up inside her.

Having said that, it hadn't been easy. She had enjoyed basking in the warm glow of shared memories. She could have been tempted to indulge herself totally in a rose-tinted view of times gone by, had it not been for the shadow falling over her whenever she remembered Matthew's misdemeanour and the future he had cruelly shattered. The future they had spent hours talking about the night before they left for college. The one with the barn conversion and the dogs and the kids. She hadn't forgotten one detail of what they had planned, or one moment of the weeks and months she had spent grieving for it. Eventually, when she could cry no more, Katy had decided that she was never going to go through that again, vowing that she would rely on herself for happiness, not a man.

When she had said goodbye the morning after the reunion, telling him to have a good life, the look on his face was all she needed to know that finally, after all this time, she was totally over it. Crestfallen and bewildered, he clearly had not expected her to be the one to call time on this brief reunion.

Ben had returned that day from his stag do visibly surprised at the renewed spring in Katy's step and her desire to bed him immediately. He protested mildly, saying he stank of lager, but she had been on a mission, keen to banish her sexual expedition with Matthew to the back room of her memory and replace it with some high jinks with Ben.

Everything had settled down again until the day Katy discovered she was pregnant.

'How the hell did that happen?' were Ben's first words

when she finally told him she was pregnant, having decided to ignore the slim possibility that it could be Matthew's.

'I think it must have been when I had a couple of really bad hangovers from entertaining clients over Christmas and I threw up. I guess it must have stopped the pill working.'

She looked at him nervously, waiting for his reaction. In the end she had to wait for it to evolve over time. He did stunned, he did aghast, he did upset, then he phoned his mum, and following an earful from her, he settled on an ongoing state of resigned and detached, with the occasional whiff of secretly excited. As for Katy, having overcome the traumatic task of telling Ben and pushing Matthew's possible input firmly to the back of her mind, she chose to treat the pregnancy as a non-event. There was no way that she would become a baby-obsessed android like every other woman she knew who got pregnant. She was determined that her personality – and Ben's – would remain intact, and it would not change their relationship. Life was to carry on as normal.

Normal, however, was not the word that sprang to mind when she arrived at work the day after the antenatal class. A second possible father turning up in week thirty-five was certainly not covered in the pregnancy guide given to her by the midwife. Nor was there any advice on how to avoid your own baby shower, which, to her utter dismay, was scheduled for that day. She knew she had zero chance of getting out of it, since everyone in her office had been surprisingly excited at the prospect of throwing her a celebration to mark the impending arrival.

'Well, a baby shower is the new wedding, darling,' declared Daniel when she had expressed amazement at the elaborate invitations he had designed.

'But it's just a bunch of people from work going for a drink and a few nibbles, isn't it?' asked Katy.

'You are being foolish in the extreme, Katy, if you think that I, Creative Director extraordinaire of this fine establishment, would pass up the chance to vent my huge creative talent on something as cheesy and far removed from the life of a gay man as a baby shower.'

'Ah, I get it now, you're feeling just a little bit left out of all this procreation stuff and so you're going to do your damnedest to gayify it. Loving the fact that I am actually giving birth to Judy Garland on the front of the invite, by the way.'

'Don't mention it. I considered Kylie, of course, but

there was no way a woman of such petite proportions was coming from your genes.'

'You are so right, Kylie would have been preposterous,' she had said at the time, not knowing that giving birth to Kylie would have been infinitely preferable to her current situation.

She heaved a huge sigh as she gathered up her bag and headed out through the door of the agency, painting a fake bright smile on her face to create the illusion of a woman in control.

The smile was knocked right off her face the minute she walked into the restaurant on the fourth floor of Harvey Nichols and saw herself in at least six-foot-high splendour, hanging from the ceiling. Actually it was a pretty stunning picture of her if you could get past the fact that her face had been superimposed onto the body of Demi Moore in the famous fully pregnant, fully nude shot that had graced the cover of *Vanity Fair* in the Nineties. Daniel was standing beneath it with an extremely satisfied grin on his face. He rushed over as soon as he saw her.

'You do love it, don't you, Katy? You have never looked better,' he gasped.

'Fantastic. So you're telling me that I am at my best with my head attached to someone else's pregnant body?' she asked in amazement.

'But look at your face. Colin in repro worked on it for hours. It took the whole of Tuesday night just to sort out your complexion. But the result is spectacular. Just see what you could look like if you took facials seriously and spent some real money on beauty products.'

'Daniel, you are a true friend. Remind me to call you any time I need convincing that suicide is the only option.' Normally her banter with Daniel gave Katy huge enjoyment, but not today. She smoothed down her designer maternity dress, bought to show her young colleagues that being pregnant did not mean she had lost her cool. To her horror, however, she could feel the tears welling up as she headed towards the table, which had been tastefully festooned with pure white marabou feathers surrounding a bobbing sea of tiny white storks on the ends of pieces of wire.

'Very nice,' she managed, as she approached the expectant faces awaiting her arrival.

'Me and Lenny did the table,' said Kim, one of the junior art directors. 'We had to fight with Daniel, though, to stop him going off on one over a drugs theme. He wanted to dangle epidural syringes from the ceiling, filled with pink and blue liquid, and then for the entertainment to get hold of a canister of gas and air for us all to have a go. Fortunately the restaurant manager put his foot down and said they weren't insured for customers to bring their own gas onto the premises.'

'Wow, lucky escape.' Katy sat down, painfully aware that she was the centre of attention just when she wanted to crawl into a hole and disappear. There was an awkward silence for a moment as she found herself at a complete loss, until her boss, the consummate professional, broke the ice to get the celebration going.

'So, Katy, tell us all about the nursery. What theme have you gone with?' he asked.

'Oh, the room was painted white anyway, so we've just left it like that.'

'Lovely, no need to go overboard, eh?' he said sympathetically. 'Can't stand those mega-themed nurseries, anyway, when absolutely everything has to be bloody Winnie the Pooh. Who needs a stupid fat bear peering at you from every nook and cranny when you've only just arrived in the world?'

'But my little Alfie loves Winnie,' said Jane the

receptionist. 'Honestly, Katy, he does. I can go with you to Mothercare if you like. You can get everything to match, it's fantastic.'

'Erm, if I get time,' said Katy, looking at her boss desperately.

'Right, why don't we get on with the formalities and then I can relax and have a drink,' he said.

He stood up and tapped a spoon lightly on the side of his glass to get everyone's attention. Christ, thought Katy. This really was turning into a wedding.

'Well, ladies and gentlemen, I have to say it's something of a surprise to be standing here today to toast Katy on her imminent launch into parenthood. I have known her for some time now, and I'm finding it pretty hard to dispel the images I have of her when she has behaved, shall we say, not exactly maternally.'

A knowing titter floated around the table.

'Sadly, I fear we will never again enjoy the sight of Katy giving a lap dancer a piece of her mind for trying to overcharge one of our clients on a night out to celebrate the success of their ad campaign. I believe your words were, "If you think you can charge a hundred quid to shake your arse in that man's face, then I think you'll find me charging double to wave two fingers in yours."

That's what I love about Katy. She always has one eye on her expense claims.'

Everyone laughed whilst Katy smiled through gritted teeth.

'Also the memory of her insisting on adjusting the position of a male model's penis for an underwear shoot, as she knew exactly how the client would want it, will probably have to be confined to the past, for fear of embarrassing her offspring.'

'She wouldn't let me get anywhere near his cock, the selfish cow,' muttered Daniel. 'If there's anyone who should know how to make a penis look perfect, it's me, surely?'

'This all goes to show how well Katy adapts to any position she is put in. I know, despite the fact that she has openly resisted any possibility of domestic bliss in the past, she will adjust just as she always does and be a very successful mother indeed.' He turned to address her directly. 'I mean that, I really do,' he said sincerely, putting his hand on her shoulder.

Katy sat paralysed. A successful mother? He wouldn't be saying that if he knew her current state of affairs.

'Now Daniel has organised an extra-special present, which he has kept a big secret, so it is with great excitement that I hand you over to him,' her boss concluded.

It was only then that Katy noticed something on the table next to them, a white cloth covering something quite lumpy and about two feet high. Daniel was hovering next to it looking surprisingly uncomfortable.

What the hell had he done this time? She really must remember to tell him she never wanted to see him again.

'Well, Katy, I'd just like you to remember that a lot of work has gone into this, so you'd better like it,' said Daniel.

He pulled the white cloth away with a flourish to reveal a pregnant torso topped by a pair of ample breasts, all made from some sort of plaster cast and mounted on a dark wooden plinth.

'I recognise those tits,' chirped Martin, one of the account directors.

'Why?' gasped Katy, her mouth wide open, her head shaking gently in utter amazement at Daniel.

'Remember I asked if I could do some shots of your belly to help with the art direction for that maternity wear catalogue?'

'Yeah.'

'Well, I lied,' he said, giggling hysterically. 'I just

wanted a good picture of you so I could get this done. Come on, Katy, you didn't really expect me to get you anything useful for the baby, did you? The overzealous use of primary colours just brings me out in a rash.'

'But to have to encounter the public display of my naked body, not once but twice, is harsh, Daniel, way harsh,' said Katy.

'Once,' corrected Daniel. 'The other one is Demi Moore, who obviously doesn't have the same stupid hang-up as you do about celebrating the gloriousness of the pregnant body.'

'Daniel, I weigh an obscene amount more than I usually do, I have stretch marks a mile long and I haven't seen my pubic hair in months. Please tell me what is glorious about that?'

'Alright, alright. Never fear, Louise is on her way with the boring presents. Don't blame me when you have to pretend to look excited about a poo bucket or something.'

At that moment Louise staggered into the room laden with gifts. She was Katy's personal assistant and resident mother hen. Her desk was full of photos of her kids and she never shut up about their latest escapades. Louise had been overjoyed when Katy told her she was expecting and was full of helpful advice on every aspect of pregnancy and motherhood, quite often knocking on her office door to share some little nugget that happened to cross her mind. Katy had begged for her to be moved to another role but her boss had refused; he was enjoying watching Katy cringe at Louise's daily account of her three labours.

'Sorry I'm late. Your bloody phone never stopped ringing.' Louise glared at Katy, like it was her fault she had been inconvenienced by having to do her job.

'Anything urgent?' asked Katy.

'Don't think so. Mostly clients, so I said you'd call them back after your baby shower, which seemed to shut them up. Oh, and some guy called Matthew something or other. Said he was an old friend and he was trying to catch up with you. I've sent his number to your BlackBerry.'

The sound of Matthew's name caused Katy to jump and she dropped a fork noisily on the floor. This gave her valuable moments to compose herself as with some effort she bent her protesting body to pick it up.

'OK, er, I think I know who that could be,' she said, sitting upright again and trying to ignore the heat rising to her cheeks.

Daniel was staring at her in shock. He was the only person she had told the Matthew story to, since her friends, whom she rarely saw, would no doubt recoil in a horrified *Stepford Wives* fashion if she told them she had screwed up something as basic as knowing who the father of her child was. Daniel, on the other hand, had applauded her spontaneity. However, confusion over who might be the father of her child had rendered him speechless. In fact he had walked away and not spoken to her again until some hours later, after he had obviously given it some deep thought. He came up to her office, shut the door behind him and told her that, after some consideration, he thought her only option was to forget Matthew. Bury him deep in a place in her mind she rarely visited and focus on being the best mum she could and help Ben to be the 'Dad of the Century'. Then he got up and left the room with Katy having said nothing. It was the only time she could remember Daniel being one hundred percent serious, and it had scared her.

'What can I get you to drink, Louise?' asked Daniel, still staring at Katy.

'White wine and lemonade please,' replied Louise.

Visibly shuddering at the prospect of having to ask

the cute barman for such a concoction, Daniel took Katy by the arm. 'Come to the bar with me.'

'What the hell,' he spluttered as soon as they were out of earshot. 'Is that the Matthew I think it is? I thought he had been confined to the back and beyond of your life?'

'I haven't had a chance to tell you yet. He turned up at my antenatal class last night. He's moved back up here,' she hissed back.

'What the hell was he doing at your antenatal class?'

'His wife is pregnant, stupid. Why else would he be there?' she said hysterically.

'You have got to be kidding me,' said Daniel, stopping in his tracks. 'You mean, he's having a baby with his wife and he could also be having a baby with you at the same time?'

'We don't know if my baby is his. I only slept with him once. We've been over this, remember?'

'I know, I know. But now that he's back in your life, that's different, isn't it? What are you going to do?'

'Well,' she said, trying to calm down. 'This can't change anything, can it? You were right the first time. I still have to ignore what happened. Even more so now his wife is pregnant. I have to assume it's not his.'

'But he's already called you,' said Daniel. 'He could be enquiring whether you have a good recommendation for babysitters of course, but I doubt it somehow. Do you think he suspects anything?'

'Well, we all had to say when our babies were due . . .'

'Oh, that is just too weird,' interrupted Daniel. 'Imagine being in a room and knowing when the last time everyone had sex was,' he mused.

'Why would it be the last time?' asked Katy.

'Oh, come on, you heteros only ever have sex over the age of thirty to procreate. The reason why pregnant women look so serene is because they have been relieved of their carnal duties. So what did Matthew do when you gave your date?'

'He went white and walked out and he didn't come back.'

'He suspects it could be his then, definitely?' Daniel pressed.

'I guess so.'

'So?' he asked.

'So what?'

'What the hell are you going to do?'

'I have no idea,' said Katy, starting to panic again. She looked around the room desperately, hoping the answer might leap out at her, only to catch sight of her two naked bodies on public display.

'This is not how it's supposed to be happening,' she said angrily.

'Hey girl, no need to take it out on me,' said Daniel. 'Let's all just keep calm, shall we? You're absolutely right. This doesn't change a thing. The plan remains, especially now you know that his wife is pregnant. Matthew is history; Ben is the father, get on with it. You just need to tell Matthew that. Then everything will be fine. You'll see.'

Chapter 8

Katy dropped a pound coin in the hat of a homeless guy begging outside the pub. For luck, she thought, in the absence of a wishing well. She pushed open the door and immediately knew there was no way she would be seen here by anybody she knew. With relief, she took in the torn gaudy wallpaper which perfectly complemented the mismatched furniture. Dirty mustard-yellow foam oozed from every padded seat onto the slimy grey carpet, battered by years of abuse. A couple of slot machines tinkled merrily in the corner, providing the only hint of cheer in the depressingly awful room. It was empty, apart from three people sitting at the bar who looked like they'd been there since lunchtime, possibly the previous day's lunchtime at that. They were slumped forward, talking in a series of high- and low-pitched noises rather than words, but seeming to understand each other nonetheless.

The only other inhabitant was a very fat old lady, dressed in a long, dirty blue raincoat and a clear plastic headscarf, sitting in the corner nursing a pint. She shouted over to Katy as she stepped gingerly over the threshold.

'He's over there, love. Made a friend already, he has,' said the woman.

Katy looked over to where she was pointing to see Matthew, looking as out of place as she must. He was dressed in a smart navy suit and tie and had a very large German shepherd dog lying across his feet.

'Is that the latest accessory you people from London wear to keep your feet warm?' she couldn't help but enquire as she sat down.

'The bloody thing won't move and I daren't kick it or it might bite me. Worse still, its owner might,' said Matthew, looking nervously across to the woman, who gave him a big, toothless grin.

'Well, I think you can safely say his bark is going to be worse than her bite,' she quipped.

Christ, where did that come from? she thought. Suddenly I'm a comedian just as I'm about to have the conversation from hell.

'Very funny,' said Matthew. 'I assumed you wouldn't be drinking, so I got a mineral water rather than a rum and Coke. But I'll get you something else if you'd prefer?'

Katy was immediately thrown. She hadn't drunk rum and Coke in years. In fact, she'd forgotten she ever used to drink such a foul concoction. Matthew clearly hadn't.

'Water's fine,' she said, taking a sip. 'So how are you?' she asked, not quite ready to enter hazardous territory yet.

'Oh, you know. Fine, considering. You?' replied Matthew.

'Yeah, OK, I guess, considering. You?'

'You already asked me.' He looked at her through eyes loaded with a thousand questions. He closed them abruptly before opening them again and shaking his head as if in disbelief at what he was about to say.

'Could it be mine?'

She was shocked. She hadn't expected the question to come so directly and so quickly. She had imagined plenty of preamble, with them hovering around the real issue for a while, allowing her time to work out how to conclude the meeting. With the absence of time to craft her words, her response was blunt.

'Yes,' she said.

He slumped back in his chair. It was out there now. No going back. Solid earth had been ripped from under them in a moment, to be replaced by something so shaky, unknown and uncharted that there was no way of knowing even how to begin to take any steps forward.

They sat there for a long time in silence, both lost in their own internal battle of what to say and do next. Eventually the German shepherd stirred, looked up at them both and, assuming they needed some time alone, got up and ambled slowly back to his owner.

It was Matthew who was finally able to make the first step into their new world.

'When you say yes, do you mean definitely yes? What about the guy at the class?'

'That's Ben, the guy I told you about at the reunion. It could also be his. I just don't know, Matthew.'

'What have you told him?'

'Nothing. As far as he is concerned, it's his. Look, Matthew, I found out I was pregnant, did the maths and worked out there was a chance that it could be yours, but surely the fact of the matter is that it's much more likely to be Ben's,' Katy babbled. 'We only spent one night together, for goodness' sake. I was trying to forget what happened between us. Why worry about something that might not be true? I convinced myself that Ben was one hundred percent the father and that was that.'

'And what do you think now?' asked Matthew.

'It's easier to forget something when you don't have any reminders. You turning up here means the tiny little doubt I had won't shut up.'

Matthew leant forward and put his head in his hands, covering his eyes. After a moment, to Katy's horror, he started to shake. When he finally lifted his head, she realised he was laughing.

'I have absolutely no idea what you find funny about this,' she snapped.

'The fucking irony, Katy. I have been to hell and back for the past five years, trying to get pregnant with my wife. Her lack of fertility turned her into a miserable cow, quite frankly, which is probably why I ended up in bed with you. But, oh joy of joys, finally it works. She's pregnant and almost the woman I married again. My life is back on track, then you drop the bombshell that after one, just one, night of sex, I could have hit the fucking jackpot and fathered another child. I guess all my Christmases must have come at once.' He slumped back in his chair, looking utterly defeated now.

'This is no Christmas for me either, you know. I didn't plan to get pregnant and not know who the father was.'

'So what were you doing then? How come you are pregnant? I admit, I'm mortified that I wasn't smart enough to use contraception, but I figured a woman of your years and experience would have it sorted or have the maturity to ask me to use a condom.'

'What on earth is that supposed to mean?' asked Katy angrily.

'That you cannot have been a stranger to that kind of situation, and there are no little Katys running around, so I guess you have previously been successful in avoiding pregnancy.'

'You make me sound like some sort of slapper,' said Katy, raising her voice. She hadn't come here to be insulted. 'I don't just sleep with anyone, you know. I only slept with you as some sort of revenge for what you did to me all those years ago. Do you think I would have looked at you twice otherwise? You're not exactly lighting anyone's fire any more, are you, Mr Boring Finance Boy? And yes, I did have it sorted. I was on the pill, but

I'd been ill and that must have stopped it working. It happens, Matthew.'

'I'm not boring,' retorted Matthew, almost shouting. 'We can't all pretend we're still seventeen, you know, working in that grown-up playground they call advertising. Some of us decide to get married, settle down and make something of ourselves, get a serious job with a future.'

'Is that what you think? That I've never grown up? It's a damn sight more mature to do a job you love rather than the dull crap you must do all day.'

'That's bollocks, Katy,' said Matthew, banging the table with his fist.

Suddenly they were aware that they weren't alone. The barman was standing right in front of them and the lady in the raincoat was peering from behind his back.

'Look, can you just keep it down. You're upsetting me regulars, who've just come in for a quiet drink,' said the barman.

'That's right. You're making my dog jumpy an' all,' said the woman.

They looked over to the bar, where the three men were slumped, virtually asleep.

'OK, mate,' said Matthew quietly.

'And that baby in there in't gonna grow up contented like, if its mum and dad are arguing like cat and dog,' added the woman for good measure.

'We're fine,' said Matthew quickly. 'Thanks.'

The barman and the old lady shuffled away, satisfied they had sorted out the posh couple.

'Great, even a daft old bat thinks the baby is mine,' said Matthew.

'Look, Matthew, this is pointless. You are off the hook, just walk away,' said Katy, deciding to put a swift end to this unpleasant encounter. She got up from her seat and found herself stroking her belly protectively as she looked down at Matthew.

'There is a slim chance, a very slim chance, this baby could be yours, but doing anything about it will only lead to heartache. You have a wife expecting twins. They need you. We have to make a pact to forget the thought of this small possibility and leave it at that. There is no other way. Now, I need a pee and by the time I come out I expect you to be gone.' She turned and strode to the toilet without a backward glance. The whole situation had given her a headache and she wanted the thinking and the talking to be over. 'Enough,' she murmured as she opened the door to the ladies' toilet.

Matthew watched her walk away and couldn't help hoping that she would at least turn around. She didn't.

'It was good to see you,' Matthew found himself saying as he gathered up his coat and walked out of the door.

Chapter 9

'The primary school down the road has an excellent Ofsted report, so we're hoping that the head is still there by the time the twins are ready for school. Unfortunately the secondary school we are in the catchment area for is pretty poor, so we think we'll have to move before they get to eleven, but that gives us plenty of time to check out which are the best schools in the area, and where we really want to live.'

Katy was staring at Alison open-mouthed. She was yet to buy a single nappy, never mind give any thought to schooling. She was actually still in shock that she was sitting there having a normal, well, normal-ish, conversation with Alison.

After her clandestine meeting with Matthew, Katy had called Daniel with the news. The deed was done. It was over. Daniel, of course, with his eager beaver nose for searching out the flaws in anything Katy did, asked immediately what they were going to do about the baby training class thing that they were both attending.

'Well, I'm sure that Matthew and Alison won't turn up again. There's no way Matthew will risk it. He'll just make some excuse.'

'Mmmmm, OK, if you say so,' replied Daniel.

'Don't say it like that. Look, he has too much to lose. You really think he's going to let his wife get within one hundred yards of me again? He got away with it last time. Letting it happen again would just be plain stupid.'

'Really stupid,' Katy murmured to herself as she glared at Matthew across the classroom. He didn't look like he was concentrating on the group discussion with the other birthing partners about support options during labour. She kept catching him glancing nervously over to her and Alison. The women were supposed to be discussing pain relief, but somehow the conversation had wound around to what Alison thought her kids might be doing in eleven years' time.

'Another idea for you to consider is a Happy Box,' cut in Joan, trying to steer the conversation back on track. 'A Happy Box is a collection of things that make you happy or smile or relax. Like maybe a favourite photograph or soft toy, or maybe even a poem. My husband read a whole poetry book to me when I gave birth to our fourth, and it was by far my best birth. Can any of you think of something that could help you in the same way? What about you, Katy, what relaxes you?'

'Erm, well, I don't get much time to relax really,' faltered Katy.

'Come on, there must be something. What about when you're really stressed after a tough day at the office? What's the first thing you do when you get home to unwind?' Joan pressed.

She wanted to say it was to pour an enormous glass of wine but didn't think that would go down too well. There was one thing she did resort to if she'd had an absolutely terrible day, but the mere thought of it made her flush with embarrassment.

'Come on, Katy, you can tell us, whatever it is,' said Joan gently, placing a reassuring hand over hers.

She looked up and saw that everyone was staring at her expectantly. 'I put my Hue and Cry tape on,' she said quickly, then looked around the group for approval of her occasional dalliance with cheesy Eighties music. 'I know it sounds stupid, but "Looking for Linda" just cheers me up for some reason.' She went bright red with embarrassment while everyone gave her blank looks.

'Who are you talking about?' Charlene asked finally. 'I've never heard of them.'

'They were a band in the Eighties,' Katy replied miserably, knowing that somehow she had really let herself down.

'Oh, I see. That was before I was born,' said Charlene proudly. 'I didn't think you were that old. I told Luke that I thought Ben was a lot younger than you, but he reckoned that Ben just looks young for his age, what with all that sport he does and everything.'

Katy was stunned. Her pregnancy-fuddled brain couldn't work fast enough to compute the amount of potential insults there were in what Charlene had just said.

'So I said to Luke, there's about ten years between them. Am I right?' asked Charlene, as if she was asking something as innocent as directions to the corner shop.

Katy still couldn't speak.

'My cousin Amy goes to Ben's school, you know,' continued Charlene, oblivious to Katy's distress. 'She says all the girls think he's dead fit. I told her that I'd met his girlfriend and she told all her mates, and they reckon they're all gonna come and scratch your eyes out. But I wouldn't worry, they're always saying stupid stuff like that at that school 'cause they're all thick.'

'Which school did you say Ben teaches at?' asked Alison, turning to Katy.

'Castle Hill Comp,' replied Katy in a trance.

'I must remember that,' said Alison.

'Well, ladies,' said Joan cheerfully. 'That's just splendid. I'll leave you to think of some other things to go in your Happy Box whilst I go and check on the men.'

'So, guys, how are we getting on here then?' asked Joan.

'Well, I reckon if in doubt, offer a banana. Can't go wrong with a banana,' said Ben, wielding the one he had picked out of the prop bag of possible things to offer your partner during labour.

'You could be right, but Katy might get sick of bananas after ten hours of labour, so you might need some other options up your sleeve to keep her calm,' said Joan. 'So who would like to take me through which item you have put next to which picture of the stages of labour?'

Matthew, Ben and Richard looked at each other furtively. Luke stared into space, as he had done for the entire session.

'OK, I'll do it,' said Matthew finally.

'Take it steady, mate,' said Ben, winking at Luke. 'We don't want you coming over all peculiar again like you did last week. There are some pretty graphic pictures here.'

'I told you, it was something I ate. I was awake all night throwing up,' said Matthew, whose top lip had broken into a sweat.

'Yeah, whatever. Come on then, fire away. There's a truly glorious pint awaiting my presence somewhere,' replied Ben, looking at his watch.

Matthew scowled at Ben, then presented Joan with his most charming smile.

'So, Joan, we thought that in the early stages of labour, whilst you are still at home, maybe the best thing would be . . .'

'A banana,' cut in Ben. 'The perfect snack. Full of energy and nutritious. Athletes swear by them, you know.'

'Actually, Ben, we decided either a bath or a favourite DVD to distract them would be good,' said Matthew through gritted teeth.

'But Katy's favourite DVD is *The Sound of* bloody *Music*. Do you really think I want my child entering the world to the sound of a load of nuns yodelling?'

'It was a goatherd,' said Richard.

'What was?' asked Ben.

'It was a lonely goatherd that yodelled in *The Sound of Music*, not the nuns.'

'Well hallelujah, that's all right then. As long as the nuns aren't yodelling, I'm absolutely fine that my son will enter the world to the sound of the gayest musical of all time,' said Ben.

'Is it a boy?' came out of Matthew's mouth before he could stop it. Katy hadn't said anything about knowing what sex the baby was.

'No idea. But if it is, he needs the right influences from day one. I'm thinking highlights of Euro '96. Shearer, Gascoigne, Seaman, beating Holland 4–1, Pearce getting that penalty, you just don't get any better than that.'

'But Katy doesn't even like football,' said Matthew. 'I mean, I'm sure she doesn't, what with her being a woman and everything. No woman really likes football,' he added quickly when Ben gave him a slightly confused look.

'Right, come on, boys, we're running out of time. A

bath or a DVD, whatever the DVD, are both good ideas. Now carry on, Matthew, please,' said Joan.

'Well, next we thought it might be a good idea to ring a friend or their mother. Someone who has been through labour and can reassure them that whatever they're feeling is normal,' Matthew ploughed on.

'Look, I'm sorry to interrupt again, but believe me, if you knew Katy's mum you wouldn't be calling her to alleviate any kind of pain. She refuses to accept that Katy is pregnant and thinks I've ruined her life. I can practically hear her nostrils flaring whenever I talk to her on the phone,' said Ben.

'She was always very friendly to me,' said Matthew.

'You've met Katy's mum?' asked Ben, confused.

'Well, er, me and Katy were in the same form at school, you know,' Matthew mumbled. 'So it must have been at sports day or speech day or something. Dove Valley was very big on parent participation.'

'Sod that. These days, the less we see of them the better,' said Ben. 'Dennis, who does careers counselling at my school, got headbutted the other week by some lad's dad. This lad said that when he left school he wanted to set up a business importing Thai women to marry British men. Dennis didn't know what to say, so he asked the lad if he thought it was ethical to treat women in such a way and commit them to a terrible life, being at the beck and call of sad old men. Turns out this lad's dad was a sad old man who'd been married to a Thai bride for eighteen months. A few hours later he marches in and just headbutts him. You want danger money to be a teacher nowadays, I tell you.'

'Which school do you work at again?' asked Matthew.

'Castle Hill Comp,' replied Ben.

'I must remember that,' said Matthew.

At the end of the class Joan gave her rallying speech.

'So, people, hopefully you've now had a chance to think about what's going to happen during labour and how you'll make the most of this glorious experience, as you prepare to welcome your new baby into the world. Remember, millions of people have gone through this before, but your birth will be totally unique and should be treasured and cherished as one of the most important experiences of your life. Think about it like that, and not as something to be blocked out at all costs by artificial means. You ladies are blessed, truly blessed, to have a body that has performed the miracle of conceiving a child – don't doubt your body now. Don't think that it can't complete this phenomenon. You can do it on your own if you really want to; I have absolute faith in all of you. Now, any last questions before we leave?'

'So if the first epidural doesn't block out all the pain, will they give me another one?' asked Charlene.

Joan stared at Charlene for a few seconds before saying, with a sigh, 'They will give you whatever you and the doctor think is necessary and good for you and the baby. OK, guys, that's enough for today. Can you just stack the chairs on your way out, and we'll see you next week.'

'I so want to have a natural birth, but I'm scared that I won't be able to, then I'll feel like I've really let these two down,' said Alison to Katy, almost in tears as they shuffled towards the door.

Katy looked at her for the first time as just another woman, petrified at the thought of giving birth, rather than as Matthew's wife who needed to be avoided at all costs.

'You'll be OK. It's twins, after all. You'll be a hero however they come out,' Katy found herself saying.

'Do you think so? You sound just like my friend Karen. She's always telling me not to be so stupid whilst being really nice at the same time,' said Alison.

'I guess you must be missing your friends at the moment,' Katy said, before realising that she was entering into conversation with the one who should not be spoken to.

'Desperately,' said Alison as a tear slid down her left cheek. 'I thought moving up here was going to be perfect. I've planned it so carefully, because you have to, don't you, when you have a family to think about. But it's hard without friends and family around you. And Matthew works really long hours now he's a partner, so I spend a lot of time on my own.' Another tear leaked out.

'Please don't cry,' said Katy, panicking for the second time that evening. 'You've only just moved. You'll make new friends once the babies have arrived, that's what everyone says always happens.' She was starting to feel desperate as more tears welled up and spilled down Alison's cheeks.

'You're right, I know you're right,' said Alison. 'Sorry to be such a cry baby. Look, I know I don't know you, but Matthew told me that he remembered you went to school together, so you know him, though not very well, he said. Why don't you and Ben come round for dinner this weekend? I think I'll scream if I don't talk to someone other than Matthew and the midwife.'

The invitation hung in the air as Katy stared at Alison in horror. How had this happened? How was she standing here being invited to dinner by the wife of the man who might have made her pregnant?

It was then that she saw something move very fast in the corner of her eye as someone or something came hurtling towards them. She turned and saw that it was actually Matthew, who appeared to be going for the record in sprinting across a hospital room.

He arrived at where Alison and Katy were standing, narrowly avoiding the embarrassment of stopping via a skid.

'What's wrong? Why are you crying?' asked Matthew, just a little bit out of breath.

'Oh, it's just me being silly, darling,' said Alison. 'I was just telling Katy that she reminds me of Karen, and then I started missing her and I just couldn't help it. Stupid, I know. Anyway, tell Katy that she and Ben must come to dinner on Saturday to stop me going out of my mind with boredom. You can reminisce about old times, and Katy can tell me all your secrets about what you were really like at school. I bet he was good-looking, wasn't he?'

'Well, they must already have plans,' said Matthew,

blind panic written on his face. 'You can't just expect them to drop everything to entertain us.'

'No – no plans,' came a voice from behind them. 'We'd love to come. You can show me that signed cup programme you were bragging about earlier,' said Ben.

'Perfect, that's settled then,' said Alison, getting a pre-printed address card out of her bag and handing it to Katy. 'We'll see you at seven-thirty.'

And with that she whisked off down the corridor, dragging Matthew behind her, leakage miraculously cured and a pleased smile on her face.

Chapter 10

'We'll have to get a move on, Rick and Braindead will be waiting,' said Ben as soon as they were outside.

'What?' asked Katy, her mind reeling after the turn of events in the last five minutes.

'Don't you remember? We're going for a beer with them so we can organise Rick's stag do,' said Ben.

'Oh God, I'd completely forgotten. Don't you want to go on your own? You don't need me there, do you?'

'Of course we do. If you're not there we'll never get it sorted. We got pissed last time and couldn't remember a thing we decided,' said Ben. 'Besides, we said we were going to the Red Lion in Otley. The guys are really looking forward to it.'

'I bet they are,' said Katy with a sigh. Her determination not to let the pregnancy affect their social life had been fully welcomed by Ben and his mates, who suddenly found themselves with a free taxi service. To her dismay, however, lately she had found herself longing to be tucked up in bed by nine o'clock, rather than having a night with the boys, even if it was usually highly entertaining.

'Let's go then,' she said, fumbling for her keys.

'You're a star,' said Ben. 'After the baby arrives I'll drive you all the time, I promise. Braindead's even offered his babysitting services to us. He says he loves kids, apparently.'

'Ben, I like Braindead, you know I do, but I doubt he even knows where babies come from, never mind being able to look after one.'

'Are you implying that my very good friend Braindead is a virgin?' asked Ben. 'April 3rd 2001, Nicola Sherwin at precisely 11.56 p.m. in a bus shelter in Headingley.'

'How did he know it was 11.56 p.m.?' Katy barely dared ask.

'Because the bus stop had one of those electronic sign

thingies,' Ben explained. 'He said as he was givin' it some when he saw the sign flash up that his bus would be arriving at 11.57 p.m. He didn't want to miss it, so he put his foot down and just managed it with one minute to spare. Don't think Nicola was impressed though. He got on the bus and just left her standing there. Braindead idiot.'

They reached the car and Ben leant over and gave Katy a quick squeeze around her shoulders.

'Come on, love, a dose of insanity will do you good. You need to relax. This pregnancy malarkey is getting you all stressed out, I can tell.' He gave her a sympathetic smile.

You have no idea, she thought as she got into the car. Still, maybe he was right. Perhaps a night out with Ben and his mates would take her mind off what the hell she was going to do about Alison's invitation to dinner.

They picked the boys up outside Whitelocks pub in the city centre.

'Alright.'

'Alright.'

'Alright.'

'Katy, when God made you, he took a star out of the sky and gave it a heart,' declared Rick.

'Then he chopped the moon in half and gave her the most glorious tits,' muttered Braindead.

'I heard that,' said Katy. 'Are you both drunk already?'

'Soz, Katy,' said Braindead. 'But you do have glorious tits now you are pregnant and everything. I was just stating a fact,' he slurred slightly.

'So what about my tits before I was pregnant?' asked Katy indignantly.

'Well, I can't say they were in my top five or anything. They were more like your kind of average, everyday tits then. But yesterday I put you in my top five.'

'Yesterday? You mean you were thinking about my tits yesterday?'

'Er, yeah.'

'But I didn't see you yesterday.'

'So?'

'You mean, you think about my tits when I'm not there?'

'Well, I'm hardly likely to think about them when you *are* there, am I? That would be, like, a bit weird, wouldn't it?' said Braindead in genuine amazement.

'No. It's weird that you think about my tits at all.'

'Ah well, it was only fleeting, if that makes you feel any better. I was in the shop at the end of my road and Mrs Rashid served me as usual. Now she has always been in my top five as sort of like a mystery guest. Mystery because she wears one of those Indian costume things, so I can't actually do a full assessment, but I liked the idea of having someone in my top five who could surprise me. Anyway, yesterday she looked somehow lacking in the appropriate potential, so I thought I'd be ruthless and ditch the mystery guest and put you in instead as a dead cert.'

'Dead cert for what?' asked Katy.

'Dead cert that you have glorious tits. Could never be sure with a mystery guest, you see,' replied Braindead.

Katy glanced over her shoulder at a contented-looking Braindead slumped across the back of her car, wearing his usual crumpled, just-got-out-of-bed look. She actually really liked the way Ben's mates only ever talked about stuff that really mattered in life, which somehow seemed to make the stuff that really, really mattered not matter quite so much.

'Well, Braindead, thank you so much for that little lesson on how not to treat your designated pregnant driver,' said Ben. 'Tell Katy you're very sorry and you promise to take her out of your top five, never think of her glorious tits again, and buy her copious amounts of J2O all night.'

'Right, I see what you mean,' agreed Braindead reluctantly. 'Offending the driver not good. Sorry, Katy. Your glorious tits are forever banished from my mind. But I am begging you, please don't make me ask for that luminous muck at a beer festival.'

'Beer festival! What beer festival? I thought we were going to that pub in Otley?' exclaimed Katy.

'We are, we are,' said Ben quickly. 'When Braindead says beer festival he doesn't mean beer festival, he means they've just got this special week with a few guest ales, that's all. Nothing major.'

OTLEY BEER FESTIVAL was written on the huge banner across the main street as they drove into the small market town.

'Well I never,' said Ben. 'They put a few extra beers on and they think they're hosting a blinking Oktoberfest. Look, Katy, I'm really sorry, I honestly thought it would be really low key. We don't have to stay long. Something to tell the little 'un, eh? First beer festival at the age of minus four weeks.'

'I suppose so, but you owe me big time,' said Katy, pulling into the pub car park.

'You got it. Come on, junior, let's go taste some ale,' said Ben, addressing Katy's bump.

When Katy crossed the threshold into the pub, however, her heart thudded to the floor. It was heaving with sweaty, overweight, middle-aged men mumbling and gurning over warm beer. There was the odd woman. Odd woman being the operative phrase. All the females present had long, shapeless hair, wore men's shirts and had a determinedly grim look on their faces that said there was no way their husbands were having a night out with the lads without them, even if they didn't enjoy it themselves.

The most upsetting thing about the chosen hostelry, however, was that there was nowhere for her to sit down and give some relief to her swollen ankles. Ben saw the look of panic cross Katy's face and seized his chance to get them all a coveted seat in the packed public house.

'Lady with a baby. Lady with a baby coming through,' he bellowed, to Katy's absolute mortification. She could feel the heat rise to her cheeks immediately as the stares of the drinking masses bored into her swollen belly.

'Would you mind if we took this table, gentlemen?'

Ben asked two solid Yorkshire men sitting in the perfect spot under a window. 'My girlfriend is due any day now and her back is killing her.'

'Of course, please, be our guest,' they replied, getting up hurriedly and scattering to the far side of the pub as if she might give birth there and then and they could get caught in the afterbirth.

'Katy, please take a seat,' he said, very pleased with himself.

Katy sat down and leant back, banging her head against something. She looked around sharply, only to come face to face with a beady-eyed stuffed puffin staring at her from the windowsill.

'What is this place?' she asked, staring around her and noticing for the first time that there was an entire collection of stuffed animals and birds lining the walls.

'Someone gave the landlord a six-foot stuffed iguana years ago and he's been collecting ever since. Cool, eh?' said Rick.

'Mmmm, maybe. Bit more of a minimalist myself,' replied Katy, thinking longingly of the clean, crisp cocktail bars she had frequented in her previous life.

'Nah, all that white and chrome everywhere, you could be drinking in a public toilet. Beer normally tastes like piss too,' chuckled Rick. Rick was undoubtedly the most image-conscious of the three, indulging heavily in the type of branded clothing that was popular on the football stands; however, he was still a northern lad at heart.

'We have to come here every so often to visit Braindead's bird,' added Ben.

'He's got a girlfriend?' exclaimed Katy. 'Where is she?' She scanned the pub for suitable candidates.

'Right behind you,' laughed Ben. 'Meet Gloria. The Puffin. Braindead took a shine to her years ago when she fell off the windowsill and landed head first right in his lap.'

'And he sat there, looked down and said . . .' continued Rick, struggling now to get the words out. 'He said, without even a pause, Katy, "Now that's my kind of bird."'

Ben and Rick collapsed, enjoying the story for what was probably the hundredth time. Katy couldn't help but join in with their infectious laughter. It was these moments with Ben and his old school buddies that she loved, when the banter and the stories were flying around in the way they only ever do between true friends. It almost made up for the fact that the time when she would have sat and had conversations like that with her old friends had somehow gone.

'I've bought Gloria some crisps,' announced Braindead, arriving back with the drinks. 'And for us, I thought we'd start with Black Gold all the way from Scotland. And for you, my darling Katy, not one, but two J2Os, to apologise again for my previous poor behaviour.'

'Thank you, Braindead, you are forgiven,' said Katy. 'What flavour crisps did you get?' she asked, suddenly realising she was famished.

'Prawn cocktail, of course. Gloria only eats fish,' replied Braindead.

'Of course,' smiled Katy, grabbing one of the bags before Braindead could commandeer it for his feathered friend.

They all sipped and crunched for a moment in silence.

'Aye well,' said Braindead eventually. 'I guess that makes up for losing my mystery guest and replacement in my top five.'

'So moving swiftly on,' said Ben, kicking Braindead under the table. 'Our spectacular lack of organisation leaves us with just two weeks to get Rick's send-off sorted. So first things first – how many are coming, Rick?'

'There's you two. Then I reckon four from work. Barry, Dave and Jacko from footie and Danny and Chris from college. So I make that twelve, including me,' stated Rick, counting them off on his fingers.

'Good. Now, home or away?' asked Ben.

'Well, I heard about this stripper boat in Prague you can hire for the afternoon. It's really efficient because you can get pissed with your own private bar and do the stripper thing all before you go out at night. What do you reckon?' asked Rick, looking eagerly between Ben and Braindead.

'Boats make me a bit queasy,' grumbled Braindead, clutching his stomach.

'I really think the combination of private bar and stripper should allow you to overcome any minor ailment,' said Rick impatiently.

'I know, but what if the stripper came on and I was really sick, just as she's doing the whole baby lotion over the breasts thing whilst gyrating on my knee. It doesn't bear thinking about,' said Braindead, shaking his head.

'Thanks, Braindead. There is no way that I can now picture a stripper on a boat without her being covered in your puke,' said Ben, leaning his elbows on the table and covering his eyes.

'Erm, can I say something?' Katy interrupted. 'I really don't want to spoil anything, but aren't you forgetting something, Ben?'

'What?' asked Ben, sitting up again, brow furrowed.

'The baby.'

'Yeah, what about it?'

'It's due less than two weeks after the stag do. Don't you think you should at least be in the country?' she said, hating herself for sounding like such a killjoy.

Ben suddenly looked his age, if not much, much younger. He pulled a face not unlike a small boy who had just had his toys taken from him for reasons he could not understand.

'She's right, you know,' Rick finally said when Ben didn't respond. 'You've responsibilities now, lad. It's coming to us all sooner or later. The minute that baby's born, that's it,' he continued, oblivious to Ben's growing distress. 'Footie? You can forget that for a start. Pub on the way home from work? No way, my friend. Poker night? Disbanded until further notice.'

Katy willed Ben to say something but he was just staring at Rick, pale-faced.

'Having a baby isn't going to do that to us,' she said firmly, reaching over for Ben's hand. She turned to Rick.

'I just don't want Ben to miss the birth, that's all. I'm not saying he's never going to be allowed out ever again.'

'Yeah, right,' said Rick. 'Have you met any parents of young kids? Too knackered to even think of having any fun. I tell you, there's no way me and Mel are having kids until we're at least thirty-five.'

Rick realised he had gone too far when Ben failed to produce a witty comeback. 'So anyway,' he said finally. 'Whatever happens, we're going to have a cracking night on my stag do. Tell you what, why don't we go to the home of this fair ale?' he said, raising his glass. 'Och aye the noo, Jimmy lad. Those wee Scotch lassies are in for a treat,' he said, in a Scottish accent with curious hints of Indian and possibly Welsh.

Ben appeared to emerge from his troubled thoughts and shot Rick a grateful smile.

'Great idea,' he said finally, his face relaxing back into the usual cheery Ben formation. 'Who wants to go abroad anyway? Weak lager and foreign language music. I can stop at home and watch the Eurovision Song Contest for that. I'll get on the internet tomorrow and get us a B&B somewhere.' He took a very long gulp of his pint, avoiding eye contact with Katy. Having drained his glass he slammed it down on the table. 'So we're all sorted,' he said. 'I'll go and get another round in, shall I?' He stood up and strode off to the bar, leaving Rick and Katy feeling rather awkward.

'Sorry, Katy,' said Rick as soon as Ben was out of earshot. 'Didn't mean to depress you both. I guess it's just that the minute anybody I know has a kid I never see them again. They stop coming out. I'm just going to miss you guys, that's all.'

Katy knew he was right. It was children that had all but extinguished most of her friendships.

'That won't happen to us,' she said, determined. 'We'll still come out, I promise.'

'You say that now,' said Rick, shaking his head.

Katy excused herself and got up to go to the toilet, unable to face Rick's slightly accusing glare and realising that two J2Os in quick succession wasn't a great idea, given the current state of her bladder. This was all her fault, she realised as she struggled to wedge herself into the narrow toilet cubicle. She was the one who'd got pregnant and was ruining it for everyone. She'd swooped in and called last orders for Ben and his mates just like her friends had done to her when they got married and had kids. She remembered how she had resented them, and there was no way she was going to do the same. This baby was not going to be a party pooper. No way.

She waddled back into the bar with renewed determination, to find Ben looking much more relaxed, chatting away to Rick and Braindead.

'That's pathetic,' said Braindead. 'We'll get much better stuff than that when we go away.'

'Rick was just telling us about Mel's hen do last weekend,' said Ben. 'Apparently all she came back with was three sets of men's underpants.'

'Underpants!' exclaimed Katy. 'That's so tame. In my hen-do days I was the queen of stealing the perfect memento. My proudest achievements included a palm tree, a male mannequin and the entire set of ingredients for a doner kebab stolen from three different kebab shops, including a full bottle of chilli sauce and a bowl of coleslaw.'

Rick and Braindead stared at Katy in silence.

'You did what?' said Rick eventually.

'I don't believe you,' said Braindead.

'Why not?' asked Katy.

'You're so . . . but you're so . . .' started Rick.

'So what?' asked Katy.

'I just can't imagine, looking at you now, you know,

in all your really smart career stuff, that you would do something so . . .' Rick paused, lost for words.

'Cool,' said Braindead.

'Thanks very much, guys. So I'm not cool then?' said Katy.

'No, that's not what I meant. I meant, so . . . so immature. You're just too sensible to do anything like that.'

Katy thought she might hit him there and then.

'Sensible?' she exclaimed. If ever there was a word that summed up her biggest fear at hitting her mid-thirties and the thought of becoming a mother, it was sensible.

'Me? Sensible?' she said again.

'Well,' said Rick, starting to look a little uncomfortable, 'since I've got to know you I've never known you do anything that silly. Maybe it was just what you were like when you were younger. Before we met you.'

Katy was so horrified she couldn't speak. So Rick thought that she must have got boring with age. She wasn't boring. She could still hold her own with the carefree and fun-loving twenty-something crowd. She wasn't past it yet. Even if she was pregnant.

She looked over at Ben for support. He'd obviously decided that he didn't want to get involved as he quickly stood up and kissed her on the forehead before announcing he was off to the gents.

Great, she thought, watching him walk away. Nice to hear some words of reassurance. So they all thought they had the sole rights on being wild and crazy just because they were male and under thirty, did they? She'd show them, she said to herself. She'd show them right now and wipe the smug, self-satisfied smiles off their faces. She looked around desperately for inspiration and caught sight of Gloria surveying the small pile of crisps that the 'oh so hilarious' Braindead had laid at her feet.

Perfect. She glanced over at Rick and Braindead, who were now debating which beer to try next.

'Watch and learn,' she muttered quietly to herself. She took a deep breath and leant forward, gripping the edge of the table really hard, enough to make her knuckles turn white. Then she let out a low groan. Rick and Braindead looked at her. She groaned again, but louder this time, causing drinkers at the neighbouring tables to turn and stare.

'I told you that J2O is dodgy stuff,' said Braindead. 'Do you need the bathroom?' he said slowly and loudly, as if she had gone deaf.

Katy groaned again, this time really loud, and clutched her belly.

'Fuck, fuck, fuck,' cried Rick, leaping up out of his chair and knocking it backwards on the floor. 'She's in fucking labour.'

'Aaaaaaaaaaaaah,' screamed Braindead as if he had seen a headless ghost. 'What the fuck do we do?' he said, grabbing his pint and downing it in one.

Katy groaned again, trying not to laugh. She grabbed Rick's arm, pulling him towards her.

'Not me, Katy,' he shrieked. 'Braindead's much better in a crisis.'

She managed to drape herself around his neck, pressing her mouth right up to his ear.

'Steal the bloody puffin,' she hissed. 'Whilst I'm distracting everyone.' She withdrew to leave a visibly shaken Rick looking nervously around. She groaned again, tugging wildly at his hand.

Finally the realisation of what was happening dawned on Rick and a smile started to emerge. He turned to a frozen Braindead.

'You get Katy to the car, we have towels and hot water there,' he shouted so the entire pub could hear. 'Can someone help them, please?' Those on the surrounding tables swarmed to surround Braindead and Katy, whilst Rick idly stuffed Gloria up his shirt before going to find Ben.

'Oh my God, Katy. Oh my God. What the fuck. Are you OK? Does it hurt? What shall I do?' panted Ben as he skidded into the car, where she was sitting quietly with a fully informed Braindead, the pub well-wishers having retreated inside.

'Got ya!' Katy and Braindead yelled in unison.

'Do we have Gloria?' asked Braindead, whilst a bewildered Ben looked from one face to another.

'Of course,' said Rick from behind Ben, pulling the puffin out from under his shirt.

'Katy, you are the absolute dog's bollocks,' said Braindead, cradling Gloria on his knee. 'And most certainly back in my top five, I don't care what you say.'

'Will someone tell me what the hell is going on?' asked Ben. 'Why aren't you screaming?'

'It's all right, there's nothing to worry about,' she said, feeling bad as well as pleased he looked so concerned. 'I was just faking labour to distract everyone so we could kidnap Gloria,' she continued. 'I thought I'd show you how I got my nickname, Queen of Steal. Not so sensible now, eh?'

Ben said nothing, just sat down on the gravel and put his head in his hands.

'You alright, mate?' asked Rick.

'I think I've just had a near heart attack,' he said eventually. He looked up to see his two best mates grinning away and giving Katy high fives.

'But I guess I can let you off, as I've never seen Braindead happier.' Finally seeing the funny side, Ben collapsed into laughter.

As they drove home, Rick and Braindead relived Katy's fake labour over and over again for Ben's benefit, who was now laughing hysterically whilst stroking her knee protectively.

That night as they lay in bed Katy felt the need to apologise for giving Ben a fright, even if it had given them all one hell of a funny pregnancy story to share.

'No, I'm sorry,' Ben said in response. 'I should have stuck up for you when Rick wouldn't believe you. I know that you're more than capable of stealing anything if you put your mind to it.'

'You must be so proud,' laughed Katy.

'I'm always proud of you,' said Ben, serious for a

moment. 'More than you'll ever know.' He leant forward and gave her a boozy kiss before turning over to fall asleep.

Katy lay there staring at the ceiling, recalling her dramatic performance with a huge amount of self-satisfaction. It was such a relief to know that pregnancy hadn't zapped her personality entirely. The real Katy Chapman was still alive and kicking and capable of anything. As sleep slowly started to claim her weary body, the thought of the dinner party invitation was the only thing to dampen her revived fighting spirit. Tomorrow she would find a way to get out of it, she resolved as she drifted off. Tomorrow she would put Matthew firmly behind her and truly begin preparations for the arrival of her and Ben's baby.

Chapter 11

Matthew had been sitting in his black leather executive chair in his home office for the past two hours, staring at a blank spreadsheet on his computer. Occasionally his hands leapt into action and hovered in anticipation over the keyboard, only to be pulled back at the last minute to rest once more on the padded arms of the chair. Alison had popped in every so often to ask his opinion on possible menu choices for the dinner party on Saturday, such was her excitement at having the first guests over to show her house off to. In fact, as soon as they had got back from the class, she had disappeared behind a fortress of celebrity chef cookbooks. It was the sight of so many patronising smiles from so many overfed, overpaid chefs on the front of these overpriced passports to social acceptability that had forced him to retreat to his inner sanctum.

Every time Alison had popped in, he had bent his head hurriedly over a copy of *Income Tax Regulations*, Volume Six, and asked her not to disturb him again.

Finally, at 11.04 p.m. he selected a box on the screen, top row, two spaces in, and typed the word 'Katy' before quickly deleting it.

Come on, he said to himself through gritted teeth. He couldn't understand it. Normally this was exactly what he needed to sort his head out. A beautifully mapped-out spreadsheet usually had the capacity to transform him from a bumbling wreck to a master of his mind and faculties.

It was Alison who had first led him to develop a fetish for this mind-altering activity. In their early dating days she had been horrified that he didn't know where he wanted to be in ten years' time. As she was a human resources professional, his lack of focus in all areas of his life had driven her demented, but eventually she had relished his indecision and taken it upon herself to turn him into the man she knew he could become.

So, one evening when he thought he was dropping by to pick her up and go to the cinema, she had dragged him into her kitchen. There, with the help of several pieces of A3 paper and a variety of coloured marker pens, she had encouraged, cajoled and dragged out of him what he should do with his life. By the end of the evening he was exhausted, if not a little emotional, having admitted things to her that he hadn't even admitted to himself.

Two days later the post had brought a beautifully typed-up chart entitled MATTHEW'S PLAN, complete with timelines and a to-do list. She had made it all seem so simple. So much so that before the morning was out he had picked up the phone and requested a prospectus from a college running evening accountancy courses. He had also rung the mate who was temporarily sleeping on his couch and told him that if he wasn't out by the weekend he would be charging rent. The feeling of progress was so good that he soon found he was doing charts on the spreadsheet function of his computer for all manner of tricky situations. Which job offer to take once he had qualified as an accountant? His criteria for selecting his first company car? How to ask Alison to marry him? How they were going to afford endless fertility treatment? He had them all filed away on the hard disc, under the title THIS IS YOUR LIFE, MATTHEW CHESTERMAN. Password protected, of course.

But tonight the magic of the spreadsheet was failing him. Tonight its special powers would not work to focus his mind in the right place. He knew deep down that he had nothing to decide. Katy had taken care of it. She had called the shots and decreed that all possible consequences of their one-night stand should be ignored. How relieved he ought to be feeling that he didn't need to construct the spreadsheet entitled TAKING CARE OF THREE CHILDREN ALL AT ONCE. But he didn't feel relieved, that was the whole point, and the damn spreadsheet wouldn't help him work out why. Or perhaps he just couldn't bring himself to do a spreadsheet entitled WHY KATY MAKES ME FEEL LIKE I GOT MATTHEW'S PLAN ALL WRONG.

In the absence of a seriously soothing spreadsheet, the following day Matthew found himself pacing up and down the pavement in front of Katy's office. After twenty painful minutes, he finally walked through the doors and strode up to the pink-haired, pierced-lipped receptionist and asked to see Ms Chapman. She buzzed through to Katy's PA via a headset and helped him negotiate with Louise the opportunity for him to wait in Katy's office until she came out of a meeting. She did this whilst also whipping him up a decaf latte from the fully equipped coffee bar that stood behind her.

He was now sitting staring at a gilt-framed *Smash Hits* poster of Patrick Swayze in his *Dirty Dancing* days in Katy's highly individual office. He could still picture the same poster on Katy's bedroom wall all those years ago. It seemed to Matthew that he'd spent a lot of time thinking about his teenage years since he'd seen Katy again. It had been bothering him as to whether the teenage boy he was then would be impressed with the man he was now.

He jumped as his phone buzzed at him from his belt clip. Unhooking it, he saw Ian's name flash on the screen.

'What do you want? I'm busy,' said Matthew under his breath, afraid that Louise, who was right outside the door, might hear.

'Where are you?' asked Ian. 'You sound funny.'

'You really don't want to know,' Matthew whispered.

'Oh, come on. The minute you say that, then of course

I must insist on knowing exactly where you are. But if you tell me you've gone down to that new lap dancing bar without me for a quickie at lunchtime, I will have to kill you.'

'Believe me, I'm not in a lap dancing bar.'

Louise looked up far too quickly, making it obvious that she'd heard what Matthew had said. Matthew turned his back on her in what he hoped was a casual manner.

'OK, so not a lap dancing bar. Are you with any attractive birds?' asked Ian.

Matthew eyed the stuffed puffin perched on Katy's desk warily. It had been giving him a very disapproving glare ever since he had sat down.

'You could say there are birds involved, yes,' he admitted.

'Interesting,' said Ian. 'Are they naked?'

Matthew switched his gaze to the filing cabinet in the corner of the room, on which stood the plaster cast of Katy's pregnant belly and breasts. He knew it was her because there was a handy plaque on the plinth stating her name and, surprisingly, her newly acquired cup size.

'Are you still there?' said Ian. 'Come on, answer the question. I'm enjoying this game.'

141

'Well, I guess you could say that at this particular moment I can see some kind of nakedness, yes,' muttered Matthew, glancing nervously over his shoulder at Louise.

'Wow, and it's only half past eleven in the morning. You rock, Matthew. So who is it? Come on, tell me. Are you watching Sue from accounts take her cycling top off through that broken window in the second-floor loos?'

'No, I am not.'

'So who is it then? Tell me now before my head explodes,' Ian insisted.

'Well, I'm actually looking at Katy's—' Matthew started.

'Katy? *The* Katy? Bonus baby Katy?' Ian interrupted.

'Shut up, Ian. That is so inappropriate.'

'Inappropriate? You can talk. You're looking at her tits.'

'They're not her real tits. Look, I'm in her office. I'll tell you why later, but there's this sort of sculpture of her naked pregnant body.'

'Wow. Just give me a moment whilst I take in what you have just said,' said Ian.

The line went quiet.

'OK, I now have the scene in my head. Now concentrate, the next question is really important. Are you alone in the office?' asked Ian.

'Er, yes. Katy didn't know I was coming, so I'm waiting for her to finish in a meeting.'

'Good. So tell me. Have you?'

'Have I what?'

'You have, haven't you?'

'Have what?'

'You know. Had a quick squeeze of the tits.'

'No, I have not,' said a shocked Matthew.

'Aw, come on. No man alone in a room with an inanimate object shaped like a naked woman is going to resist a quick grope.'

'Not all men are like you, Ian.'

'Don't give me that. I just have the guts to say what everyone else is thinking,' said Ian. 'So come on. Don't you at least want to know if they feel different now that she's pregnant?'

Matthew peered over his shoulder to see if Louise was still sniffing around. Her chair was empty.

'Go on. Just a quick one for the boys, Matthew. Are you a man or a machine? I'll never let you live it down if you don't,' Ian continued.

'Oh, for goodness' sake,' said Matthew as he got up and strode over to the figure. 'I'm doing it, OK? Satisfied now?' he barked down the phone as he cupped the left breast with his right hand.

'Oh, totally and utterly,' purred a voice from the doorway.

'Shit!' Matthew threw his phone on the floor and pulled his hand away with lightning speed.

'Don't you think it's just marvellous,' continued the perfectly posed man, one hand on out-thrust hip whilst the other rested against the door frame. 'And to have such a fine specimen as yourself truly appreciate my handiwork is such a compliment. I'm Daniel by the way. Creative genius behind the object of your admiration.'

'Hi. I'm Matthew. I'm so sorry, I was just, er . . .'

'Matthew, you say?' asked Daniel.

'Yes, Matthew. I'm just waiting for Katy.'

'I see,' said Daniel, not hiding the fact that he was giving Matthew a good look up and down. 'I'm impressed,' he said finally. 'She never said you were so handsome.'

There was an awkward silence, interrupted only by the sound of Ian squeaking from the phone lying somewhere on the floor.

'The brand manager for Crispy Bix is a complete and

utter bitch,' said Katy as she swept past Daniel into her office.

She stopped in her tracks at the sight of Matthew still hovering next to her naked body.

'Matthew, what the hell are you doing here?' she said, glancing nervously between him, Daniel and the plaster cast.

'He was just admiring your baby shower present,' said Daniel with a smug smile. 'You see, some people appreciate true art, Katy.'

'No really, I wasn't doing anything,' said Matthew. 'I was just seeing what it was made of. Such an interesting texture. Yes, really interesting. You must tell me how you did it, Daniel.'

'Actually he was touching your breasts,' Daniel told Katy. 'As if that didn't get him in enough trouble last time.'

'Daniel!' Katy exclaimed.

'So, must dash. I have other meetings to gatecrash,' said Daniel. 'I shall speak to you later,' he said pointedly to Katy as he left.

Katy shut the door firmly behind him.

'My God, why on earth did you have to tell him?' asked Matthew, making his getaway from the proximity of the plaster cast and picking up his now silent phone.

'Well, I had to talk to someone, and despite appearances I know I can trust him.'

'Really? Looked like your typical gossipy gay guy to me,' said Matthew as he perched on the edge of the desk, causing the puffin to wobble alarmingly.

'Be careful of Gloria,' said Katy, leaping over to steady the bird.

'Gloria? It has a name? Why exactly have you got a stuffed puffin in your office, Katy?'

'We stole her last night.'

'Who did?'

'Me and Ben and a couple of his mates.'

Matthew stared at her, saying nothing.

'What? What's the matter?' asked Katy.

Matthew found he couldn't get any words out.

'Matthew, why are you standing there with a disappointed look on your face?' Katy asked eventually, eyeing the copy of Gina Ford falling out of his briefcase.

Matthew hastily stuffed *The Contented Little Baby Book* back in his bag.

'Alison gave it to me this morning and told me to memorise the nought-to-six-weeks routine over my lunch hour,' he explained.

'How super,' said Katy. 'Very sensible, of course. But please can you wipe that disappointed look off your face.'

'I'm not disappointed in you,' said Matthew, turning away from her. 'I'm actually disappointed that in no part of my life would I ever get caught up in stealing a stuffed puffin.'

Katy looked confused.

He spun back round to look at her. 'I would have stolen a stuffed puffin, though, wouldn't I? When I was younger, I mean? I was fun then, wasn't I?' he asked with a slightly desperate tone in his voice.

'I don't think you should be judging your life by your ability to steal a stuffed puffin,' said Katy, clearly at a loss.

'It's just that I go to work and talk about stupid bloody tax all day and I come home and talk about baby routines and whether we should be bathing at 5.45 p.m. or 6 p.m. and other bullshit like that,' he said, kicking the side of his briefcase where the baby boot camp bible lurked.

He was quiet for a moment, lost in thought. Katy fidgeted with her Post-it notes.

'And I don't even have a plant in my office, never mind a stuffed puffin or a cast of my naked body or a picture of Patrick Swayze,' said Matthew, pointing at the faded poster.

'Well, I will always love Patrick Swayze,' said Katy quietly.

'I know you will,' said Matthew, banging the desk with his hand, making Katy and Gloria jump. 'I've been sitting here thinking about us driving down to Devon and you making me listen to that bloody *Dirty Dancing* tape the whole way.'

'I didn't make you. You were singing your head off,' said Katy.

'I know I was, and that's just it, Katy. I never sing any more. What's happened to me?' Matthew slumped in the chair. He was starting to think MATTHEW'S PLAN had some serious omissions.

'So sing now,' said Katy.

'What?'

'Sing now.'

'Don't be ridiculous.'

'Oh, for goodness' sake, Matthew. You complain about never singing any more and now you won't. Come on, we'll do it together.'

Katy stood up and cleared her throat. Thrusting her bump out proudly, she began a shockingly bad attempt at the opening bars of 'I've Had the Time of My Life'.

Suddenly he was back in his dad's Rover; windows wound right down, wind in his hair, music blaring and one hand on Katy's bare knee as she sang at the top of her voice.

He found himself laughing at Katy as she got more confident in her memory of the lyrics and began to sway a little as she built up to the chorus.

'Come on then. Join in. Don't be shy,' she gasped between lines.

Matthew started to mumble the lines he couldn't believe he could still remember. At the end of the chorus Katy fell back in her chair, laughing.

'You're still crap at singing,' she said. 'Good job you don't do it any more. So anyway, what do we do about this dinner date then? I assume that's why you're here?'

'What? Oh yeah, of course. That's what I came to talk about,' said Matthew, trying to get his mind back on track. 'So I know this is going to sound strange, but the thing is, Alison is really excited about it. She got home last night and was straight into Gordon Ramsay and has the whole menu planned already. It's the most cheerful I've seen her since we moved here. And there's no way she'll let you get out of it. Believe me, once Alison has the bit between her teeth there's no stopping her. I know the whole situation has disaster written all over it, but do you think we could go ahead? Life's so much better when she's cheerful.'

'God, Matthew, we're really pushing our luck here you know.'

'I know, but if it makes her feel like she's settling in she might relax a bit, which would be such a relief. I know this is a crazy situation and I can't believe I'm asking, but please come. I dread to think what she'll be like if you call with an excuse.'

'You do realise we can't be friends,' Katy said slowly.

'I know, but this might just be the thing to inspire her into making an effort to make some other friends rather than obsessing about the babies. Though not with you, of course. Please come round just this once and then I promise you we'll never . . .' Matthew trailed off.

He got up and walked around her desk towards her.

'What are you doing?' she asked as he got closer.

'Is that the baby?' he said as he went past her and peered at the scan photo she had pinned to the notice board behind her desk.

He couldn't stop his fingers from reaching up to touch the image. He traced the shape of the baby, just as he had done with the twins' picture. He felt the world stopping, or at the very least slowing down.

Katy stared at him in horror.

'Yes it is,' she said quietly.

He swallowed, then turned to look deep into her eyes. Before she could say anything else, he muttered, 'I'll go now. See you on Saturday.'

He scurried back round the desk, picked up his briefcase and walked out of her office without looking back.

Chapter 12

The morning of the dinner party dawned and Katy decided that, rather than spend the day fretting, she should finally get round to buying some baby gear. To her surprise, Ben reacted with a degree of enthusiasm. Armed with a list from Louise – who couldn't believe Katy's lack of preparation – they set off to the out-of-town baby store.

'Brilliant, there's a Currys,' said Ben as soon as they got out of the car. 'I need camera batteries so I can get some embarrassing pictures on the stag do. I'll just pop in now, love. Won't be long, you just carry on.'

He was gone before she could protest, and walking far

152

too fast for her pregnant body to catch up with him. Sighing, she turned to contemplate the enormous baby store, remembering previous unnerving visits to buy gifts for other people's babies. The sight of so many pregnant women in one place always disturbed her. She felt as though she had landed on a different planet, where all women had to be pregnant all the time. She shivered at the thought before forcing herself to go in and get on with it.

She'd start with clothes, she thought. She was good at buying clothes. She had been doing it practically all her life. All confidence vanished, however, when faced with her first difficult decision. What size? Newborn or 0–3 months? What was that all about? Surely they were the same? What was the difference? Why didn't she know about this? Was it a conspiracy to confuse her? She looked up in a panic, only to see lots of other mums-to-be effortlessly gliding around her looking totally in the know. She hastily stuffed half a dozen of each into her trolley before deciding to move on to something less stressful.

She consulted the list. Monitors. That had to be easy. She took a deep breath and attempted her own calm glide off to the safety section.

Is somebody having a laugh? she thought as she looked in a daze at the row upon row of listening devices blinking at her like evil little aliens. The level of equipment required made her think the baby must be expected to do a complete Beatles medley at least before it went to sleep. She reached out a now slightly shaking hand and took one off the middle shelf, then attempted to read the sales blurb – but it might as well have been written in Dutch for all the sense it made. She flung it into the trolley before stalking back to the relative sanctuary of the clothing section.

After an hour and ten minutes she was in a sweat, utterly confused, distraught and angry. She looked up from the Templeton Deluxe Pushchair Travel System, which had kept her in mortal combat for the last twenty minutes, and hoped no-one saw her give it a good kick. The shop assistant had made it all look so easy when, with a flick of the wrist, she had morphed it from what appeared to be a complete tangle of silver chrome and flappy black canvas into a robust, if complicated-looking, baby carriage.

'What about this one?' said the assistant, appearing again and pointing at another pram that looked like Tupperware on wheels. 'This one is really simple to use, especially if you haven't got a man who can get it in and out of the car for you.'

Katy stood with her mouth open. How dare she assume she was a single mum? Ben would be here any minute, she said to herself again, looking desperately towards the door for the umpteenth time.

She sat down on the edge of the display to try and pull herself together and watched in a haze as a smartly dressed couple wandered over to look at the pushchairs.

'I can't believe that twenty minutes ago we were at the garage selling your convertible and now we're in here buying a pram,' said the heavily pregnant woman. 'Life's never going to be the same again, is it?' she continued, looking almost as shaken as Katy felt.

'You're right,' replied the man, putting an arm around her shoulders. 'But I wouldn't trade with anyone in the world right now. And do you know what? I loved that car, you know I did, but I bet you I'm going to love our new pram a million times more, especially when it's got our little princess in it.'

Katy watched, mesmerised, as they both turned to face each other, huge smiles on their faces. Then they kissed, quite passionately for the middle of a Saturday afternoon in an out-of-town store. When they had finished, the man reached inside his jacket and pulled out several sheets of paper.

'So,' he said. 'I printed all this stuff off the internet last night, after you'd gone to bed. Now the best one, according to this website, is that one over there . . .'

Katy turned away. She couldn't bear to watch the perfect partnership any more. She looked again towards the door. Still no sign of Ben.

She hauled herself up and trudged to the checkout, gulping back the tears which had suddenly threatened to engulf her. In the middle of her purchases being scanned and packed, the sales assistant leant over and gave her a tissue.

'Hormones,' she said kindly. 'Happens all the time.'

Absolutely mortified, she hurled the bags into her trolley as fast as she could and virtually ran out of the store, as if the building were on fire.

'Bloody hell, are there wild tigers in there or something?' she heard Ben say, just as she was careering through the automatic doors.

'Where the hell have you been?' she managed before bursting into floods of tears whilst trying not to hyperventilate.

'Hey, it's OK, calm down. Did the other pregnant ladies not play nicely?' he said, grinning.

'Stop!' she shouted. 'Just stop,' she repeated angrily, looking up at him, bright red in the face. He stared back at her in shock. They didn't do angry with each other. 'I don't need you to do funny, OK? Just stop doing funny.'

'OK,' he replied, the grin wiped off his face. 'So what do you need?' he asked slowly.

'I don't know,' she said desperately. 'Just not funny, OK? I need . . . I need . . . I need you to just be there sometimes. You know, like when I'm going through hell trying to make a stupid pram stand upright.'

'I see,' he said quietly. 'You need me. That's a new one.'

'Yep, well, you know, just sometimes,' she replied. They both stood for a moment staring at the ground, lost in their own thoughts, until Ben gently prised the trolley out of her fingers and took it to the car to unload.

That night the atmosphere was so chilling that it could have been made for horror movies. Pitch black, driving rain, a howling gale, and all manner of sudden bangs and crashes to make you leap out of your skin.

Which was exactly what Katy did when Ben jumped into the car, a flashlight illuminating his face.

'Don't go on the moors, lassie, don't go on them moors now,' he moaned as he hovered in her face.

'Don't, Ben,' she said, swatting him away. She had managed to calm down a little since the afternoon shopping trip. Ben had apologised profusely on the way home, explaining that he'd got caught up with an old pal who was working in Currys and could get him a discount. She was trying very hard not to be pissed off with him still, especially as she needed every drop of positive energy she had to get her through the dinner party with Matthew and Alison.

Ben switched on the radio to listen intently to the afternoon's football activity. Katy, her heart still thumping wildly, was busy trying to clear her head of the image of Alison hacking her to death with a bloody axe whilst Matthew dug her grave in a misty forest in the middle of nowhere.

'We're crap. They all want sacking,' Ben declared eventually, pressing the tuning button repeatedly to try and find some decent music.

'Leave it alone, will you?' said Katy.

'Sorry,' he said, skulking down in his seat. There was an awkward silence before Ben dared speak again.

'Well, I don't know about you, but I'm on the edge of

my seat with excitement at the prospect of a night with Dull and Duller. Wonder how long the tour of the famous nursery will take? I actually feel as if I have decorated it myself, Lady Alison has described it in so much detail.'

'Don't remind me,' said Katy, her heart sinking at the prospect. 'I'm going to feel so inadequate.'

'No way. You listen here, Katy,' said Ben, pulling himself up in his seat. 'You will not be an anal mum who turns her children into serial killers. You are going to be as cool as fuck and this baby is going to love you for it.'

Katy allowed herself to smile. 'Do you know what, Ben? That might have been the nicest thing you have ever said to me.'

'Well, I aim to please,' he said. 'I do try,' he added when Katy looked sideways at him, then abruptly changed the subject. 'So where the heck are we going then?'

'It should be just up here on the right.'

Ben let out a long, low whistle as the large, detached, new-build house came into sight.

'Wow, it's a mini mansion. No more Lady Alison, it's Lady Alison of WAG Towers from now on,' he exclaimed.

The wheels of Katy's car scrunched on the neat gravel

TRACY BLOOM

drive as they pulled up to the door. They were instantly bathed in a welcoming pool of orange light as ornate wrought-iron lanterns came to life, illuminating them and the enormous front porch. Two beautifully manicured miniature trees in shiny copper tubs stood guard on either side of an imposing glossy black door with a very large moulded brass handle in the centre. The effect was more high-end restaurant than family home, thought Katy.

'It's bigger than school!' exclaimed Ben as he helped Katy ease her fit-to-burst body out of the car. 'They must be minted. Perhaps we should consider actually being good mates with them. There could be fringe benefits.'

'Here, let me,' said Matthew, appearing at Ben's side and grabbing Katy's hand.

Katy jumped at the physical contact and withdrew her hand sharply. There had been no touching since the reunion.

'I'm pregnant, not disabled,' she said as she wobbled upright and slammed the door behind her.

'Of course,' said Matthew. 'Sorry. Look, get inside quick. Don't get wet.' He rushed forward and held open the massive black door, inviting them into an imposing double-height hall.

'Sorry, but do you mind if you take your shoes off? New carpets have just been laid,' he said as Katy crossed the threshold.

Katy looked at him to see if he was joking, but he was obviously serious. She had a thing about people who asked visitors to take their shoes off. It always made her feel like something the cat had dragged in. She kicked off her shoes, refusing to put them neatly on the shoe rack supplied for the convenience of guests.

'Are you sure Al would rather have my smelly, holey footie socks?' Ben piped up, waving his left foot in the air, revealing a worn-out sock with a big toe sticking out.

'Come through,' said Matthew, ignoring Ben. 'Alison is just finishing off in the kitchen.'

'Hey, mate, do you want to show me that programme now, just in case I get too drunk to truly appreciate the piece of history I'll be holding in my hands?' said Ben as they moved into the sitting room.

'I guess so,' said Matthew, as if he had only just noticed that Ben was there. 'Come into my office. We'll be back in a minute, Katy.'

Katy stood in the middle of the sitting room, which must have been at least twenty-five feet long, feeling lost and unsure what to do. She slowly looked around, admiring first the beautiful low-slung designer sofa with its soft camel suede cushions symmetrically placed in each corner. She then noticed the state-of-the-art floor lamp she had seen in a very expensive designer store in Leeds, which arched gracefully into the centre of the room to hover over a perfectly weathered coffee table. A super-sleek Bose hi-fi system sat on a glass shelf and emitted wonderfully calming sounds as she walked to the other end of the room and stroked her hand down the swathes of deep chocolate slubbed silk that hung from a thick wooden pole. She gently pushed the curtains aside and peeped behind them at the illuminated, perfectly manicured lawn. Turning round, she wandered back into the centre of the room, and was just wondering what she could spy on next when her eyes rested on two impressively tall, sculptural candlesticks that book-ended the obligatory row of photographs on the mantelpiece.

She took a sharp intake of breath.

This was it, Matthew's life. The life he had lived without Katy but with Alison, summarised in half a dozen images staring back at her, framed in matching brushed silver chrome.

She went slowly towards the mantelpiece, a little unsure whether she really wanted to look.

They were pretty predictable. Crazy young dating couple at a party. First summer holiday together. First skiing holiday together. First black-tie do together. First professional shot, which was probably an engagement picture. And of course, a glorious wedding photograph. Katy found herself scrutinising Matthew's face in each shot. She looked at his eyes and his mouth and then his body language. She realised she was trying to see if he looked happy. Happy in his post-Katy life.

She jumped as Alison came into the room.

'Sorry about that, just finishing off some little nibbles,' she said as she placed two dishes on the coffee table.

'Nice photos,' Katy finally forced out, at a loss as to what to say.

'Oh, thank you. I do love our wedding photograph, it's just so us.'

Katy looked again at the largest frame and took in the artful black-and-white image. Matthew and Alison stood gazing into each other's eyes on the steps of what looked like a castle.

'So where did you get married?' she asked tentatively, not sure she liked this subject.

'Well, we found this brilliant castle in Hampshire with its own chapel. It was so perfect. It was hard work finding the right place though. We seemed to be viewing venues for weeks before we were satisfied. I still have a file this thick of everywhere we went to see, so if you are ever thinking of taking the plunge, you know where to come. You're not married, are you, you and Ben?'

'No, maybe one day, who knows?' Katy said, unable to meet Alison's eye.

'I was wondering if you were waiting until the baby is born?' she asked.

'No. We haven't really got that far yet.'

'Well, you never know, Ben might have it all planned. The minute you give birth, he'll pop the question,' Alison ploughed on.

'Pop what question?' Ben asked as he strode into the room.

'I was just being nosy, Ben. I was asking if you have any plans to get married. I'm good at organising weddings, you see.'

'I don't think that is really anything to do with us, Alison,' said Matthew sharply.

'Don't worry. Me and Katy don't worry about such formalities,' said Ben, falling onto the sofa. 'I reckon one day we'll just wake up and say, you know what, let's get married. We are more a spur-of-the-moment, fly-by-the-seat-of-our-pants kind of couple, aren't we, love?'

'That's right,' said Katy, looking anywhere but at Matthew. 'Definitely.'

'My word, Al, is this tea?' asked Ben. 'We'll have to have a chinese on the way home at this rate,' he continued in a stage whisper to Katy.

'No, no, they're just some nibbles before we sit down to eat properly.'

'I'm just pulling your leg. Right, did someone say go? I'm starving,' he said, picking up an entire plate and helping himself.

Finally, after half an hour of embarrassingly awkward small talk, Alison announced that dinner would be ready in ten minutes.

'Would you like to see the nursery before we sit down?' she asked.

Katy and Ben looked at each other. Katy knew that it was the last thing she wanted to do.

'Love to,' said Ben, with a shrug to Katy. 'Which wing is it in?'

'It's ridiculously big, isn't it?' said Alison as she led

them upstairs. 'But Matthew got such a good package when he was made partner that it meant we could afford this.'

'Say, big guy, you're quite a catch, aren't you?' said Ben.

'He is now,' said Alison, smiling proudly at him. 'But it hasn't always been like this. You should have seen the mess he was in when I met him.'

Katy was beginning to feel really weird. She felt all clammy and a bit sick. Something was wrong.

'So here we are,' said Alison, as she opened the door at the top of the stairs. 'Our nest.'

Katy stepped into the room and felt her jaw drop. She had never seen such a beautiful room. It was a wonderfully serene sea of creams and greens that felt so soft and gentle that she wanted to curl up on the sheepskin rug in the middle of the floor and go to sleep. She stood in the doorway in absolute awe, before finding herself drawn to the two cribs that stood side by side on the far wall underneath an enormous arched window. Delicate flowing canopies cascaded protectively over the perfect little havens, and as she got closer, she had to fight back the tears when she caught sight of a small green teddy bear placed in each one, waiting patiently for its new owner to arrive. She was aware that Alison was talking to her but she couldn't concentrate. She turned around slowly and spotted an antique, dark oak rocking chair with a pretty patchwork cushion nestling on its seat. Again she couldn't help herself but walk over and stroke its long arched back before easing herself down into it. She closed her eyes and gently rocked backwards and forwards.

She let her mind drift off until suddenly her composure was shattered. She thought of the bare white room back at her flat with cardboard boxes stacked haphazardly in one corner and carrier bags strewn in another, belching out the random baby purchases made in a panic earlier that day.

Filled with dismay, she realised what was wrong. She was jealous. And to her horror, a vivid image popped into her mind of a picture-perfect barn conversion with roses trailing up the wall and her with Matthew and their two kids waving from the front door.

She started to try and scramble her way out of the chair but found that her belly thought it had found its perfect resting place and was reluctant to let go. Matthew came over to rescue her, touching her for the second time that evening as he gently took her hand and put his arm around her shoulder.

'You OK?' he asked. 'You look a bit pale. Can I get you anything?'

'No, I'm fine. Absolutely fine,' she said, looking at him wide-eyed. 'Let's eat now, I'm starving.' She bolted to the door.

She could hear Alison prattling on as she came down the stairs, but all Katy could think about was how she was going to escape this nightmare as quickly as possible so she would never have to look at Matthew's life again.

Chapter 13

'So we have rocket, fennel, watercress and pear salad. Enjoy,' said Alison as she laid down the delicate white starter plates which were most certainly not of IKEA origin.

Ben eyed the foliage in front of him suspiciously, then picked up his fork, took a deep breath and dug in.

'I've found starters particularly hard during pregnancy, haven't you, Katy?' said Alison. 'Everything seems to have shellfish, soft cheese or cured meat in it.'

'I guess I normally end up having soup and I hate soup,' said Katy miserably.

There was an awkward silence.

'Soup is always such a conversation killer, isn't it?' said Ben. 'Soup and death. They should both be banned from discussion whilst eating.'

Alison stared at Ben and then turned to ask Katy a question. 'So, Katy, do you think you will breastfeed or bottle-feed?'

'Forgot to add breastfeeding,' muttered Ben under his breath.

'Well, I don't really know yet. Depends on what the baby goes for, I guess,' said Katy, kicking Ben under the table.

'Well, we've discussed it – haven't we, Matthew? – and I really want to breastfeed, but obviously with two that could be exhausting, so I've bought a breast pump. Matthew will be able to feed them when it's too much for me. I went for the expensive electronic one. Apparently hand pumping is really hard work.'

'Breast pump?' questioned Ben, perking up. 'You mean you can buy something to milk your breasts?'

'Oh yes, they're very common these days, what with working mums,' Alison told him.

'But how does it work?' he asked.

'Well, there's a suction cup that goes over the breast and it's attached to a pump,' said Alison. 'The suction pulls the nipple in and out, just like a baby sucking. And everything can be sterilised so it's very hygienic,' she added, suddenly aware that Ben was looking slightly aghast.

'Oh, I have no doubt it's all very clean, it's just that the thought of you ladies attaching yourselves to a machine that sucks your nipple in and out is a bit weird . . . isn't it?'

No-one said anything.

'Come on, don't look at me like that. It's hard on us men. We're programmed to fantasise about the female body, right, Matthew? From puberty we dream of seeing boobs in the flesh, never mind touching them. Then as we get older we're allowed to become more familiar with the female form, then suddenly, just as you think you've got your hands on the damn things, bang, you have to forget every dream you ever had. Now the object of your affection has been taken over by a baby who has no idea how lucky they are, or worse, a damn machine. A machine is allowed to fondle your woman's tits but you're not.'

Matthew, Katy and Alison all stared at Ben when he had finished.

'That was lovely, Alison. Shall we move on to the

main course?' said Katy after a pause, now even keener to hurry the evening along.

'Of course,' said Alison, getting up immediately. 'Matthew, would you help me clear away?'

'Ben, you might want to wind it down a little,' said Katy after they had left the room.

'Why? What did I say?'

'I don't really think the whole boob fantasy gone wrong thing was entirely appropriate.'

'I was only trying to make conversation and break the ice a bit. Trouble is, I think the ice has frozen up her ass. Boy, does she need to relax. And can she only talk about bloody babies? We have got to get her off the subject, or else I'm going to have to get very, very drunk.'

'Sssssh, they're coming back,' hissed Katy. 'Just tone it down, *please*.'

'Here we are. Now this is pot-roasted poussin with honeyed parsnips and mustard mash. Hope you like it,' said Alison.

'Looks wonderful,' said Ben with a huge grin aimed directly at Alison's now rather frosty smile.

Alison thawed slightly as she watched Ben dig his knife into his poussin's chest with gusto.

'So, have you got your route to hospital all planned

out, Ben?' she asked. 'We've tried several options at different times of day, just to check which is quickest.'

Ben stared at her in amazement, still chewing. 'Depends,' he said finally.

'On what?' she asked.

'On whether I'll be travelling from home or from Edinburgh.'

'Edinburgh?' she said, her turn to look amazed. 'Why on earth would you be travelling from there?'

'I'm going there on a stag do in a couple of weeks' time.'

Alison almost dropped her knife and fork in shock.

'You're going on a stag do just before Katy gives birth?' she said.

'Yes,' said Ben, as if he expected that to be the end of it.

Alison turned to direct her line of questioning at Katy.

'Aren't you worried, Katy? I have to say, if Matthew asked if he could go on a stag do just before I was due to give birth I'd tell him not to go.'

'It's only in Edinburgh, it's not that far,' said Katy defensively. 'I don't tell Ben what he can and can't do,' she added, glancing over at Matthew.

Alison stared at her for a moment as if she had just arrived from another planet, before getting up from her chair. 'Well, good for you,' she said, clearing away the plates. 'I just hope you have someone on standby if those contractions start. I wouldn't want to be on my own for that.'

Matthew, Katy and Ben sat in silence, listening to the kitchen door squeak quietly back and forth behind Alison.

'I suppose she does have a point really,' said Matthew. 'You wouldn't want to be on your own, would you?'

'Look, let's change the subject, shall we? It's not going to happen. It's nearly two weeks before my due date, and if I do start I'll have to call Daniel,' said Katy, realising that, worryingly, he was her only option.

'Does it have to be Daniel?' said Ben. 'I like the guy, I really do, but if it's a boy in there I'd like to give him half a chance of coming out on the right side.'

'Well, you won't have much choice, will you, if you're not there?' said Matthew, a bit too quickly and sharply.

'Hey, I thought you'd be on my side, mate,' said Ben, slightly taken aback.

'Well, I am, but . . .' Matthew paused. 'I know if it were my child I wouldn't take any risk at all that I might not be around.' He looked down quickly, knowing he had crossed a line.

'It's my best mate, I can't miss it. I can get the train

back in about five hours or I can get a flight that takes an hour. I've got all the details and Katy's cool, aren't you, love?'

'Yeah, sure,' said Katy, somewhat shocked at the mention of a five-hour travel time but even more disturbed by what Matthew had said.

The kitchen door recommenced its squeak as Alison swept back into the room with a large tray.

'I've done something really simple for dessert. Hope you don't mind, but it's one of my favourites.'

Matthew jumped up to help her and unloaded four small glass plates onto the table, each holding an assortment of frozen berries.

Ben looked at Katy with a questioning look on his face, almost as if to ask permission to speak. Katy looked back quizzically, not sure what he was up to now.

Ben looked at the plate in front of him again. Then he picked up a raspberry, put it in his mouth and crunched down hard.

'Christ, that's cold,' he said, clutching his jaw.

'No, Ben,' said Alison. 'Look, you pour this melted white chocolate over the berries to thaw them. Now try.'

Ben tried again, swirling the food around in his mouth several times to ensure adequate defrosting.

'Nice,' he said finally. 'Reckon even I could do that.'

'So, Katy, I'd love to know what Matthew was like at school,' said Alison, having clearly decided whilst in the kitchen that they needed a change of subject. Katy's heart sank even deeper. This was really hard work and she was tired. How was she going to get out of this one alive? The image of Alison with the axe on the moors reappeared in her mind.

'Well, he was just a regular kind of guy, really. I remember he did have long hair, but that was kind of common back then.'

'Oh, I know. I have seen the dreadful pictures at his mother's. And those fingerless gloves. I never would have dreamed that he was such a fashion victim,' said Alison, screwing her nose up.

Katy had a sudden flashback of her and Matthew spending the day trawling an indoor market, trying to find the perfect gloves. They were essential for their outfits as they were going to a gig together, she remembered. Their first real grown-up gig in the back of some pub somewhere. It was dark and smoky and heaving and they had loved every minute of it.

'Well, that's what you do at that age, don't you, follow fashion? It's all part of being a teenager,' said Katy, feeling dizzy from the effort of walking on so many eggshells.

'But it was the Eighties,' said Alison. 'The fashion was so awful then. I drew the line at padded shoulders. Thank goodness it's calmed down these days and we never have to go through that again. Anyway, come on, you must remember something else?' she persisted.

'No secret snogging behind the bike sheds you haven't told us about?' sniggered Ben, nudging Katy. 'Come on, you can tell us, did he ever try it on with you, Katy?'

'God no, never,' Katy laughed hysterically, trying not to show the complete panic that had gripped her insides. Matthew joined in, laughing way too heartily.

'What a ridiculous idea!' he said. 'She was so not my type.'

'Hang on a minute,' said Ben. 'Didn't you go to some reunion last year? Remember, when I was at Paul's stag do?'

'Bollocks,' exclaimed Matthew in a very high-pitched voice as he leapt in the air, spilling his coffee right down his front.

'Oh Matthew, take it off quick, you'll burn, and it's your best shirt. Come on, quick. Look, here's some ice, darling.'

Alison was pulling frantically at Matthew's shirt, trying to get the tails out of his trousers as the coffee stain crept rapidly across the fabric.

His shirt was halfway over his head now. He was trying to undo the buttons from the top whilst Alison desperately tried to pull it over his head. Eventually she won and dragged it off, revealing Matthew's completely hairless chest. This instantly reminded Katy of the sex. She looked away, fearful that Alison would read her mind.

Matthew held a damp napkin wrapped around some ice to his lower belly. He was breathing very hard and looking nervously from one person to another.

'I'm OK,' he puffed. 'It was just hot, that's all, made me jump. Shall we open some more wine? Alison, there's some more Merlot in the rack, you go and get it and I'll just go and put another shirt on.'

'Why don't you put the green and taupe one on? It's hanging in your wardrobe,' shouted Alison as he left the room.

She turned back to Katy and Ben. 'How embarrassing. You've seen his guilty secret now. That cupid tattoo is another unfortunate legacy from his school days. Hideous, isn't it? He said an old girlfriend talked him into it. I keep telling him to have it removed. I hate staring at a reminder of an ex, wouldn't you?'

Ben was sitting very quietly, his brow furrowed. He didn't reply to Alison's question, just looked at Katy and furrowed his brow even more.

Katy felt sick. Disaster had well and truly struck. She couldn't breathe. They had to get out and get out now.

'Alison, I'm so, so sorry but I'm dead on my feet. It's been wonderful, but we're really going to have to go home; I can't keep my eyes open. Is that alright with you, Ben?'

He nodded.

'I understand perfectly. We must make the most of all the sleep we can get at the moment, mustn't we? I'll go and get your coats,' said Alison, getting up.

They were all standing in the hall by the time Matthew came back downstairs. Ben had shoved his hands in his pockets, pulled his hat over his ears and was staring at the floor. Katy was trying to act normally towards Alison whilst shooting warning looks at Matthew.

'So, thank you so much, it's been great. Sorry, Matthew. Gotta go, suddenly really tired,' said Katy as she awkwardly shook Alison and Matthew's hands. Ben had already opened the front door, letting the wind come howling in. He walked straight out without saying anything, head down, chin in his chest.

'So, bye then,' she said, rushing out to follow him after a final glance at Matthew's confused face.

'Shit, shit, shit, what have I done? Stupid, stupid, stupid,' she cursed before opening the car door, the wind and driving rain more alluring than what might greet her inside.

She dropped into the driving seat.

Ben said nothing.

She had her usual battle with the seat belt as it protested at the expanse of her belly.

Ben said nothing.

She sat for a moment watching an abundantly overflowing hanging basket swing precariously on a wrought-iron hook, looking like it might fly right off. Was this the moment, she wondered, when everything came tumbling down?

'Why?' asked Ben.

'Why what?'

'Oh, come on, Katy. There's a bloke who you were at school with who has the exact same tattoo as you. I have to ask why.'

The tears were already flowing. They came the second

Ben opened his mouth. She sniffed hard and swallowed.

'I'm so sorry; it's just that, well, we used to go out together, just at school. It was a stupid dare, the tattoos, I mean. Really stupid.'

'But why didn't you say so?'

'Because of Alison. Apparently she's so jealous that if she knew I was the ex-girlfriend it would freak her out, and Matthew doesn't want to upset her at the moment. And I didn't mean to lie to you as well, Ben, but it just seemed easier. It meant you didn't have to lie too. Stupid, I know, I'm so sorry. He means nothing to me, I promise.'

For the first time since they had got into the car Ben raised his head to look at her.

'I never asked if he meant anything to you.'

It was Katy's turn to stare at the floor.

'Oh right, yeah. I just wanted to make sure you knew, that's all.'

They sat in silence until Ben reached back to put on his seat belt.

Katy leant forward and started the car and they drove home to the sound of the moaning wind.

Chapter 14

Katy stared gloomily at the phone for a good five minutes after she had put the receiver down. It was the longest conversation she'd had with Ben since Saturday night, which was something. The fact that he'd said he wouldn't be going to that evening's antenatal class because he was playing football, however, was not a sign that he was in a good place with everything yet. She wanted the old Ben back, not this quiet, awkward, monosyllabic stranger. Not that she had seen much of him since the dinner party.

On Sunday he had left the flat in the early hours and not returned until after she had gone to bed. The following morning she had got up to find him passed out on the sofa, fully clothed. A half-eaten pizza lay spilling out of its box on the rug and empty bottles of beer littered the floor, making the whole place smell as bad as his over-indulged breath. As gently as possible, she had shaken him awake, not daring to kick off about the debris surrounding him. She had made him some breakfast and then they sat at the breakfast bar in silence, chewing toast. Unable to bear Ben on mute mode, Katy had finally dared to raise the subject of Matthew, apologising again for lying about their school days relationship. Without looking her in the eye, he had grunted a 'Fine. Stop worrying about it' before getting up abruptly to go to work, leaving her to tidy up his mess. This is what it must be like living with a sulky teenager, she thought, getting mildly pissed off as she sponged crusty tomato sauce off the rug. She would have hoped he would be mature enough to talk to her about it, but obviously not. He didn't come home before she went to bed again that night and as she walked into the lounge the next day she braced herself for the aftermath of yet another night of heavy drinking and late-night takeaways. But he had already left, crumpled sticky foil cartons from the Chinese crammed into the bin under the sink and an empty bottle of red wine put ready for recycling. She had seen this as progress, evidence that he was less angry with her, but now she felt utterly deflated that he could not even bring himself to go to one last class.

Finally, in desperation, she picked up the phone again and dialled Daniel's extension.

'Meet me outside in ten minutes with a blindfold. I have a surprise for you,' she said before Daniel could speak. She put down the receiver and stared at the phone miserably. She started to gather her things and wondered if she was making a big mistake.

'This is so exciting I can't even begin to tell you,' said Daniel, bouncing up and down with glee in Katy's car. 'I love, love, love surprises. You will tell me when I can take the blindfold off, won't you?'

'Don't worry,' replied Katy. 'We're just arriving. You can take it off as soon as I've stopped the car. And it's not really a surprise. More a thank you for the wonderful baby shower you threw me.'

'See, I knew you'd come round in the end. It was marvellous, wasn't it?' said Daniel. 'I bet I can guess where you're taking me. You've rung all my friends and gathered them for cocktails at Norman's Bar. I'm right, aren't I?'

'Not exactly,' said Katy as she parked the car. 'OK, you can take it off now.'

Daniel peeked over the top of the blindfold. His excited grin faded as he yanked it off his head and recognised where he was.

'Hospital? What the hell are we doing here?' he said, turning to look at Katy.

'Daniel, I knew you wouldn't come if I asked first, but this is serious. I need you to come to my last antenatal class with me,' Katy pleaded. 'You're the only person who knows what's going on, and there's every chance that I might need you with me at the birth.'

'Are you out of your mind? You already have two possible fathers. To get me involved as well is just plain greedy, Katy.'

To Katy's horror, she started to cry.

'Are you crying?' asked Daniel.

Katy nodded whilst fumbling for a tissue in her bag.

'If you are pretend crying just to get me to go in there, then it won't work, Katy. You've been very cruel and brought me here under false pretences and I am nobody's fool.'

'Daniel, I need you, OK? I need you to help me,' said Katy, tears coming thick and fast now.

'They're not pretend tears, are they?'

'Of course they bloody aren't!'

'Oh Katy, I'm no use to you here. It's Ben you need, not me.' Daniel took Katy's hand in his.

'But he's not here, is he? Since the dinner party, he's shut me out completely. I can't get a word out of him. He spends hardly any time in the flat. He goes out every night straight from school and comes home after I've gone to bed.'

'You've got to talk to him, Katy,' said Daniel.

'I know, I know. But he won't talk to me.'

They sat in silence for some time.

'Can I ask you something difficult?' Daniel said finally.

'Do you have to? My brain hurts as it is.'

'Well, no, of course not, but as your friend and confidant on this matter I feel that now is probably the time to ask the difficult questions. You'll never have another chance.'

'What do you mean, I'll never have another chance?'

'Well, I have this theory. Only when things are really bad do you force yourself to ask the difficult questions.

Well, I say questions, but I really mean one, since there is only one really, truly difficult question.'

He paused.

'Well, come on then, what is it?' asked Katy impatiently.

'The difficult question always is,' said Daniel, pausing again for dramatic effect. 'Do I really love him?'

'That's it? That's the one really, truly difficult question?'

'Yes.'

They sat in silence again while they both considered Daniel's theory. When Katy failed to speak, Daniel decided to expand on his thoughts.

'You see, when things are OK with a man, not fantastic but OK, the really, truly difficult question hovers at the back of your mind and occasionally threatens to break through and present itself. But to try and answer it would inevitably drive change in the relationship, which is too much effort, so you don't answer it. Which is fine, but if everything continues as OK, not fantastic but OK, you could end up in a long-term relationship without ever tackling the really, truly difficult question and therefore you could end up with someone you don't love. Are you with me so far?'

Katy nodded.

'So you see, you have to hope for a bad patch, because then you're more open to answering the really, truly difficult question, and change can only be good. So, in summary, this trauma is great news because now you get to answer the really, truly difficult question. Do you get it?'

'I think so,' sniffed Katy. 'The logic is a bit messy, but I guess there is a point in there somewhere.'

'Good. So do you?'

'Do I what?'

'Have you been listening at all? Do you really love him?' urged Daniel.

'Which one?'

'You are kidding me, right?'

'What? Oh, stop it, Daniel, I can't think straight,' said Katy, the tears starting to flow again.

'Are you trying to tell me it's not just your feelings for Ben that are in question here, that Matthew is also back on the dance floor?'

'No, of course not. Oh, I don't know. It's just that . . . it's just that we were singing the *Dirty Dancing* soundtrack in my office last week . . .' Katy started to say.

'Which song?' Daniel interrupted.

'"I've Had the Time of My Life", obviously,' replied Katy.

'You disappoint me. "Hungry Eyes" is far superior.'

'I really don't think that's relevant at this point, Daniel.'

'Sorry. Continue.'

'Well, it's just that it all came flooding back, you know, that first love feeling. When it's just so damned uncomplicated,' said Katy with a sigh.

'I'm not sure I agree with you there. I mean, Baby really did think Johnny had got Penny pregnant. I wouldn't call that uncomplicated.'

'I don't mean *Dirty Dancing*,' said Katy, getting frustrated. 'I mean me and Matthew. I was in love with him once. And it was great. Really great. I thought he was the one, Daniel, I really did. I thought I was going to be with him for the rest of my life. Then when we went for dinner and I saw him in his house, in his life, I couldn't help thinking that could have been me, you know. With the gravel drive and the hanging baskets and the beautiful nursery and his and hers bathrooms and the goddamn wedding photos on the mantelpiece.' A fresh wave of tears came.

'Hanging baskets?' questioned Daniel. 'I cannot

condone a man who gets you thinking that hanging baskets are aspirational. That's not you, Katy. There's more to you than that, surely? Come on, you stole a puffin last week. That's better than picking out bedding plants.'

'You're right. I know you're right,' she said. 'Ben and me have a great time, but I'm having a baby, Daniel, and I'm starting to wonder if that is entirely compatible with a relationship that is no more developed than that of a couple of students who only just met at freshers' week.' She turned away from him and stared into the distance. 'And as for the really, truly difficult question. We have never discussed the L word. Never. Here we are, having a baby, and we have never talked about what we really mean to each other.'

'Christ, Katy, I never realised how screwed up you are,' said Daniel.

'Thanks. I've worked hard at it,' she said sadly.

'Well, my darling, this does mean you really have to talk to Ben. And I'll tell you something else. You need to know what you want before you do, because quite frankly, this is a mess just waiting to explode, and when it does you have to know what you want to grab out of the fire.'

'It all seemed so clear a few weeks ago, and now I'm so confused,' said Katy.

'Well, let's get you through this last birth class thing. Then you know you never have to see Matthew again. Perhaps that will help clear your mind.'

'So you'll come with me?' she asked. 'I can't go in on my own. Especially not with Matthew and Alison being there.'

'What, miss the drama? No way. I just wish you'd told me earlier so that I could have dressed down, though.' Daniel climbed out of the car.

'Well, as you know, this is our last antenatal class, I am very sad to say.' Joan actually did look genuinely sad. 'It has been such a joy spending this special time with you and getting to know you all. We will, of course, exchange emails and phone numbers at the end so that we can form a support network. Some of my groups meet for coffee once a week. Very helpful for getting out of the house into a baby-friendly environment during those first few weeks.'

Extremely unlikely, thought Katy, as she tried to dodge Matthew's questioning stare and Alison's fake sympathy smile that had been beaming across to her ever since she had arrived without Ben.

'But now, before we start, I do have some very exciting news,' said Joan. 'You will notice that Richard and Rachel are not here tonight. That's because Rachel gave birth to a bouncing little boy yesterday.'

The entire room gasped in shock. It was one thing sitting and talking about having a baby, but it was quite another to actually do it. And if Rachel had done it, then that meant they all had to do it, and soon.

'Is everything OK?' asked Alison, recovering first.

'Oh, fine. Richard is beside himself and apparently Rachel did a wonderful job. He said the Happy Box really helped. Especially the ticket stub from the concert they went to on their first date.'

'What was the concert?' asked Katy, knowing that Ben would have, had he been there.

'He did tell me, actually, and I remember because they were my favourites too. It was Robson and Jerome. Isn't that lovely?' sighed Joan.

'Robson and Jerome!' Katy exclaimed. 'No wonder that worked. Enough to anaesthetise anyone.'

'Now, now, Katy, that is a little harsh,' said Daniel. 'Robson and Jerome were pretty special, weren't they? I'm sorry, we've not been properly introduced.' Daniel stood up to shake Joan's hand.

'Oh, I'm Joan,' she replied. 'And you are . . . ?'

'Daniel, I'm with Katy,' said Daniel.

All eyes turned questioningly to Katy.

'He only likes them because he loved *Soldier Soldier*,' Katy said.

Joan furrowed her brow.

'It was the uniforms,' added Daniel helpfully.

'Oh, oh, oh my, oh yes, of course,' stuttered Joan. 'Oh, how wonderful, oh super, so good of you to come, I mean, you know, in the circumstances, because you know, not really your thing really, yes, good, lovely to meet you, I have a very good friend who is, you know . . .'

'Also a fan of Robson and Jerome?' asked Daniel.

'Yes, that's it exactly, a big fan, I imagine. Well, anyway, we must get on. Please sit down and we shall begin. Good, yes, right, let me see. So what I usually do at the beginning of the last class is ask if anyone has any burning questions left or absolutely anything they want to say. Because now is your last chance.'

Charlene jumped up from her chair as only a pregnant woman under twenty could.

'Can I say something?' she virtually squealed.

'Of course, Charlene, you go right ahead,' said Joan.

'Well, it's not a question really; we just have something very exciting to ask you all. You see, me and Luke were talking, and we think you're all so ace that we would like to invite you to our wedding party on Saturday,' gushed Charlene, struggling to keep any of her limbs still in the excitement. 'I know it's really short notice, but loads of people have said they won't come because they don't think we should get married. Mostly Luke's family, not mine. They think I've trapped him or something. Dickheads. Anyway, we wanted to ask you all, seeing as we've already booked the buffet and everything. Here's a proper invite, and I've put a little map in so that you can find it alright. So say you'll come, won't you? I can't wait to see Luke's mum's face when you turn up.' She went around the room, pushing sparkly pink envelopes into each couple's hands.

'So you're really getting married?' asked Matthew, incredulous as he opened the envelope and watched multicoloured confetti scatter all over his work suit.

'Yeah, we can't wait, can we, Luke?' said Charlene, looking over her shoulder at her husband-to-be, who was studying his fingers.

'How old are you again?' asked a clearly quite freaked-out Matthew.

'Eighteen. But Luke will be nineteen twenty-three days after we get married. The baby should be here by then, so he's going to have the best birthday ever with just me and peanut,' replied Charlene.

'Bloody hell, poor bastard,' muttered Matthew under his breath.

'Matthew,' hissed Alison. 'Be quiet.'

Charlene swung round to face him.

'I heard that,' she said, glaring at him.

'Charlene,' intercepted Joan. 'I don't think he meant—'

'No, Joan,' Charlene interrupted, still glaring at Matthew. 'I know what he meant.'

The room went silent and everyone looked at the floor. All except Charlene and Luke, who for once had looked up to stare at Matthew.

'We love each other, OK?' she said, walking right up to Matthew and pointing an evil-looking blue false fingernail right in his face. 'I love him and he loves me. End of. You can be in love at eighteen, can't you?'

Matthew was forced to lean back in his chair to avoid the lethal weapon hovering dangerously close to his left eye.

'Can't you?' she shouted, prodding her fingernail firmly in his cheek.

Katy had been watching, mesmerised, and now found herself holding her breath waiting for Matthew's answer, images of their teenage romance swirling around in her head.

'Of course you can, sweetheart,' said Daniel, breaking the silence. He got up and moved towards Charlene in slow motion, gently moving the offending fingernail away from Matthew's face. 'Of course you can,' he repeated gently as he led her back to her chair and sat her down. Luke moved to stroke her hand before resuming his finger study.

'This is so much better than *EastEnders*,' Daniel whispered to Katy as he positioned himself back in his own seat and smiled attentively at Joan.

'Shall we continue?' he said to her, as if nothing had happened.

'Of course, we should, shouldn't we?' she blustered. She stood up and riffled manically through the sheets on her flip chart before finally resting on the one she was looking for. The group was completely silent. No-one dared speak.

'Let's try this one, shall we?' she said, turning around with a fixed smile on her face. 'So, people, we are going to write two lists. One will be a list of what a typical day looks like for you now, pre-baby, and the other will be what a typical day could be like after you've had the baby. Does that make sense?'

Blank looks all round.

'Perfect. Now, let's see. Might I suggest that we mix it up a bit, seeing as it's our last class together? Daniel, why don't you help Charlene with this exercise? Would that be OK?'

'Of course,' said Mr Charming himself. 'It will be a pleasure.'

'Excellent. Now, Alison, why don't you do this with Luke and you can give him some tips on how to enjoy his wedding day. Is that OK, Luke?'

''Spose.'

'So that leaves Matthew and Katy. Good. OK then, here are some pens and paper. You have a few minutes to work on this and then we'll discuss it in the group.'

Matthew got up without saying a word, grabbed a pen and some paper and went and sat in the corner furthest away from the rest of the group. Katy trudged after him.

'Why didn't you answer the question?' she couldn't stop herself from asking when she sat down.

'What question?' he said sulkily.

'The question that Charlene asked you.'

'Because I was bloody petrified. She could have had my bloody eye out.'

'I see,' said Katy, snatching the paper from him and rapidly folding and unfolding it in her hands.

'Who cares about Charlene anyway?' said Matthew. 'What the hell happened on Saturday? Why did you leave so quickly?'

'Because, you idiot, Ben saw your tattoo,' said Katy, folding the paper even faster.

'Oh my God,' exclaimed Matthew, clamping his hand to his mouth.

'Exactly.'

'How could we be so stupid? What did he say? What did you say?'

'I had to admit we used to go out together at school, so of course he wanted to know why I hadn't told him. I said it was because Alison was very jealous and you didn't want to upset her in her condition. I said I didn't tell him so he wouldn't have to lie as well.'

'Did he believe you?'

'I think so. But we've barely spoken since. Ben doesn't do relationship talks, so I have no idea what he's really thinking.'

'This is a disaster. What if he tries to get in touch with Alison? He could ruin everything,' said Matthew, looking over to Alison, who was talking at a silent Luke.

'*Ben* could ruin everything? This is hardly his fault, is it?' Katy hissed. 'We got ourselves in this mess, Matthew. Ben would never do anything as deliberately nasty as to talk to Alison. You have nothing to worry about. It's my relationship that's on the brink here, not yours.'

'Katy, people do stupid things when they think they've been let down. And Ben is hardly a model of maturity, is he?'

'What's that supposed to mean?'

'Come on, Katy. He's just a kid, isn't he? And I'm sorry, but I have to say this. I cannot believe he is going to a stag do just as you are about to give birth. Talk about avoiding responsibility. Are you sure he's going to grow up in time to be a father?'

'That's really unfair,' she replied as the tears started to sting her eyes again. Really unfair, she thought, especially now she had seen Matthew in all his 'perfect provider' glory. She had to admit, she'd found herself thinking that having a man like that had some appeal, despite her years of dogged independence and determination to stand on her own two feet. Maybe more appeal than one who at the end of the month could often only afford to take her to the unlicensed Indian restaurant at the end of their road, where he would cheerfully hand over a can of own-label supermarket lager from a carrier bag. She and Ben had had some good nights there though, she reminded herself, particularly when they had invented the highly technical skill of naan bread mask-making.

'You have no right to judge him,' she said, trying to convince herself as much as Matthew. 'He may not have achieved your level of success, but he will come through. I know he will.'

'But I can't help but worry about you,' said Matthew, glancing nervously over at Alison again. 'Look, I've been thinking. If you ever need anything, you can always call me, you know.' He reached into the inside pocket of his jacket and pulled out a silver engraved business card holder. He took one out and offered it to Katy.

She stared down at the stiff white card quivering in his hand.

'No thanks,' she said finally. 'I think it's best if we never see each other again after tonight. Don't you?'

*

'Well, I'd just like to wish you all well,' said Joan at the end of the class. 'Let's give ourselves a big round of applause. Well done, everyone.'

They all looked at each other, slightly bewildered. That was it now, nothing else to complete before the big day itself. Eventually they got up and hugged awkwardly, wishing each other luck. Charlene even managed a hug with Matthew at Daniel's request. Since doing the exercise with him she had been transformed back into her usual Tigger persona, bouncing up and down like a teenager should.

'Daniel has given me the best ever idea for a wedding present for Luke,' she told Katy and Alison, clapping her hands in excitement. 'And he says he's coming to our party, so all of you have got to come now. You will, won't you, Alison, perleeeeeeease? Matthew and me are totally cool now.'

'We'll do our best,' Alison managed to say, almost without moving her lips.

'And you'll come with Ben, won't you, Katy? Since he's gone back to football, Luke's talked to him loads about being a dad. He's been great. I'm sure he'll want to come,' said Charlene.

'Well, I'll see if he can make it,' said Katy, surprised

that Ben had had a conversation with anyone about being a dad, let alone an eighteen-year-old boy.

When Alison hugged Katy goodbye she held her back for a moment and asked earnestly if things between her and Ben were alright, given his abrupt change of mood at the dinner party and his absence at the class. Katy swept aside her concern, saying they had both just been tired and everything was great.

'Still, Katy, if you ever need to talk, just call me, OK?' said Alison, giving Katy one last sympathetic squeeze.

Katy had to get out then. She turned and fled to the door without saying goodbye to Matthew.

Chapter 15

Matthew shook the ball again. The words INDI-
CATIONS SAY YES glowed mysteriously from the
hidden depths of the black plastic sphere.

One more time, he said to himself, now shaking
vigorously with both hands. ASK LATER appeared.

Matthew shoved the Decision Maker Magic Ball,
purchased from a gadget shop earlier that week, into
his desk drawer under a file. It had rapidly become an
obsession, and he found himself consulting it on all
manner of subjects. Who needs spreadsheets? he
thought, grateful that he had found a new way of
guiding his life. This was much more spontaneous,

much more fun and much more likely to lead to adventure.

Already he had derived great satisfaction that it had decreed a NO DOUBT ABOUT IT, when he had asked whether he should go to Charlene and Luke's wedding party. He was so pleased he had immediately informed Alison that they would be going. This had transported her into possibly the worst mood he had seen her in for some time. It was rare that something was deemed so bad that it destroyed their normal evening routine. But gone were the carefully prepared three-course gastronomic experiences that Alison usually spent endless hours preparing during the day. Gone were the perfect place settings taken from their treasured twelve-piece dinner service, a wedding present from a rich aunt. And most certainly gone were the long, leisurely if sometimes tedious meals during which Alison would regurgitate her latest thoughts on her master plan for her first few weeks of motherhood. This had all been unceremoniously replaced with a tray on the kitchen table, on which stood a supermarket ready-meal soggily defrosting, knife and fork strewn to one side.

He needed to say goodbye to Katy properly, he had concluded. Sadly, he could not explain that to Alison, who could see no good reason on this earth why she should attend the party, given that it would no doubt be celebrated in some 'godforsaken hovel'. She had dismissed Matthew's decision, assuming that an 'over my dead body' would have changed his mind. But as the week wore on and it became apparent that Matthew was going to remain uncharacteristically firm against her opposition, she proceeded to punish him with minimal, terse conversation and plastic food. More worryingly, as Matthew became increasingly distracted by his torment over the need to gain closure with Katy, he sensed Alison's growing disappointment that he was not delivering the level of support necessary at this stage of the pregnancy. And her inability to fully engage him resulted in her completely severing his involvement in the remaining preparations. She was clearly determined that she wasn't going to let Matthew or anyone else prevent her from being the best-prepared mother of twins there had ever been. Purchases were made, appointments set and nurseries reorganised without Matthew being called upon for any consultation whatsoever. His abrupt redundancy made him uneasy. However, he was unable to muster any power to address it until after the wedding party.

And so, as they pulled into the car park of the Miners'

Welfare Hall & Institute that Saturday, Alison's first comment was unsurprising.

'I told you we shouldn't have come,' she declared.

To be honest, there wasn't much that looked hopeful about the exterior of the 1960s, single-storey, flat-roofed building on the opposite side of the potholed car park. The lurid green concrete cladding contrasted unattractively with the red tin roof. A broken window that had been patched using bright yellow electrician's tape was barely holding on to a flapping Sugar Puffs cereal packet, and a sign above the door had been obliterated by graffiti. All of which did nothing to heighten one's anticipation of an enjoyable evening.

'Charlene and Luke must be really popular,' said Matthew, trying to ignore the fact that Alison had just pressed the lock down on her door. They sat in silence and surveyed the lively group of about thirty people that were hanging around outside what must be a very packed hall. Clearly at the end of a good day's drinking, the crowd was noisily standing in small, boisterous clusters. A group of middle-aged women sat on the ground with their backs against the wall, sipping from plastic pint glasses filled with wine, stilettos discarded, revealing grubby feet. A small cloud of smoke hovered above the happy crowd, curling its way up from numerous cigarettes.

Matthew and Alison were interrupted by a loud rap on the window.

'What the . . .' said Matthew as he reached for the button to lower the window.

'Boss car, man,' said a young lad of no more than twelve, poking his head right through the window and causing Matthew to jerk his head back to avoid a shower of spit.

'You 'ere for Charlene's wedding?'

'Er, yes, that's right,' replied Matthew.

'I'm Scott, Charlene's bro'. I'm in charge of that valley parking thing, so you just give us your keys and I'll park this baby and keep it safe and sound till you're ready to go, alright?'

'But we are already parked.'

'You're right, boss, but you see, all the wedding cars have to be parked over there.'

'Why?'

'Because they'll be safer over there.'

'Why?' Matthew asked again.

'Because.'

'Look, son. How about we leave the car here and you take us to where the party is instead?'

'So I'd valley park you?' asked Scott.

'Exactly.'

'I'd still have to charge, though. You're still asking for the valley parking service,' said Scott seriously.

'OK, how about a bag of crisps and a tip? It's valet parking, not valley parking.'

'Yeah, that's what I said.'

'No, valet, like . . . ballet,' said Matthew.

'Ballet? I ain't wearing no pink dress just so I can drive a flash car.'

Matthew looked at Alison, who had her arms clamped tightly over her belly as if afraid someone might steal the twins from under her nose at any minute.

'Come on,' he said to her. 'Just for an hour.'

Scott ran off and stood waiting for them by the door, punching away at three saggy pale pink balloons that must have been taped to the door.

'If I inhale one breath of smoke I may never forgive you,' said Alison as she reluctantly lifted the door lock and heaved herself out of the car.

She held Matthew's arm in a vice-like grip as they crossed the car park, clutching her other hand to her mouth and nose.

'Coming through, coming through,' shouted Scott

above the noisy chatter as they got closer to the door. 'Lady with a baby. Come on, let her through.'

They eventually managed to push their way through the lively bustle and were surprised to find a scene of relative calm inside the hall. Rainbow-coloured disco lights skipped and swirled across a dusty, almost empty dance floor. The DJ's efforts to get everyone up were going mostly ignored, apart from two small boys doing knee slides. Plastic chairs that reminded Matthew of school were lined up all around the outside of the hall, already bagged by a sulky-looking older generation. No lively chatter here as they sat with their arms firmly folded or fingers drumming impatiently on tables, looking hopefully towards the kitchen door, wondering when the buffet was coming out so they could have a good tea and head off home in time to watch *Casualty*.

What must have been the friends of the bride and groom were all standing huddled in one corner, also quiet and drumming their fingers, but this time with eyes focused down on mobile phones, concentrating hard on whatever urgent message had to be sent, probably to the person standing next to them.

Without daring to look at Alison's face, Matthew took her hand and pulled her over to the bar area. Or rather, the hatch that linked the hall to a brightly lit kitchen manned by two students dressed in gothic-style clothes, made up with way too much eyeliner, serving drinks and wearing black lace fingerless gloves.

'This is hideous,' hissed Alison. 'What are we doing here?'

'Oh, for God's sake, Alison,' said Matthew, finally snapping. 'If you stopped being such a bloody snob for just five minutes you might enjoy yourself.'

Alison looked completely taken aback by Matthew's outburst. 'What on earth has got into you? Enjoy myself here? Don't be ridiculous.'

'You came, you came! I can't believe you really came!'

An oversized cloud of brilliant white rushed past them out of nowhere, almost knocking Alison off her feet. For a moment a storm of netting and taffeta obscured the view until Charlene turned and revealed Daniel standing in the doorway with Katy and Ben. Charlene immediately dragged him over to the group of teenage texters. The girls flocked around him, whispering urgently whilst looking over their shoulders and bursting into giggles. The teenage boys in the crowd drew back together in a defensive stance, clearly discussing how they were going to deal with this new, alien threat to their patch.

Katy and Ben were left standing alone at the door, Charlene having totally ignored them. Ben took one look at Matthew, said something to Katy then walked back outside without even saying hello.

'I wonder what on earth has got into Ben,' said Alison. 'He was so moody when he came to dinner, and his manners, well, non-existent. Then not turning up to the class. There's something really weird happening there. I think he can't handle the thought of becoming a father, you know. Poor Katy. She's so lovely and deserves so much better, don't you think?'

Matthew didn't trust himself to reply so pretended not to hear her.

'Are you listening?' she persisted. 'Don't you think Katy deserves better?'

'Yes,' was all he could whisper, trying hard to suppress the desire to run over and comfort a very forlorn-looking Katy.

'I'm going to cheer her up,' said Alison, striding away. Matthew trailed behind her, wondering whether it had been a big mistake to come.

'So, no sign of the baby yet?' Alison asked Katy when they reached her.

'Er, no, not yet,' said Katy, looking nervously at Matthew. 'I'm surprised you're here.'

'Not as surprised as me,' said Alison. 'Matthew insisted we come. I still have absolutely no idea why.'

Matthew could not decipher the look that Katy gave him.

'Ben really wanted to come,' Katy said eventually. 'Turns out he and Luke have bonded over their impending fatherhood.'

'Well, I guess they do have a lot in common,' said Matthew.

'Because they're both too young, you mean?' Katy shot back. 'Ben's not that young, you know.'

'You're right, he's actually very mature,' said Matthew, unable to withhold the sarcasm.

'Matthew,' said Alison sharply. 'Just ignore him, Katy. He's in a foul mood. I'm so glad you're here, so at least I can have a sensible conversation with someone before we make our apologies and leave this excuse for a wedding.'

Katy was shocked at Alison's visible disdain. 'As long as Charlene and Luke are happy, that's all that matters, isn't it?' she said.

'Well, I guess if you get married at eighteen, what can you expect? But seriously, Katy, would you be happy if you and Ben ended up having your very first dance as a married couple in a *shed*?' asked Alison.

'Katy and Ben aren't getting married, they told you,' said Matthew firmly.

'They might,' said Alison. 'They might change their minds after the baby arrives.'

'Who knows?' replied Katy, looking around desperately. 'Oh look, here's Daniel coming back,' she said with considerable relief.

'Hello, one and all,' he said as he approached. 'What a marvellous party.'

'You seem to be an instant hit,' said Katy. 'What on earth did you find to talk about to teenage girls?'

'Music and dancing, of course,' he said. 'The two greatest obsessions that teenage girls and gay men share. That as well as being in love, of course,' he added, giving Matthew a sly smile.

'And also public toilets, it would seem,' said Katy, digging Daniel in the ribs and pointing out Charlene and her gang of friends trooping into the ladies' toilets.

'There's no need for such vulgarity, Katy. For your information, they've gone to change for the first dance,' said Daniel.

'What, all of them?'

'Yes, all of them. Now I suggest we go and find a seat with a good view, because you don't want to miss this, trust me.'

Daniel hustled them to the edge of the dance floor and found seats for the pregnant ladies. Shortly afterwards Charlene emerged from the toilets, followed by her entourage dressed, or rather not dressed, in metallic-blue frighteningly short miniskirts and bra-tops. Charlene herself was in a slightly more demure but nonetheless pretty offensive bright red frilly number, which was knee-length at the back but sadly only just crotch-length at the front, owing to her bump. She staggered across the dance floor in ankle-breaking high heels to the front door of the hall.

'You lot. Put your fags out and come in here now,' she shouted to the puffing throng outside the door. 'If you don't I am shutting the bar, because this is my wedding and you have to do what I tell you.'

She strutted back across the hall towards the DJ as the rowdy smokers trickled in and headed straight for the bar.

Charlene's mates were now all standing in a vague line in the middle of the dance floor doing some bizarre limb wriggling as if preparing to set off for a sprint.

Charlene spent a few moments shouting in the DJ's ear before he gave a thumbs up. She then picked her way back through a maze of cables and speakers until she was in the centre of her assembled crew. She shouted something and they instantly formed a rigid straight line with about two feet between each of them.

'OK, ladies and gentlemen,' said the DJ, interrupting his utterly predictable Motown section. 'If I could have your undivided attention, we have something very special for you tonight. Apparently our handsome groom Luke didn't want to do a first dance because he's too shy. Let's hear a big aaaah for Luke, everybody.'

The room was silent apart from a small child shouting, 'Get off my ninny,' from underneath a table.

'Come on people, a big aaaah for poor old Luke,' begged the DJ.

A feeble aaah came from the old fogeys' corner, who were now taking it in turns to go into the kitchen to ask what time the buffet was being served.

'So anyway, our Charlene, not being the shy type herself, decided that she would still have a first dance, but with her mates instead, and dedicate it to her brand-new husband. So here for one night only are the Hussycat Dolls of Leeds, performing for your delight

"Don't Cha Wish Your Husband Was Hot Like Mine".'

'Bravo, bravo,' cheered Daniel wildly. 'Just inspired. Fan-bloody-tastic. You go, girls.'

The line of girls were all gently nodding at each other in time to the music as the intro bars to the song came pounding over the speakers. Then they all seemed to draw breath in unison before launching into flamboyant, not quite synchronised arm waving, which took them through the entire first verse. This was followed by a moment's respite before they braced themselves for the chorus. As the first line came up they all jumped forward in the air in unison then stood and gyrated wildly whilst shouting the adapted lyrics at the top of their voices.

Don't cha wish your husband was hot like mine?
You really shouldn't wish 'cause from today he's all mine.
Don't cha
Don't cha, baby
Don't cha wish your husband was right like mine?
If you try and steal him I will fight you 'cause he's mine.
Don't cha
Don't cha, baby.

The effect was very disturbing. Some of the girls had clearly spent hours perfecting their gyrating, whereas some of the more physically challenged looked like clay on a potter's wheel in the hands of a very poor potter.

By this time Daniel was hysterical.

'You couldn't pay for this,' he said as he wiped his eyes. 'Even my creative genius couldn't make this up. Although I have to admit, I did give Charlene the idea, but I never dreamed it would turn out like this. I think I might sign them up. They would be best in show at Gay Pride, I'm sure.'

To their credit, they kept it together right until the last chorus, when Charlene lost it. The little kids in the room clearly thought that the all-singing, all-dancing troupe had been brought in for their entertainment and were now standing in line in front of them, attempting to copy their every move. It was not this, however, that upset Charlene. It was Scott, who had stuffed two balloons and a cushion down his front. His bright blue and red cleavage could be seen bursting out of the top of his shirt whilst a gold tassel dangled jauntily out at the bottom. He was standing directly behind Charlene, mimicking her every move as well as stopping every few moments to clutch his back and pull a pained face, pretending to be heavily pregnant. Charlene finally caught sight of people laughing at something behind her and whirled round to find Scott in mid-flow.

'Mum, get Scott away!' she wailed. 'Why does he have to ruin everything? It's not fair! Muuuuuuum, now!'

Charlene's mum appeared from nowhere, attached herself to his ear and dragged him off.

This took only a moment, then Charlene returned to the routine as if nothing had happened.

'What a pro, what a pro!' shouted Daniel as he leapt up for the final line of the song to lead the standing ovation. 'Brilliant, just brilliant!'

'She's quite a performer, your wife,' said Ben, loitering by the bar with Luke, who was trying to be as inconspicuous as possible.

'Tell me about it,' he muttered.

'What do your parents think of her?' asked Ben, trying not to stare at Charlene's too-short skirt bouncing up and down to reveal way too much underwear.

'Don't care.'

'Where are they? I've not seen them yet.'

'Gone home.'

'I see.'

Ben took another long slug of his extra-strong lager,

the third pint he had managed to down since he had arrived.

'So, Luke, you OK with all of this marriage and baby stuff?' asked Ben.

'Yeah.'

'Petrified, right? You don't have to tell me, I can relate to that. Boy, can I relate to that,' said Ben, shaking his head before draining his glass. 'I mean, we're two young guys in our prime, right? Our whole lives ahead of us. We could do anything, go anywhere, be anything, and look at us. One minute you're thinking that with a bit more practice you could still be a pro footballer and the next minute all bets are off because someone tells you that the next eighteen years of your life have been taken from right under your nose. Just like that. I sympathise with you, man. I'm there with you, Luke. We're in this together, mate, you and me.' Ben flung an arm around Luke's shoulders and picked up his next pint.

'And another thing,' said Ben, spilling lager as he waved it in the air. 'And I'm sure you'll agree with this one, Luke. So you have a baby, right, and suddenly you and the mother are supposed to get married and stay together forever, just like that. I tell you, I take my hat off to you, mate. I'm young but you're a bloody child. I know I shouldn't say this, but I can't believe you're doing this. I really can't.'

Luke stared at the ground and started to kick the wall.

'Look, you can tell me, man to man, like,' said Ben, bending over to try and get Luke to look at him. 'Is this what you really want?'

Luke kicked the wall extra hard then raised his head, looking Ben in the eye, probably for the first time ever.

'Yes, I do,' he said steadily. 'Because my dad is a shit. He hates my guts. Just because I'm not like him, he thinks I can't do anything right. He's made my life hell. And it's not the kid's fault, is it? Every kid deserves a good dad. Every kid does, don't they?'

Ben stood open-mouthed. He had never heard a sentence from Luke, never mind a whole string of them.

'Don't they?' Luke repeated, much louder.

Ben reeled back from the force of Luke's question and the lager that had got the better of his legs.

Luke grabbed a chair and managed to get Ben to sit on it.

'They do, don't they?' Luke asked yet again.

Ben looked up at him, thinking.

Eventually he said, very quietly, 'They bloody well do, Luke, they bloody well do.' He pulled himself unsteadily to his feet and staggered outside.

Chapter 16

Katy watched Ben get up and go outside from across the room. He'd barely said two words to her the whole evening and she was getting sick of having to make awkward conversation with Matthew and Alison, and even more sick of watching Matthew massage Alison's swollen feet, even if he didn't look too happy about it. Alison's smug smile was getting to her in a way she couldn't bear to think about. She looked away, only to be confronted by the sight of Charlene and Luke locked in a snogathon. She stared at them as they kissed hungrily before participating in some weird ear-biting ritual. When they surfaced for air, Luke took Charlene's hand

and led her to a seat. They both sat down and Luke put his arm around her and sat stroking her belly tenderly.

Ben had never stroked her belly. No, that was a lie, she realised. He had done it once when she had first started to show. They had been watching a DVD one night and he'd leant over and, in one of the most intimate moments they had ever had, he had nudged her top up and gently stroked her bare, swollen belly. But it had been way too intimate for her. In her opinion that wasn't the relationship she had signed up for. They did laughing, they did fun, they did great sex, they did ridiculous conversations way into the night, but they didn't do intimacy. She'd spent years using intimacy as her warning signal that she was in the potential heartbreak zone, so she had pushed his hand firmly away and got up to go and make a cup of tea.

Just as she was starting to wonder what the hell she had been thinking, the DJ's voice boomed over the loudspeaker to introduce the next song.

'For all you lovers out there we have a seriously smoochy blast from the past, requested by the mother of the bride herself. So come on, you men, get those ladies on the floor and press some flesh.'

Katy shuddered at his turn of phrase then felt her

entire body droop as she recognised the opening bars to the Eighties hit 'Right Here Waiting' by Richard Marx. The dance floor filled instantly and she watched through blurry eyes as a sea of floral dresses squirmed against creased and sweaty blue and white shirts. The song had been a big hit in her first year at university and she remembered painfully how this song in particular had the power to reduce her to a quivering wreck after her break-up with Matthew. As she sat there alone watching the love-fest sway in front of her eyes, it reminded her far too closely of similar nights she had spent on the edge of the dance floor at the Student Union watching her friends copping off, as she pined for Matthew.

She realised, with heart-crushing clarity, that she didn't want to be the one sitting on her own at the edge of a dance floor any more. And most certainly not at a wedding, nearly nine months pregnant. Actually, to her amazement, what she really wanted was to be the one having her belly stroked, just like Charlene.

Just as she sensed that her thoughts were about to take a horrific downward spiral, Ben plunged into her eyeline, obliterating the picture of wedded bliss before her.

'Katy,' he said.

'Ben,' she replied.

He dragged his fingers through his untidy mop of hair whilst he looked around wildly, as if at a loss as to what to say. Then he took a deep breath and wiped his eyes. If Katy had not known him better, she could have sworn he'd been crying.

'Please will you dance with me?' he asked finally, holding out a slightly shaky hand.

She was completely thrown. This couldn't be happening. Dancing was in Ben's top five least favourite activities, along with cleaning up his own sick and eating quiche.

To her surprise he took her hand, pulled her out of her chair ever so gently and led her to the dance floor, where he pulled her in close to his slightly sweaty body.

'Are you pissed?' she asked cautiously.

'What makes you say that?'

'We've never slow-danced before,' she said.

'Well, I just . . .' he began, before engulfing her in a huge hug and breathing lager-soaked fumes heavily in her ear.

'Oh Katy,' he murmured.

Katy hugged him back as hard as she could,

224

wondering what this was leading to. Unable to stand the suspense, she pushed him away to arm's-length and looked at him nervously.

'Ben, has something happened?' she asked.

Ben looked as if he actually might cry before he gave an enormous sniff and squared his shoulders.

'Yes, Katy, it has. I have just realised I've been a prick,' he said before pausing briefly for thought. 'Not that I have always been a prick, you understand,' he continued. 'In fact, my previous record is somewhat prickless, I like to think. It's just recently I've found a certain aptitude for it.'

'But it's my fault,' she said. 'I shouldn't have . . .'

'No, you shouldn't,' he interrupted. 'In fact, that does put us on a par on the prick scorecard.'

'Well, yes, but don't forget you always have a prick in hand,' she couldn't help but reply. She was slipping into their normal banter mode, which she realised always irritatingly happened when they should have been talking seriously.

'True, true, always useful I find,' he responded rather dejectedly.

They both looked at each other awkwardly, hands clasped firmly between them.

Katy could stand it no longer; she had to find out what direction this conversation was taking.

'So, so . . . are we OK?' she asked cautiously.

'Yes,' he said, nodding seriously, his brow furrowed. 'Yes, we are.'

Katy held her breath, waiting for more, but Ben appeared to be still processing thoughts behind a tormented-looking face. Finally, after a very long pause, his face softened and a smile slowly started to appear. Katy allowed herself to breathe again and braced herself for Ben's next words.

'We're having a baby,' he said, almost as if it was the very first time he had actually taken it in, a slight look of amazement on his face.

'We are,' she said slowly. 'Is that OK?'

'It's fucking brilliant,' he replied, a watery but proud grin fully illuminating him at last. 'And I'm going to be a fucking brilliant dad,' he continued, now grinning from ear to ear.

Katy felt her legs buckle as a shot of sheer joy surged through her entire body. She stumbled but Ben grasped her arms firmly, allowing her to steady herself.

'Hey, you alright?' he asked, looking worried again whilst he gently stroked her hair.

'I'm more than alright,' she said, beaming up at him. Ben wanted to be a dad. He wanted to be a dad to her child. He wanted a future with her and the baby. She wasn't alone on the edge of the dance floor. She was right in the middle, clinging to Ben. She realised her entire world had just changed, because for the first time in a very long while she wanted to stop being a 'me' and start being an 'us'. An 'us' with Ben and the baby. She gulped for air as her tears changed into laughter, both their shoulders heaving up and down in unison as they continued to slow-dance.

They clung to each other for the rest of the dance, not speaking, Ben rhythmically rubbing her back and rocking her gently.

'There is one thing, though,' he said, pulling away as the song drew to a close. Katy felt her heart drop like a stone. 'After tonight, do we ever have to see Matthew and Alison again? It's not the ex-boyfriend thing, although imagining you with such a stiff does nothing for your street-cred, Katy. It's just that they are so horribly perfect that they make me feel like daddy dunce. And I want to be a good dad, I really do. Because every kid deserves a good dad, don't they? But you'll have to let me do it my way,' he said earnestly.

Ben's way would be a great way, Katy thought, impulsively reaching up to stroke his cheek. 'Let's just forget all about them,' she said. 'After tonight we can pretend they never existed. Agreed?'

'Agreed,' he replied, looking relieved.

'Can I ask you something now?' Katy said, feeling suddenly shy.

'Anything, my love, apart from dancing to George Michael, that is,' said Ben.

'Will you stroke my belly?' she asked.

This time a tear did escape from his eye.

'That would make me the proudest man alive,' he said as he gently nudged up her top and rested his hand on her warm belly. They shared a long, lingering kiss until Katy felt a tap on her shoulder.

'So sorry to disturb this tender moment but I am desperate,' said Daniel, looking nervously around him. 'Old biddies keep coming up and asking me to dance. You have to rescue me.'

'Why don't you dance with Katy while I go for a slash?' said Ben, before kissing Katy on the forehead and disappearing off to the gents, waving cheerily as he went.

'So what's with love's young dream then?' asked

Daniel, observing the very smiley Katy.

'Oh Daniel, it's all going to be alright. We made up and he says he's excited about being a dad,' Katy beamed. 'And this has to be the absolutely last time I ever have to see Matthew, so I think I have weathered the storm and calmer waters are approaching. I can finally get on with the rest of my life.'

'Really, so all those emotions and feelings are where they should be, hey?' asked Daniel.

'Exactly.'

'And you got the answer to the really, truly difficult question?'

'What question?' she asked.

'Christ, Katy, you never listen to a word I say, do you? Do-I-really-love-him?' Daniel spelled out. 'Remember? That question.'

'Well yeah, I guess I must do.'

'Have you told him? Has he told you?'

'Well no, but we're really not that kind of couple,' said Katy with a shrug. 'It's fine, honestly, Daniel, we're back on track. We're going to be absolutely fine.'

'OK, OK, if you say so. Just be happy, OK? Promise me?' asked Daniel.

'I promise,' reassured Katy.

'And another thing. You make sure you tell that Matthew never to rear his ugly head again.'

'Sure, sure. Now can we please sit down, my feet are killing me.'

'Good idea. I need a decent drink,' said Daniel, taking her hand and leading her off the dance floor.

By the time Ben had come back from the toilets, Daniel had miraculously produced a very expensive bottle of vodka he'd sneaked in, knowing that the bar was probably going to be a strictly cash and carry affair.

'I'll have a bit of that,' said Ben. 'That lager is doing no good to my insides.'

'Be my guest,' said Daniel, feeling generous given that Ben had obviously made Katy so happy.

'Watch out, stand by your beds,' muttered Ben as Matthew and Alison came to sit with them, having been to inspect the buffet and decided to abstain. Katy couldn't help but notice the displeasure spread over Matthew's face as he observed Ben nuzzling contentedly into her shoulder whilst he rotated his hand over and over her bump under her shirt, occasionally revealing a peek at her naked pregnant belly.

The look didn't go unnoticed by Daniel, either, who

shoved the vodka bottle at Matthew and told him to take a swig in an effort to distract him.

Matthew looked at Alison, who immediately placed her hand firmly on his arm.

'Don't mind if I do,' Matthew said, shaking off her hand before taking the bottle from Daniel and jamming it firmly in his mouth, downing several gulps.

'Matthew!' exclaimed Alison. 'You don't know where it's been.'

Matthew took another very large swig whilst holding eye contact with Alison.

'Matthew, stop. It's not funny,' she protested.

'It's just vodka,' said Matthew.

'But what happens if the babies come tonight and you are blind drunk?'

Matthew gave a big sigh and stared at the bottle in his hands. 'Just one more,' he muttered, this time not looking at Alison and taking an extra-long slug.

'Right, that's it. We're going,' said Alison. 'Don't move. You just sit there. I'll go and say goodbye to Charlene and Luke and thank Charlene's parents. I want you to be capable of getting into the car by the time I'm back. Excuse me, everyone. And don't let him have any more of that vodka.'

As soon as her back was turned, Matthew took another slug of vodka before handing the bottle back to Daniel.

'I owe you a drink,' he said but made no move to go to the bar, preferring to stare after Alison.

'Tell you what, I'll get a round in,' said Ben. 'Won't be a tick.'

Daniel looked at Katy and coughed, nodding vigorously towards Matthew.

'Yes, and I need some air,' Daniel said. 'I'll be outside.'

Katy and Matthew sat in silence until Matthew reached forward and grabbed the vodka and took yet another swig.

'What's with you?' asked Katy.

'Nothing.'

'Come on, you've hardly had a civil word for anyone, and what's with the vodka?'

'It's all just too weird for me, Katy,' he said, looking far into the distance. 'Just too weird.'

'What's weird?'

'This is. Don't you think it's weird that this is the last time we'll ever see each other?'

'Guess so, but it's not exactly been a barrel of laughs, has it?'

'No, but it's been good, you know,' he said, turning to

face her. 'Apart from making me sing stupid songs. We were good once, weren't we? Really good. And I screwed it up.' He paused. 'Ever wonder what might have been? You know, if I hadn't been such a dick.'

'No, never,' Katy lied.

'I do.'

'Don't.'

'I can't help it,' said Matthew, letting his head sink into his hands. Katy wasn't sure what to say. She hadn't expected this.

Suddenly Matthew's head shot up and he looked at Katy.

'Let me see you and the baby. Just once, I promise. I think I need to see you both, so I can get closure or something. Say a proper goodbye and then draw the line. Then I'll be able to move on. I think that will make me feel better.'

Katy stared back at him, completely dumbstruck.

'Make you feel better?' she said finally through gritted teeth. 'That sums it up, doesn't it? You just don't get it, do you?' She was shouting right in his ear now to make sure he could hear her. 'Listen carefully. This is not about you. This is about the baby and me and Ben, and us somehow making this work. And it is about your wife and your two kids on their way any day. You have to do what's right for other people now, Matthew, not what might make you feel better.'

'But I can't help the fact that I care about you and what happens to the baby,' he said, rocking himself backwards and forwards.

Katy closed her eyes and tried to slow down her rapid breathing.

'The time to care was right about when you were shagging the Virgin Mary, not now. You missed it, Matthew. Well and truly missed it.'

Matthew looked utterly defeated for a moment and then his face hardened.

'I was stupid and I'm sorry, but you slept with me and I didn't see you worrying about Ben. Now you're planning the rest of your life with him, despite the fact he's an idiot.'

'Leave it, Matthew. It's nothing to do with you and you have absolutely no right to say that.'

'But he could be bringing up my child.'

'Stop. That's enough. How dare you talk like this now? We dealt with this weeks ago, remember? Ben will be the father of this child, end of story. Now just leave it alone.'

Matthew stared at her briefly before saying, 'Fine, if that's the way you want it. Just don't come running to me when he walks out on you because he can't take the responsibility.' He got up and walked unsteadily in the direction of the gents'.

What a twat, she thought. How dare he ask to see the baby and how dare he say Ben was going to let her down. Deep down, however, she knew Matthew might be right. Despite Ben's sudden upturn in attitude, come crunch time, he might not be able to take the pressure. She looked around for him, frantically needing some immediate reassurance. He was talking to some of Luke's friends by the bar. She breathed heavily, trying not to cry, and made her way over. Just as she got within a few yards of him she felt the tears spring up like a sprinkler on a late-night timer. She tried sniffing vigorously but there was nothing she could do; they were off and running. Ben looked horrified at the blubbering mess advancing towards him. He muttered some words to the three boys talking to him, who took one look at Katy and backed away in terrified awe.

'What is it? What's happened?' asked Ben, putting his arm around her.

Katy breathed in hard again, trying desperately to regain some control.

'Katy, my love, was it the trifle?' asked Ben. 'Did Charlene's mum make you eat it? I know it tastes like rat poison, but I really don't think anyone who names her children after *Neighbours* characters would deliberately try to harm you. Although I did hear she wants to kill off all the guests so they won't have to return the presents come divorce time.'

Katy couldn't help but smile, then slowly but surely her shoulders began to shake with laughter as she buried her head in a tissue. She dried her eyes and gave a big sigh. God, it was good to have Ben back on form.

'So what did the tosser say this time? I saw you talking to him,' said Ben, turning serious. 'He wasn't giving you grief about your telling me about you and him, was he? Because if he was, I'll have to have a word with him. It's his lie, not yours. It wasn't your idea not to tell her.'

'No, Ben, it wasn't that. He was just a bit worried that, well, you had taken it badly and were taking it out on me. That's all, nothing really.'

'You what? He thinks *I'm* giving you a hard time over *his* stupid bloody secrets? Christ, he's got a nerve. Who the hell does he think he is, playing all these games?'

'It's not a game, honestly, Ben, just a stupid lie that got out of hand, that's all.'

'A stupid lie that was ridiculous in the first place. What kind of crazy relationship do they have that Matthew is scared shitless of confessing previous girl-friends?' said Ben, getting worked up.

'Ben, please just forget about it, it's really not worth it.'

'Back in a minute,' he mumbled and walked off.

Katy was about to reach for her tissues again when she noticed where he was going. Within moments the gents' door shrieked then slammed with an ominous bang.

Matthew was standing unsteadily at the urinal with his back to the room when Ben walked in. It was empty, apart from whatever non-human inhabitants were encouraged by decades of grime and stale piss. There were two cubicles to the right but only one had a door, and a bare bulb flickered distractedly in the middle of the room, making everything look like a scene from a B-movie.

There were three urinals and Matthew had taken the one to the far right, allowing any newcomer to leave the one in the middle free, in accordance with male toilet etiquette. Ben could sense that Matthew was therefore somewhat surprised when someone brushed up right next to him.

'So Katy tells me you're worried that I'm giving her a hard time because it somehow slipped both your minds that you used to go out together. That is despite the fact you've had a reminder tattooed to your shoulders for the last God knows how many years.'

The shock of the intrusion caused Matthew to halt mid-flow. He looked up at Ben and puffed his chest out.

'No, Ben. I was just checking she was alright. She needs looking after. She is about to have a baby.'

'Don't you think I know that? I'm doing it. I'm doing it and then you come along and upset everything,' said Ben.

'Doing what?' Matthew let out a small laugh. 'What *are* you doing exactly, Ben? Because, to be honest, I don't see you doing that much.' He gave up on his interrupted stream and tucked himself away before turning to face Ben head on.

'All you ever did was arse around at the classes. You're out all the time with your mates and you still think it's a good idea to go to a stag do when the baby is due. Honestly, Ben, I don't think you're up to it. You need to grow up or leave Katy to it. No father is better than a father who doesn't give a shit, and Katy deserves better than that.'

The door burst open and Scott came hurtling in.

'Mister, mister,' he said breathlessly to Ben. 'Your girl-friend is outside and she says I've got to get you out right now and she'll buy me a half of shandy if I don't tell me mum.' Scott grabbed Ben's hand and started pulling for all he was worth.

Ben's stony gaze did not move from Matthew's face.

'If you get out now I'll buy you a pint,' said Ben.

'What, of shandy, or do you mean a real pint?'

'Whatever you want. Now get out.'

'Yes sireee sir, whatever you say, sir,' said Scott, disap-pearing as suddenly as he'd arrived.

'You think I'm not worthy to be a father? That's where you get your snotty-nosed attitude from, is it? Well, I'll be honest, Matthew. It's taken some getting used to. And yes, there have been many times that I've felt like running away, but I haven't, have I? And just because I've got Katy and you've got a woman with a broom stuck up her arse, well, that's your fault, isn't it? Now you listen to me, mate. You had your turn and now she wouldn't look twice at you, so get lost, you stuck-up twat.'

Matthew gripped hold of a broken towel rail to try and steady himself, visibly shocked at Ben's verbal attack.

'Pathetic, just pathetic,' laughed Ben.

Next thing he knew, Ben was reeling back, his chin feeling like it was on fire. He collided with the toilet door, stumbling back into the crowded room and onto the edge of the dance floor. He hit me. The bastard hit me, he thought as his head thudded to the floor. Next thing he knew, Matthew was on top of him, pulling him up by his collar.

'Wouldn't want me, you say? Wouldn't want me?' he whispered angrily, right in Ben's ear. 'I think you'd better ask her about that. She sure did want me the night of the school reunion. Nice flat she's got. At a stag do, weren't you? Amazing what you miss going on a stag do, isn't it?' Matthew shoved Ben's head back to the floor again, got up and started to stagger across the dance floor to the door.

The excitement hadn't gone unnoticed by the old biddies, who were nodding genteelly to an Eminem track. They rushed over to where Matthew had left Ben.

'What are you doing down there, love?' said one.

'Do you want a sherry?' said another.

'Go on after him, the brute, give him one from me,'

said an overexcited lady who had spilt pickle down the front of her polyester frock.

Ben got up and fought his way through his devoted crowd to reach Matthew just as he got to the middle of the hall. He grabbed him by the shoulder, spun him around and flattened him with an extremely well-targeted left hook. Matthew fell to the ground as if he had been shot. Then lay there, not moving.

'Ben!' came the first cry. 'What are you doing?'

Katy pushed through the crowd of teenagers who had beaten her to the scene and who were looking extremely impressed by Ben.

Ben stared at her, not knowing what to say or how to feel. He opened his mouth to speak but closed it again when she dropped to her knees and knelt beside Matthew, who was still out cold.

'Matthew, wake up, please wake up,' she pleaded to the blank face.

'How could you?' She turned to Ben, giving him an icy look and shaking her head.

He opened his mouth again to speak, or shout, but no words came. He took one last look at the scene in front of him then turned and walked away, out of the door and into the night.

Chapter 17

Katy was watching *The Deadliest Catch* on the Discovery Channel. Fishermen were wrestling hundreds of live crabs as they came tumbling from nets onto the frantic deck of the fishing boat and it was all making her feel a bit sick. She wasn't sure why she was watching these men go through hell, but she suspected it was mainly because it was of some comfort to see someone with a worse life than hers. It was only her second day of maternity leave and daytime television had worn thin already, especially as her remote insisted on leading her to baby programmes depicting wonderful loving couples going through a wonderful loving experience together. This had almost caused her to cancel her subscription in disgust and sue Sky for mental cruelty until she chanced upon *The Deadliest Catch*. It had cheered her up enormously as she watched the men battling in such desperate conditions. It also happened to be Ben's favourite programme, and she suspected she was subconsciously keeping it on in the hope that it might act as a homing call back to her flat.

She had not seen Ben since the night of the wedding party, three days ago. Thankfully Matthew had opened his eyes when Scott had helpfully chucked a pint of cold lager over his face. By this time Alison had been alerted to the altercation and was at the scene, sitting uncomfortably on a chair in the middle of the dance floor next to his head.

'What happened, ask him what happened?' she had shrieked at Katy.

Katy looked down at Matthew, who had come round but was not making any sense. She looked up for Ben but he was nowhere to be seen.

'That other bloke punched him,' said Scott. 'Right in the gob. Perfect hit, it was. I tried to stop 'em, honestly I did. I went into them toilets, you know, when I knew there was trouble, and I stood between 'em and told them to pack it in, but that other bloke told me to get lost. Obviously didn't want me to see him thump him.'

'Who are you talking about? Who hit him?' Alison shouted in Scott's face.

'You know, her bloke, tall, a bit scruffy,' replied Scott, pointing at Katy.

'Katy, he doesn't mean Ben, does he? Why would Ben do this to Matthew?'

'I don't know, Alison. I didn't have a chance to ask him and now he's gone.'

Alison stared at Katy then slowly pulled herself up before asking Charlene's father if he would help Matthew to their car.

'Of course,' he replied. 'Shall I see if we can get hold of some hot towels?' he asked, confused by alcohol and the sight of so many pregnant women and someone flat on their back.

'No, I don't think we'll need those. Just get him into the car and I'll take him home.'

'Can I come with you and help you get him into the house?' asked Katy as Charlene's father hauled Matthew up onto his shoulder.

'No,' Alison replied. 'I think that you and Ben have done enough, don't you?'

*

Katy had been shocked at how quiet a phone could be. In her normal life phones trilled constantly, demanding her attention. She found she couldn't get used to the eerie silence, especially as her entire body was poised on red alert for the slightest possibility of a call from Ben.

And so, with just two weeks to go before she was due to give birth, Katy could feel herself falling apart. She was like one of the crabs on the TV, hopelessly scrabbling around, trying to find a way out but not making any progress in any direction, all the while knowing the inevitable was looming. For the crab it was certain death, but for Katy it was certain life. The life of a new baby who currently didn't have the possibility of one father, never mind the option of two. Every time she remembered Ben stroking her belly in the middle of the dance floor it triggered a wave of uncontrollable sobbing. It killed her to think that for the first time since Matthew, for what was all of half an hour, she had allowed her mind to explore the fantasy of a long-term future with a man. Whilst Ben merrily shared Daniel's vodka she had surprised herself by picturing the two of them at a simple but beautiful marriage ceremony, on a beach, with their child clinging on to Ben's hand, holding a ribbon on which dangled their wedding bands. It had been blissful to finally let her mind wander confidently forward and it felt shockingly cruel that yet again it looked as though her future hopes were not to be.

She put the now desperate crabs on mute and crawled under the duvet which had taken permanent residence on her sofa. She realised that nothing in her life was where it should be. Duvet always on the sofa, pyjamas always on her body, dirty crockery in the sink, empty hospital bag at the back of the wardrobe, babygros still in plastic wrappers in carrier bags and Ben somewhere else entirely.

Somehow, through the fog of her despair, she decided she had to do something. If she got everything back where it should be then maybe that would help. That had to be a good plan. Better than no plan. Better than sitting crying in front of death-row crabs.

So she hauled herself off the couch, which hissed in relief, and bent down to begin to gather the debris of the truly depressed off the floor. Damp tissues, chocolate wrappers, takeaway menus and back copies of *Hello* magazine. She got on all fours and methodically tramped up and down the length of the lounge like some sort of human vacuum cleaner, stuffing rubbish into pockets and up sleeves to save her going backwards and forwards to the bin. A glimpse of a long-lost DVD remote control behind the sofa finally gave her something to smile about as she set off in hot pursuit, trying to cram herself between the couch and the wall. Just as she thought she might be permanently wedged, she heard the front door click and footsteps across the hall. If it was armed robbers, she thought, it would be best to stay hidden, but her legs sticking out could be a giveaway. However, it could be Ben, so she heaved herself up, popping out suddenly like a rabbit out of a hole.

Ben was standing in the middle of the room with one eye on the muted and now very dead crabs and one eye on her.

'It's a good one, this. One bloke loses a leg,' he mumbled as Katy pulled herself to her feet, noting that he made no effort to help her.

'Where have you been? I've been worried sick,' she said.

He took both eyes off the crabs and looked at her blankly.

'At me mum's.'

'What happened, Ben? Why did you leave like that?'

'Well, you didn't want me to stay, did you?'

'I did, of course I did.'

'No, you didn't. I'm going to get my stuff.'

'Ben, stop. Sit down. Please. Just tell me what happened,' said Katy. 'Did Matthew wind you up? You shouldn't let him get to you, you know. We can forget about him now.'

'Can we?' Ben sat down and stared at the TV screen, not saying anything.

'Yes, Ben. Please, let's forget it all and think about the baby. That's all that matters, isn't it?' she begged.

He stood up again abruptly.

'No, it's not going to happen. It can't happen.'

'But why?' pleaded Katy, grabbing at his wrist, beginning to panic. 'Come on, Ben, we can do this.'

Ben spoke quietly and carefully.

'No, we can't. It's him you really want, isn't it? Well, maybe not exactly him, but someone like him. Not someone like me. I get it now. I can see how you see me. I just arse about all day, playing stupid games with stupid kids, and then I arse around all night, playing stupid games with my stupid mates. What is there in that for you? You and your posh office and your secretary and your posh lunches and your expense account. How could I ever think that I was anything more than just a bit of fun? No wonder you slept with Matthew.'

Katy sat down abruptly. So that was why Ben had hit him. Matthew had told him. Tears streamed down her face.

'I'm so sorry,' she sobbed into her hands. 'It was a stupid, stupid mistake. I never meant to hurt you.'

'It's not like we'd made any commitment or anything, is it?' he continued, not seeming to have heard a word Katy had said. 'We hadn't said we weren't going to sleep with other people. I just wish you'd told me, that's all. So I'd have known where I stood. Because now I feel really stupid for thinking this was all going to work out.' He looked down at the floor and started kicking the side of the sofa methodically.

'And you know what?' he continued. 'I can see the attraction in a guy like Matthew, honestly I can. I mean, he's got it all, hasn't he? A guy like that can take care of a woman. Good job, big house and he's sensible, you know, good dad material. He wouldn't lead his kids astray, like I would. Security, that's what it is, isn't it? That's what you need now. What can I offer? A crappy old Ford Focus and a Leeds United season ticket is all the security I have.'

'Ben, stop, please stop,' Katy begged. 'You've got it all wrong, honestly you have.'

'No, Katy,' he said, finally looking at her. 'I think for the first time I haven't got it wrong. I've been thinking about this and I realise I was an idiot. I was batting way above my league with you, and at some point a guy like Matthew was bound to come along who was on a level with you. And even if you did only sleep with him once, there are a million other Matthews out there who are worthy of you and a million times more capable of taking care of you than I am.' His voice broke and he turned away quickly to hide the tear sliding down his cheek.

'But, Ben, there aren't a million more of you. There's no-one else that would make me feel the way that you do,' sobbed Katy.

He wiped his eye wearily before responding.

'And how is that exactly?' he asked.

'Well,' she said, sensing a chink of hope. She desperately searched for the right words but she had no idea where to start. 'Ben, you're different from all the other guys. You make me laugh and, and . . .'

'Precisely. It's not enough,' said Ben grimly.

'No, wait, listen. It's much more than that. How do I explain? You're the one who stops me being my own worst nightmare. Oh God, I'm crap at this,' she said, waving her arms about in desperation. 'It's like when I tell you we've been arguing at work over how to describe a toilet cleaner, you're the one who says we should just say it cleans up shit.'

'Well, that's what it does.'

'Exactly. But only you could say that.'

'What, that toilet cleaner cleans up shit? Yeah, I sure am proud of that. Thinking of nominating myself for the Nobel Prize with words of wisdom like that.'

'No, Ben, I'm trying to explain,' she said, getting up and grabbing hold of his wrists. 'I've been thinking about it too, and it's because we're so different, that's what makes it right. I don't want someone who's like me, because I would turn into one of those hideous middle-class suburban housewives who lusts after hanging baskets.'

Ben looked confused.

'But, but . . .' he stuttered. 'But you're just better than me,' he said finally with a heavy sigh.

'That is so not true,' she said, reaching her hand up tentatively to stroke his cheek, feeling his wet tears on her fingertips. 'You, Ben King,' she said softly, 'are the funniest, kindest, most loyal, most greatest person I know and I am the luckiest girl on earth to have you.'

Ben stared down at her, looking completely stunned. He started to blink very fast, trying to prevent a barrage of tears.

'Really?' he asked, looking deep into her eyes for any sign of pretence.

'Really,' she replied, nodding her head firmly and clenching every single part of her body, willing him to believe her.

'I think I need you to repeat that,' he said quietly.

'I said, you are the funniest, kindest, most loyal, most greatest person I know and I am the luckiest girl on earth to have you,' she repeated breathlessly. A smile started to struggle through at the corner of his mouth. It must be working. She tried hard to remember what else she had been thinking in her foggy state over the last few days that might convince Ben they still had a future. 'And you are worth ten of Matthew or any other guy like him and I will regret sleeping with him for the rest of my life,' she said, knowing she had never said a truer word. 'Ben, I know I don't deserve your forgiveness, but I want you. More than anything, because you stroking my belly is not something I can live without any more.' She reached down, picked up his hand and pulled it up to her lips for the lightest of kisses before placing it on her belly.

Ben looked deep into her eyes again before looking down at their hands entwined on her stomach. Suddenly he lurched forward, enveloped her in his arms and sobbed uncontrollably.

Katy held him as tightly as she could, breathing heavily. She was absolutely exhausted from her unprecedented emotional outpouring, and with the relief that the future might be back on after all.

But then suddenly, without warning, Ben pulled away, wiping his hand across his dripping nose.

'But Katy, I'm not sure I can be a good dad,' he said, shaking his head. 'And you can't take that risk, saddling yourself with a crap dad.'

Katy sighed. She wasn't sure she had any energy left to tackle his insecurities about being a good father. But she had to keep going, the end was in sight.

'Ben, I know you'll be a great dad, I just do. And I know it must be so hard to think there's a tiny possibility that the baby isn't yours, but that doesn't matter. I think of you as the father. End of story.'

Ben staggered back as if someone had hit him.

'What? What do you mean, it may not be mine? What the hell are you talking about?' he asked, his eyes wide in disbelief.

'What . . . you mean . . . oh my God,' Katy buried her head in her hands.

'What do you mean, Katy?' Ben repeated.

Rocking back and forth in shock, Katy couldn't raise her head.

Ben reached down and pulled her hand roughly away from her face.

'What do you mean?' he asked again, almost shouting.

'I thought you would have worked it out. Oh Ben, I'm so sorry.'

'About what, Katy? Explain what you mean. *Now!*' he shouted.

With considerable effort Katy blurted out an explanation. 'When me and Matthew had sex, we only did it once, I promise, but it was about the time I got pregnant, so there's a very small possibility that Matthew could be the father. But Ben, it's tiny,' she said, looking up at him pleadingly. 'You and I had sex so many times around then that the baby must be yours. It's got to be, Ben. This baby is yours, I promise you.' She gripped his shoulders with her hands and shook him as if to drill it into him.

'But I don't understand,' said Ben, backing away from her. 'Are you telling me you've always known this?'

'Well, suspected. But as I say, it really is such a tiny possibility that . . . that . . .'

'That what? You thought you wouldn't tell me. Have you spoken to Matthew about it?'

'Well, yes, but only because he suspected too, so I had to. And we agreed that the chance is so small that everyone would be better off if we just forgot about it.'

'When did you talk to him?'

'Ages ago, I can't remember.'

'When, Katy?' asked Ben aggressively.

'Well, Christ, I don't know,' said Katy, totally flustered. 'I guess it must have been after we saw them at the first antenatal class. I thought I'd never see him again after the reunion, but then when he turned up at the class I had to talk to him.'

'So you and him have been having these talks for weeks, and all along you've let me think that the baby was mine.'

'Ben, please, you make it sound so terrible. I was trying to do the right thing, I promise you. I wasn't trying to deceive you on purpose.'

'What? Making me think all the way along that this was my baby when you knew it might not be? Don't you think I had the right to know? You obviously thought that Matthew did.'

'No. It wasn't like that. I didn't choose to tell Matthew, he guessed, and I had to talk to him to stop him ruining everything. I couldn't let him ruin it for nothing. Please listen, Ben,' begged Katy. 'You are the father.'

Ben was silent, staring through the window into the distance. Katy didn't dare to speak for fear of saying the wrong thing yet again. She silently prayed for a miracle. Finally Ben made his parting shot.

'It doesn't matter how small the chance is, Katy, there's still a chance, and I don't know how I can live with that. But what is certain is that you lied to me. Not only about the baby but also about Matthew. You're not who I thought you were, Katy. And to think I thought I wasn't good enough for you.'

Tears were streaming down his cheeks now, almost as fast as down Katy's.

'Of course you're good enough for me, of course you are, Ben. And you're right, I'm not good enough for you. What I've done is terrible, but I was trying to do the right thing. I never wanted to hurt you.'

'Well, you just did.'

Ben turned and headed out of the room.

'Don't go. Please don't go, Ben,' said Katy, stumbling after him. 'I need you. I can't do this alone. Ben, please. Please don't leave me.'

Ben turned around briefly, almost unrecognisable in his despair, lines having suddenly appeared on his young face. He stared at her for a moment. Then turned again and walked out of the door.

Katy slumped to the floor and wept like she had never wept before, just as the dead crabs tumbled, still muted, onto a pier somewhere in Alaska in the middle of the night.

Chapter 18

She wasn't sure what time it was. She looked up and the crabs were gone, probably already having their insides ripped out by some surly Alaskan. Katy felt like her own insides had been wrenched from her body. This was no normal crying. It was a torrent, an almighty avalanche, a wild typhoon of a cry that threatened to drown and quite possibly deafen her. Every time she felt she might be mastering the storm another front came from nowhere and flattened her without mercy.

She was still slumped in the hallway where Ben had left her, unable to summon up any purpose to moving. Her hands and her forearms were soaked with tears, since she had long ago drenched the tissues she had stuffed up her sleeves from her earlier clean-up.

Finally she managed to comprehend that she needed help. This was not going to die away without some kind of external effort. She hauled herself onto her hands and knees and made slow progress towards the phone, which sat on a side table on the opposite side of the hall. She collapsed against the wall when she reached it, as though she had just run a marathon, and sat for a few moments trying to regain some sort of steady breathing. She took a deep breath and picked up the phone to dial Daniel's mobile.

Of course it went straight to voicemail. She slumped again, listening to Daniel's message whilst trying to summon up the energy to speak.

'Hi, guys. I must be doing something really important, or screening my calls and just don't want to talk to you. Anyway, leave me a message and I'll call you when I've finished collecting my award for creative genius in advertising.'

'Daniel. Pick up the phone. Please pick up the phone,' she said in between the sniffs.

Eventually she remembered that she was talking to a mobile answer machine so he wouldn't be able to hear her.

'Daniel, call me now. Ben knows everything and he's gone, for good. What am I going to do? Just stop everything and call me, Daniel. I need you.'

She put the phone back then winced as the baby gave an almighty kick. She looked down to see some kind of limb desperately feeling the very edges of her belly for any kind of gap that might lead to daylight.

This is really happening, she thought, staring at the small mole hill travelling across her front. I'm really going to have a baby alone.

The tears started to flow again, not a storm this time, more an irritating drizzle, the type that never seems to end.

The drizzle continued whilst Katy miserably contemplated her life as a lone parent. When the phone finally sprang to life, Katy answered before the second ring.

'What am I going to do? Ben's gone. Gone for good,' she blurted out before Daniel could even say hello. 'He came and it was fine, and then stupid, stupid me thought he must have worked it out that he might not be the dad. But he hadn't worked it out, had he? And he kept shouting at me to explain, and so I had to tell him everything, and so he stopped shouting but he wouldn't say anything. Nothing. He just stared and looked so sad. I have never seen him look so sad before. Then finally he said that I was not worthy of him. That he couldn't get over the lies. And he's so right. Of course he's right. I've been so, so stupid. And now what am I going to do? How am I going to tell the baby what I've done? That it's my fault it doesn't have a daddy. That I totally screwed it up. That I've ruined its life even before it was born.'

'I'm on my way,' replied Matthew.

The line went dead before Katy had time to drop the receiver on the floor. There was an unhealthy crack as it struck the wooden floorboard, followed by the sound of a soft purr, confirming that the caller had moved on. The shock of Matthew's voice left Katy numb. Almost on auto-pilot, she picked up the phone and dialled 1471 then returned the call. It went straight through to voicemail.

'Hello, you're through to Matthew Chesterman. I'm sorry I can't get to the phone right now, but if you leave your name and number I'll call you back as soon as I can. Please wait for the beep. Thank you.'

'Pick up the phone,' muttered Katy, realising full well this time that he couldn't hear her.

The beep sounded.

'I thought you were Daniel. If you get this, I don't think you should come here. Just stay away, Matthew, please.'

She replaced the receiver, shuffled back through to the lounge and collapsed on the sofa. The Discovery Channel had moved on from the crabs and was now showing wild moose mating in some remote-looking wooded area. The ritual looked particularly unjoyful conducted in mute. Katy watched as the male finished, clambered off, shook himself then surveyed the rest of the females before wandering nonchalantly over to his next target.

Typical man, she thought, before realising that she had behaved exactly like the detached-looking male moose. Had she not wandered from mate to mate without any fear of the consequences?

The action changed. Now the male moose was running quickly through dense forest. The screen went black before showing a scene of the moose lying dead on the ground as two hunters reloaded their guns.

I so deserve to be shot, thought Katy.

The baby gave her another almighty kick.

'My God, there's a baby, a real baby,' she cried. 'I can't even wish to get shot in peace.'

The baby kicked her again.

'Alright, alright. Enough already.' She flew up from the couch, marched into the nursery and surveyed the cot in bits on the floor and the pile of plastic carriers full of untouched baby retail.

Grabbing the nearest carrier bag, she emptied it onto the floor, knelt down and began tearing cellophane and cardboard as though her life depended on it. She flung packaging into one corner and its contents into another, shrieking in frustration every time an item appeared not to want to be parted from its wrapping.

By the time she had finished ransacking the plastic bags she had worked up quite a sweat. She caught sight of the screwdriver left in the room by Ben, ready to make up the cot. She seized it and began attaching screws to pieces of wood with no idea if they were in the right place. Before long she somehow had a cot that resembled an avant-garde tepee for dwarfs. By now she was breathing very fast but she didn't dare stop or slow down, because that would allow her mind to wander away from her artistic construction towards something much more destructive.

When she could no longer find any screws to screw, she flung the screwdriver across the room and hauled herself up. She walked over to the corner of the room and scooped up an armful of vests, babygros, sheets and blankets and waddled out of the room towards the kitchen, tripping occasionally as her feet got caught in trailing garments.

Just as she approached the hall the doorbell rang. Incredibly, in her crazed fervour, she had forgotten that Matthew had called and wondered in surprise who it could be. For a moment her heart leapt as she wondered if it was Ben, then she recalled her mistaken outburst at Matthew and realised that he obviously hadn't got her message.

She hovered in the hallway, burying her head in the pile of clothes. She felt her shoulders start to heave yet again as a fresh wave of despair engulfed her.

'Let me in, Katy. Please. Let me look after you, just for a minute. Let me see that you're alright,' Matthew called through the door. He sounded so gentle and soothing that she lunged for the door with relief, managing to open it despite her loaded arms.

Matthew peered around the pile of washing that greeted him as the door opened.

'Where are you?' he asked.

'I'm here,' she sobbed, trying to hide her puffy red face deep in the washing.

'Look, why don't we just put this all down here on the floor? We can go and sit down and you can tell me what happened.'

'No,' said Katy, her head flying out of her temporary mask. 'I have to get these in the wash now. They can't go on the floor. They have to be washed now. The baby could come any minute.' She tugged the pile back from Matthew and strode off to the kitchen.

'You're not in labour, are you?' asked Matthew.

She turned in the doorway.

'Don't be ridiculous. Do you think I'd be here if I was? These have to be washed straight away, no time to lose. I have to be ready, because there'll be no-one to help me now.'

Matthew caught up with her in the kitchen trying to stuff at least two loads of washing in at once.

'Why don't you let me help?' he said, gently attempting to pull away from her some of the cream cotton babygros.

'No, I can do it. I have to do it. Ben has gone. I'm all alone. I have to learn to do everything on my own now.'

She was frantically squeezing anything she could lay her hands on into the washing machine. She had just about managed it when the corner of a blanket refused to budge. She tugged and tugged but it would not move.

'Just let go, Matthew, you're not helping,' she screamed, but when she looked up, Matthew was a few yards away, leaning against the wall, waiting patiently for her to finish. She looked down at the corner of the blanket and gave it an enormous tug, which almost threw her off balance.

'Katy, you're trying to put your dressing gown into the machine whilst you're still wearing it,' said Matthew, kneeling down beside her and stroking her back. 'Please sit down and let's just be calm for a minute, shall we?'

'Stop hindering me,' she shouted in his face. 'I don't have time for this, I told you. Nothing's ready and I have to do it on my own.' Suddenly she stared at Matthew in horror. 'Oh my God, oh my God, I haven't even packed my hospital bag. That's what I should be doing first.'

She pulled herself up and left the washing spilling out of the machine to head back to the nursery.

Matthew followed her and watched as she tried to get her overnight bag off the top shelf of the cupboard. He noticed the dwarf tepee, which remarkably was still standing in the middle of the room. He contemplated asking what had happened but thought better of it. He walked up behind her and reached over the top of her head to pull down the bag.

'Thanks,' she puffed. 'I'll have everything down low soon so I won't need anyone to get things down for me.' She strode off again, this time to the bathroom. He thought he might go and wait in the living room until this whirlwind had died down, but he heard a crash and decided he had better continue his shadowing.

'It's alright, it's alright, just go away. Leave me alone. It's just some bubble bath broken in the bath. I'll wash it away later. Just leave, Matthew, please.'

Katy was throwing every bottle of fancy fragrance she owned into her hospital bag. Matthew looked around and remembered with a sharp pang his feelings in this room all those months ago on the night of the reunion. It had seemed like Katy's calm little oasis that he was intruding on. It had an exotic air, just as Katy had had on that fateful night when he had dared to behave as a free man. Who would have thought that the next time he was in this room it would be with a mad woman throwing bottles everywhere?

Katy pushed past him roughly. Dejectedly he followed her into the bedroom, not quite sure of his next move. She was now elbow deep in a chest of drawers, throwing every item onto the floor.

'I bloody didn't, did I? God, I am absolute crap. The

one thing I had to get and I didn't. I am useless and not fit to be a mother. I'll just have to go now. Before the shops shut, before it's too late.'

She opened the wardrobe, pulled out some boots, then sat on the bed attempting to put them on, despite the fact she was still in her pyjamas and laces are damn near impossible to tie at nearly nine months pregnant.

Matthew knelt down on the floor in front of her and gently lifted her head. 'Where are you going?' he said as calmly as he could.

'I have to go and get a nightdress to give birth in and it has to have buttons down the front because that's what Joan said at the class because then you can hold the baby to your skin without having to take anything off and you're supposed to hold your baby to your skin because that helps you bond straight away and I have to bond straight away you see because if I don't who will, because it will be just me. Only me.'

The tide of tears returned and she fell into Matthew's arms as the sobbing racked her body. They sat on the edge of her bed as he rocked her slowly and she buried her head in his ironed, monogrammed handkerchief.

They didn't speak for a good half-hour, until Katy was completely spent. She sat twisting his sodden handkerchief in her lap, sniffing occasionally, whilst he gently rubbed her back.

'Do you want to tell me what happened?' Matthew asked, when he considered the tears to have completely dried up. Katy tried to start to tell him but was hit by yet another wave of despair, rendering her unable to speak. She threw herself on the bed and pounded the pillows.

'I am shit, so shit,' came a muffled howl. 'What have I done? I don't deserve anyone, I've made such a mess of things,' she said, finally raising her head.

'So has he left you?' asked Matthew.

'Yes, of course he has. Wouldn't you? He knows everything, Matthew. He knows you could be the father. Why did you tell him we slept together?' she said angrily. 'Why, Matthew? He had to know, I realise that now. He made me realise that, but *I* should have told him, not you. What right did you have to tell him? You bastard. You absolute bastard.'

She started beating his chest with all her strength until he managed to catch her wrists in his hands.

'I'm sorry, really I am. I was drunk and I was upset with Alison for treating me like a child in front of everyone, telling me off over the vodka. Then Ben came into the toilets and he was taunting me, telling me that you would never look twice at me now because I was too boring, so . . . so I couldn't help myself. I had to go and put him straight, didn't I? I was stupid and I was wrong. I'm sorry, Katy, really I am.'

She went limp and buried her head in her hands.

'You know what, it doesn't really matter. He would have found out somehow. How on earth I could have thought that I could keep a secret like that I don't know. I made my bed, and now I've got to lie in it. It's my problem.'

'No, it's not just your problem, it's mine as well,' he said, putting his arm around her and putting one hand over hers. 'We started this, both of us. I'm not going to leave you to cope with this on your own. I'll figure something out. I'll take care of you, Katy, somehow. I let you down all those years ago and I'm not going to do it again. There has to be a way. You are not going to do this on your own.'

Silent tears were now pouring down Katy's face as she looked up at Matthew.

'But you have a wife and twins on the way.'

'Let me worry about them. You could be having my baby, Katy. I'm not going to walk away from that. You can't make me. I'll look after you, I promise.'

He bent to give her a peck on her hot, wet cheek which, to his alarm, appeared to make her silent tears flow even faster.

'I'm sorry,' she said quietly, apologising for her lack of control over her emotions.

'No, I'm sorry,' he said, bending forward again and this time placing his lips firmly over hers. She resisted for a moment then gave in to the reassuring warmth of his mouth. His hands continued to rotate on her back, making her feel drowsy and deliciously sleepy. Suddenly an image of Ben's face popped into her head out of nowhere and she sprang back as if she had been struck by an electric shock.

'Stop! Stop now! Get out! What am I doing? Oh my God, have I not destroyed enough today?' She leapt up and ran out of the room, screaming at Matthew to get out. She had the flat door open by the time he stumbled into the hall.

'Just go. Go now. Leave me alone.'

'Katy, please, just . . .'

'Go now!' she screeched.

'But Katy—'

'Now!' she screamed.

Chapter 19

Katy half opened one eye to find herself lying on her couch surrounded by darkness, apart from the flickering silent TV screen. Where had everyone gone? Why was it so quiet and why was it dark? It hadn't been this quiet the last time she was conscious, she was sure.

Then it happened. She felt her body start to tense all on its own without her mind telling it to. Then the tension wasn't just mildly irritating, it was all-consuming, like someone was inside her with a million cattle prods. The prods roamed for a few seconds around the insides of her belly, leaving no patch untouched before retreating as quickly as they had emerged.

'Bloody hell, what was that?' she cried out, clutching her belly, the pain causing her to pant. As she felt the tense, swollen globe still encased in her pyjamas, the events of the day came flooding back, as well as the dawning realisation that she might well have just experienced a contraction. She waited for the panting to calm down before easing herself upright and turning the TV off, plunging her into bleak darkness.

She scrabbled for the table lamp at the end of the sofa, feeling absolutely washed out. She didn't have the energy to go into labour. Not after the day she'd had. It was probably just the baby moving. Or one of those pretend contraction things. Hicks or something. She sat very still, willing the pain not to return. A few minutes passed and all appeared to be normal.

Bath, she thought. Bath then bed, then sleep, then tomorrow things may seem less dire than today. Surely she had well and truly hit rock bottom.

She went to move, but just as she did, the cattle prods hit her again, causing her to double up and cry out, just like an old cow.

She rocked herself and breathed as best she could in between the pained mooing. When it finally subsided she sat down heavily on the floor in shock.

Not now. Please not now. I can't do it now. I'm not ready. My head isn't ready, she said to herself.

'Dear God. I know I only talk to you when I want something, or at Christmas when I hear small children singing "Away in a Manger" and it makes me cry. But this time I'm really desperate. I promise, if you help me, I will talk to you every day and I will put money into those little envelopes old ladies leave rather than throwing them in the bin. I will do loads of other good things as well, I promise, but please, God, give me a break. Even if it's just until tomorrow, please let it not be now.' Katy was on her knees with her hands pressed firmly together, eyes squeezed tightly shut when the next contraction came.

'So you want to teach me a lesson, is that it? For getting myself into this in the first place? Well, I'm telling you, you'll be sorry. You leave me with no option,' she huffed.

Katy pulled herself up and staggered out to the hallway, picked up the phone and dialled.

'This had better be good; you have no idea the wonder I have put on ice to pick up the phone to you.'

'Daniel,' she said through gritted teeth. 'Get here now. You are about to witness the wonder of childbirth.

I'm in labour.' She slammed down the phone, took the front door off the latch and waddled into the bathroom.

She was aware that there was some substantial leakage going on somewhere below. Had her waters broken, or was it normal to wet yourself in panic when you first had a contraction? She desperately tried to remember what Joan had said in the classes. All that kept coming back was that you might have contractions for a while before it was time to go into hospital. She sat with her head in her hands on the toilet, trying to summon the energy to get up and get changed before the next contraction took its toll. She hobbled back into her bedroom, and managed somehow to get herself into another pair of pyjamas and onto the bed before the next one overtook her.

She had no idea how many times the cattle prods had returned by the time she heard a loud knock at the door.

'It's open,' she shouted.

There was a pause, followed by a louder, more insistent knock.

'Katy, it's me, I have hot towels and tequila. Let me in,' came Daniel's voice.

'It's open,' she shouted, even louder.

Another pause.

The knock came again.

'Katy, are you alright?'

'For God's sake, just open the bloody door!' she screamed.

'Can I help, dear?' she heard her neighbour say to Daniel out on the landing.

'Yes, it's Katy. She rang to say she'd gone into labour and now she's not answering. Do you know if she left already?'

'Not recently, it's been dead quiet. Mind you, there's been men coming and going all day. Making a right racket they have, shouting and screaming. I said to my Dave at one point that he should come over and see what's happening, what with her condition and everything. But he's bloody useless. Can't get his arse off the sofa for love nor money. Do you want me to go and knock on our living room wall? It connects to her bedroom and the walls are like paper. We have to turn our telly up some nights, if you know what I mean.'

'Really,' replied Daniel. 'Have you had to do that recently, then?'

The door flew open.

'The door was unlocked, you useless poof. Get in here and do something. Goodnight, Mrs Jenkins.'

Daniel ran like a startled rabbit into the apartment and the door slammed shut behind him.

'Useless poof? Useless poof? Katy, I normally find your insults entertaining, but please use a little creativity. The obvious is so beneath you.'

Katy was holding on to Daniel's shoulders and puffing like a forty-a-day smoker who had just run up the stairs.

'What's with the white suit?' she finally managed to puff out.

'You mean my labour partner outfit? Well, I figured white was really the only option given the medical nature of the event. But we must be careful not to get baby gunk on it, as I need to wear it again to Alan and Chris's civil ceremony next week.'

She gave a low, guttural growl.

'Is that really necessary? I've left a strippergram I met last night at Steve's birthday bash, gagging for it at home, so stop being so mean to me.'

'It's coming,' she grunted.

'It was, but you put a stop to that, darling.'

'Not you, stupid, a contraction. It's coming just about . . . now.'

She howled. Then swore. Then howled a lot more.

'Oh my God, what is that thing doing to you?' said

Daniel, looking petrified. 'Shit, Katy, is this really normal? Jesus Christ, I'm not supposed to be doing this. I've made a lifestyle choice that entitles me to have nothing to do with childbirth. What the hell am I doing here?'

'Just help me,' said Katy weakly. 'Help me back to bed and then just hold my hand or something.'

'Back to bed? Are you mad? We're going to the hospital now. I can't be alone with you in this state. You need to be near people with knives and things, for your own safety.'

'No, Daniel. The contractions aren't close enough together yet. I need to wait a bit longer. Call the hospital and tell them I've started and that we'll call them when the contractions are five minutes apart.'

'OK, OK.' Daniel was already breathing as fast as Katy.

He took Katy's arm and started to lead her back to the bedroom.

'Don't do that thing again just yet, will you? You know, the wailing thing,' he asked.

'I'll try,' she said, plopping back down on the bed. 'The number is by the bed in the front of that book. You have to ask for the labour ward.'

278

He picked up the phone and dialled with his back to Katy, hoping that if he ignored her she wouldn't start making horrible noises again.

'Labour ward and be quick,' he barked.

Katy could vaguely hear the gentle ring at the other end as Daniel was put through.

'They're not picking up. What are we going to do? Let's just go down there, Katy, please. I can get you there really quick.'

'Labour ward,' said a woman's voice on the end of the phone.

'Christ, you are there, are you? Right, I have a woman here screaming blue murder. Tell me what to do.'

'Is she in labour?'

'No, she's in Timbuktu. Of course she's bloody well in labour, why else would I be talking to you?'

'Hey now, just calm down. I know it can be very frightening, but you need to be calm for your wife now. You getting upset will not help.'

'She is not my wife,' said Daniel angrily.

'I am sorry, sir, girlfriend.'

'She is not my girlfriend. I have more sense. Now, please tell me what to do.'

'How far apart are her contractions?'

'How should I know? I just got here and she's scream-ing so hard I can't even hear myself think.'

'About twenty minutes,' interrupted Katy.

'She says twenty minutes. That's close enough, right? I'll bring her straight in.'

'Just hang on one second. Ask her if her waters have broken.'

'Some mucussy discharge,' muttered Katy, bracing herself as the next contraction approached.

Daniel leant over and held the receiver to Katy's mouth.

'I love you, Katy, but there ain't no way on this planet those words are ever gonna pass these lips. Say it again.'

He pulled the receiver back as soon as Katy had explained what had been going on in the wet stuff department.

'She gave you the right answer, right? I'll get her in the car pronto, shall I?'

'To be honest, home is where she should be at the moment, where she's most comfortable. She's only in the very early stages of labour, and if you bring her in we'll probably send her straight home again. She is definitely in the right place.'

Katy chose that moment to let out her next yowl.

Daniel held the phone up to her mouth again so that the full force of her contraction could be heard.

'Does that sound anything like a woman who is in the right place? She sounds like someone who is in as wrong a place as anyone could be. That is just not normal.'

'Sir, I promise you, it is normal and you'll help your friend the most by keeping her where she is and nice and calm. Now call us again when the contractions are five minutes apart or when she thinks her waters have broken fully.'

Daniel stared at the phone.

'Fuck you,' he shouted before slamming it down.

He sat on the edge of the bed, shaking slightly.

'I can do this. This is easy. I have achieved great things with my life. I can get through this. Daniel, this is easy,' he said to himself before taking a few deep breaths and turning around to face Katy with a large, fixed smile on his face.

'Fancy a cocktail?' he offered.

'No, I'm pregnant, you idiot, I can't drink.'

'Mind if I have one?'

'Daniel, this is about me, not you. Being my labour partner is about you forgetting what you need and being there for whatever I need.'

'It's just that you usually say I'm more fun when I've had a few. Thought I might cheer you up more if I had a drink.'

'Daniel, you do have to drive me to the hospital later.'

'Good point,' sighed Daniel.

Katy shifted her body.

'Don't move too quickly, it may start you off again.'

'I'm fine; my back was just hurting a bit.'

They both stared at the wall for a while.

'You can talk to me, you know. Labour doesn't make you deaf or mute,' said Katy.

'Sorry. I'm just holding my breath waiting for the next contraction thingy.'

'They seem to have gone off a bit.'

'Right, right. So what do we do when that happens?' asked Daniel.

'We just wait, I guess.'

'For what?'

'For them to start up again.'

'OK, so we just sit and wait. I can do that. That's fine. We will sit here and chill.'

Both of them fell into silence again.

'For God's sake,' hissed Katy. 'There's a bottle of

brandy in the kitchen cupboard. A small one each shouldn't do us any harm.'

'Wise, very wise. Good for the circulation. I will be back shortly,' said Daniel, scuttling off.

Daniel returned and they both sat sipping their drinks, deep in thought. The contractions seemed to have stopped completely for the time being.

'So, are you going to tell me why I'm sitting here being your not very good labour partner rather than one of the two possible fathers?'

'Do I have to?' asked Katy, not sure if she had the energy.

'Well, yes, I think you do, seeing as you're putting me through this. I need to know I'm doing it for good reason.'

She reached over to grip his hand, praying her contractions would give her respite for just a little longer.

'It's over with Ben,' she said, breathing heavily and increasing the grip on Daniel's hand.

'How come?' he managed to utter, despite the pain he was in.

'He knows everything,' she said. 'Now he's gone for good and I hate myself.' She released Daniel's hand and rolled over onto her side to let the silent tears fall unobserved. Daniel shook his hand vigorously to try and restore some sense of circulation.

'Then Matthew came and he kissed me,' she muttered, barely audible.

Leaping up, Daniel ran around, threw himself onto the bed next to her and thrust his face right into hers.

'You are kidding me?' he said.

'No,' she said, shaking her head slowly, tears dripping off the end of her nose.

'What did you do?' Daniel was almost bouncing up and down on the bed with the excitement of the drama.

'Kicked him out.'

'Come on!' he said, punching the air. 'Serve the toerag right, what an utter slut.'

Katy thrust her head in her pillow and wailed.

'Not you, him,' said Daniel. When she refused to look at him he lay down next to her and pulled her towards him.

'I am a slut,' she cried into his shoulder.

'No, Katy. You're not. One night of unfortunate sex does not make you a slut,' replied Daniel. 'Believe me, I know a slut when I see one.'

Eventually the tears subsided and Daniel heard a faint snore. Heaving a huge sigh of relief, he gently laid her back against her pillow, then picked up the bottle of brandy and his glass and left the room.

In the kitchen he guiltily poured himself a very large drink and downed it in one before pouring another one, this time taking his time over the amber liquid, deep in thought. After maybe half an hour he made a decision. He got up a little unsteadily and started to search the flat systematically, until he eventually found Katy's phone under a chair in the living room. He returned to the kitchen, shut himself in again and started to scroll through her numbers until he found Ben's.

He pressed the call button and tried to steady his rapidly beating heart.

'Just calm down, Daniel,' he said to himself. 'It's not like you're calling to ask him out.' He shuddered at the image of him and football nut Ben as a couple.

The phone seemed to ring endlessly until finally going through to voicemail. He left a fairly abusive message, telling Ben that if he didn't call back within the next five minutes he would personally nominate him for 'Perfect Partners' in next month's bestselling Leeds gay magazine.

He sat there drumming his fingers, willing the phone to ring. At five minutes on the dot he picked the phone up again and started to scroll down Katy's phone book.

First he looked to see if 'Ben's Mum' came up or even 'Ben's Dad'. Nothing. He racked his brains, trying to remember if Katy had ever mentioned a brother or a sister as he kept scrolling, desperate for some inspiration. He got all the way through the list without finding anything. He started again, praying he might have missed something, and stopped as a name caught his eye.

'Braindead.'

Either Katy had a particular dislike of one of her clients or this had to be a friend of Ben's. His thumb hovered over the call button. Worth the risk, he thought. He took another swig of brandy and pressed down hard.

After a couple of rings someone picked up.

Chapter 20

'I'm havin' a piss, hold on,' came a voice at the other end of the phone, followed by the unmistakable tinkle of urine falling at speed into a tin urinal.

'Sorry about that, who is it?'

'It's Daniel here. I'm a friend of Katy's. Ben knows me and I need to speak to him urgently. Are you with him?'

'Who?'

'Daniel. I know Katy and Ben. I need to speak to Ben. Do you know where he is?'

'He's sitting here. What you calling me for?'

'Because I can't get through to him.'

'I can give you his mobile number. Call him tomorrow, though, 'cause he's shit-faced.'

'No, wait, it's urgent, I need to talk to him now. His girlfriend is in labour.'

'What? Hang on a minute,' said Braindead. 'Shut the fuck up, will ya? I'm trying to be Ben's secretary and I can't hear what this posh bloke is saying,' Daniel heard Braindead shout.

'Say again?'

'I said, it's imperative I speak to Ben now, about Katy.'

'And how would you be spelling that?'

'Look, it doesn't matter. Just let me speak to Ben.'

'Well, you see, I would, but he's kind of in mourning like. Mourning of the getting-utterly-hammered variety, owing to Katy totally throwing him over a bridge this morning.'

'I know that, but I need to speak to him, it's urgent.'

'Well, I'll try. What did you say your name was?'

'Daniel.'

'Oi, Ben. Some bloke called Daniel needs to speak to you about Katy.'

'Tell the gay bastard to fuck off,' Daniel heard in the distance at the other end of the line.

'He said, tell the gay bastard to fuck off. No offence

like, mate. He doesn't actually think you are gay, he's just saying that because he's pissed.'

'That's charming. Just tell him that Katy has gone into labour, will you?'

'He says Katy's in labour.'

'Katy who? I don't give a fuck.'

'Did you hear that?' Braindead asked Daniel.

'Look, I know what Katy did was wrong and she feels terrible, believe me, but she needs him right now to compartmentalise his anger and be with her.'

'You want me to tell him that?'

'Yes.'

'This bloke says you need to compost your anger and be with her.'

'Tell the gay twat that none of his advertising bullshit is going to work now.'

'I assume you heard that. Again, don't take offence at the gay thing; he calls everyone gay when he's pissed.'

'He *is* gay, you idiot,' Ben bellowed in the background.

'No, is he? Are you?' asked Braindead.

'Yes, but it's not exactly relevant at this moment, is it?'

'It is if someone's calling you a gay twat when you're not. But now I know you are, that's fine.'

'Thank you, I think. Anyway, look, you have to help me. We have to get Ben back here to be with Katy at the birth. She wants him, I know she does. You have to help me persuade him. He'll regret it for the rest of his life if he's not there.'

'Why?' asked Braindead.

'Because . . . because of course he will. Because what if it really is his child and he misses the birth because he's out getting pissed?'

'Ah, but what if it isn't? As he has actually been saying all day. What if it isn't? What if he spends hours with a wailing woman for nothing, only to see someone else's baby born? Man, there is no way I would do that, would you?'

'But, but, but it still could be his,' said Daniel, on the verge of a nervous breakdown. He took another swig of brandy, this time straight from the bottle.

Come on, Daniel, he said to himself. You do this all the time, this is your job. You have to sell people thoughts, ideas, images. You have to convince them that your opinion as a creative director is always right. You do this every day. Come on, think.

'Look, Braindead. Tell him to imagine this tiny, help-less, pink little bundle has just arrived in the world, looking for its father. Crying desperately because there is no-one there to hold him.'

'You want me to tell him that?'

'Yes, go on, you can do it.'

'Right, he's now saying it will be small and pink and wanting its dad and you won't be there.'

'Tell him to call its other bloody dad then.'

'Don't think that was the right thing to say somehow,' said Braindead to Daniel.

'OK, just bear with me. Tell him to imagine a beautiful little girl who sings like an angel and dances like a butterfly and makes him so proud it makes him want to cry. Can he really walk away from that?'

'Are you sure you want me to tell him that?'

'Yep, go on, and a bit more emotion this time, yeah?'

'Emotion? What, you want me to cry?'

'If you can, great.'

'Who is this guy?' Braindead said to Ben. 'Anyway, he says you'd be proud because she's like an angel and a butterfly.'

'No, no, no,' said Daniel. 'I said she sings like an angel and dances like a butterfly.'

'Look, I'm trying, mate, but you're not really selling it, are you? Have you ever met Ben? Angels and butterflies aren't really his thing. Yours, maybe, but not our Ben.'

'Right, right, yes, you're right. Not his thing. I'm not thinking who my consumer is. Always bring it back to the consumer. I'm forgetting my fundamentals.'

'Look, mate, I'm sorry, you probably mean well, but I don't think this is really doing any good, is it?'

'No, don't hang up. Give me one more shot. Just hang on. I am thinking Ben now. What would it take? Come on, it's coming, it's coming. Got it. Are you ready, Braindead?'

'Come on then, but that's it, no more after this.'

'Imagine in a few hours' time the next great England striker could be born here in Leeds. Ben's son playing for England. And how would Ben cope whenever he watched his son play in a match, knowing that he didn't even bother to turn up at his debut appearance? Now, he might not be Ben's son and he might not play for England, but then again, he might, and isn't might enough?'

Braindead was silent at the end of the phone.

'Did you get that? Do you want me to say it again?' asked Daniel.

The next thing Daniel heard was Braindead literally shouting at Ben.

'Get your arse out of this pub and back to Katy. This

might be your son coming and he might play for England one day, and I want you to get me tickets if that happens. So stop worrying about what he might not be, and start worrying about what he might be, and get yourself back there.'

'Come on, Braindead, that's brilliant. I really like the shouting bit. Keep going,' urged Daniel.

'Keep going? I don't know what else to say.'

'You're doing great. Just tell him what you really think. Go on, speak from the heart, you know him best.'

'Right. OK,' said Braindead. There was a short silence before he spoke again. 'And Ben, listen. Katy's ace.'

'Beautiful, concise, to the point, wonderfully executed. Well done, Braindead,' said Daniel, raising his fist in victory.

'Is she really in labour?' Suddenly Ben's voice was on the phone.

'Well, if she's not she sure is doing a good impression. Look, Ben, she knows what she did was wrong and she feels awful, but you have to get here and see this. Don't walk away now. Maybe later if you can't work it out, but not now. Not now you've got this far. She needs you. The baby needs you.'

'I'm in Edinburgh.'

293

'*What?*'

'In Edinburgh. Me and Braindead decided to throw a sickie and get up here early for a stag do because I just couldn't face anything.'

'OK, keep calm. This is a minor blip we can overcome. Think, Daniel, think. Right, I don't think you'll get a flight this late, so I'm just checking on my BlackBerry for train times. Give me a sec. OK, there's a train at 12.30 a.m. and it gets into Leeds at . . . just hang on. Jesus Christ – are you coming from the moon? – it doesn't get you in until 8.30 a.m. Right, put Braindead back on.'

'Yep.'

'Right, I need you to listen carefully. You need to ask the barman to call a taxi firm and ask them if they'll drive you and Ben back to Leeds tonight. You have half an hour to try and get someone to drive you, but if no-one will, you need to get to the station and catch the 12.30 a.m. train. Have you got that?'

'Yeah, why me and Ben?'

'Because you need to get the father of the next England striker back here to see his baby born.'

'Oh yeah.'

'Now, don't worry about the cost. We'll sort that out

when you get here. Just get back as quick as you can by whatever means. Call me when you're in a taxi or on the train, OK?'

'Got it, Danno.'

'It's Daniel.'

'Yeah, but I was being, you know, concise and to the point.'

'Just get him here and you can call me whatever you like.'

'What, even something like Puff the Magic Danno?'

'Only if you're here in less than five hours.'

'Well, now you've laid down the challenge, we'll see you in four.'

Chapter 21

7.12 a.m.

'I can't believe you,' Katy said to Daniel through gritted teeth as she sat on a chair in the hall, her discomfort clearly visible via the white knuckles wrapped around the wooden arms.

'Shush, please don't talk too loud,' said Daniel, who was slumped on the floor, his head resting on Katy's hospital bag.

'Do you not think that I'm coping with enough without you having the mother of all hangovers?' Katy kicked the bag from under Daniel, causing him to bang his head on the floor.

'Ow,' he yelled, pulling himself up and rubbing his head. 'Was that necessary? Do you really think I could get through an entire night of you screeching and wailing without some medicinal aid? It's hardly my fault that the only thing you had in the house was cheap brandy. And I'm telling you, when I see those bitches who answer the phone at the labour ward, I'm going to give them a piece of my mind. What do you have to do to make them understand that we had a crisis going on here and needed to be in hospital?'

'It wasn't a crisis. Women go into labour every day,' said Katy, looking nervously at her watch.

'Not with me they don't. I even told them if they didn't help me I was a suicide risk, but they just laughed and told me to pull myself together.'

'Just go and take some paracetamol, and while you're at it bring me some,' said Katy, sensing pain rapidly approaching.

'Paracetamol? I'm not really thinking suicide, Katy. You and the world need me,' said Daniel sincerely.

'For your hangover, you idiot,' said Katy. 'And for the torture I am going through. Go on, quick; the taxi should be here any minute.'

TRACY BLOOM

7.30 a.m.

'Daniel, get out here now,' shouted Katy. 'The taxi's here.'

'After you, you lovely, charming lady,' said Daniel as he emerged from the bathroom.

'Bag. Carry. You,' said Katy before she took a deep breath and started her painful descent down the stairs.

'So you think you'll be in hospital a long time then?' Daniel asked from behind her.

'Hope not, why?' she puffed.

'This bag is bloody heavy. What the hell have you got in it?'

'Clothes for me and the baby and stuff for clearing up mess in general. Nappies, wipes, cotton wool, sanitary towels, bra pads, you know, that sort of thing.'

'Why do you insist on making this as difficult as possible for me? Such items should never be spoken of within my earshot. Mess is just so unsettling.'

Katy stopped at the bottom of the stairs and turned to face Daniel. 'You are about to witness me giving birth. The messiest, most disgusting process you could ever be part of. If you don't think you are man enough, let's halt this pretence now and you can go back to bed whilst I face the most important and most difficult moment of

298

my life all alone.' She stopped and her face screwed up in pain. 'Aaaaaaaaah. Christ, another contraction. Aaaaaah, just get me into this damn taxi. Aaaaaaaaaah, and then go.'

Daniel and the taxi driver stared helplessly as she writhed in pain, grasping the stair rail as if her life depended on it.

'You, lad, in that taxi now,' said the taxi driver gruffly when Katy's contraction appeared to be calming down. 'Come on, get a move on. If you're man enough to do the necessary to make a baby, then you sure as hell are man enough to be there when it arrives. You young lads think you can run around like rampant rabbits and never have to face the consequences. Well, today is consequence day, so stop your moaning and get in.'

Daniel stared open-mouthed at the taxi driver then looked at Katy.

'You heard him, get in,' she said through clenched teeth.

Reluctantly, Daniel got into the cab, followed by a panting Katy. He slammed shut the partition window between the driver and the passenger cabin.

'Good God, how can he not recognise that I am most definitely not one of those losers who go out every weekend, get smashed and then shag anything that moves.'

'Sounds like you to me,' replied Katy, the puffing slowing down slightly.

'Love you too.'

'Likewise. Thanks for getting in the cab,' she said, leaning back slowly.

'The fact that he's bigger and uglier than me had nothing to do with my decision.'

'Hasn't he called you yet then?' she asked as Daniel got his phone out of his pocket.

'Who? No-one. What, sorry?' he bumbled as he quickly stuffed it back in his pocket.

'The strippergram? You keep checking your phone,' Katy persisted.

Right on cue the phone emitted four loud beeps from Daniel's pocket.

'What's he said?' asked Katy.

WILL BE AT LEEDS STATION AT 8.30 A.M. BIG KISS BRAINDEAD, read Daniel. He allowed himself a small sigh of relief.

'Er, he says he has to leave the flat and get to work. We'll catch up later.'

Katy screwed up her face, thinking that another

contraction was coming, but it appeared to be a false alarm.

'He has a job at this time in the morning?' she asked in an attempt to distract herself.

'Oh yes, very common, you know, with shift workers and farmers apparently.'

'Farmers?'

'Yeah, that's right. Big demand for cow strippergrams whilst they're milking, you know. Really switches them on, apparently. So anyway, how far off do you think you are now from the actual birth thing? Just so I know.'

'Who knows?' she said wearily, leaning over to rest her head on his shoulder. 'They'll tell me how far dilated I am, which should be an indication.'

'But it will still be a little while yet though? Like at least an hour?' said Daniel, starting to feel anxious.

'Probably.'

'Good, good. Why don't we talk about something else? Might relax you, slow you down a bit.'

'Tell me about this cow strippergram. Is it for the cows or the farmer?' asked Katy sleepily.

'Well, the farmer, of course,' said Daniel, rolling his eyes.

'Do they do it to music?'

'Katy, I have no idea, it's just one of those weird new things, OK? Why don't we talk about something else?'

'Fine, you start.'

'So, Katy. Who do you think I should call first after the baby has arrived?'

'Oh Daniel, I don't know. I'm trying not to think about how I've screwed this whole thing up, and how my life is a mess, and then you go and say something like that and . . . my God, here comes another contraction. Oh my God, oh my God, oh my God . . . Danieeeeellll.'

'OK, OK, just be calm,' said Daniel, stroking her hand vigorously. 'Let's go back to strippergrams, OK? Let's just think what the most appropriate song would be for a stripping cow. Can you think about that? Can you focus on thinking up the all-time, top five cow stripping songs?'

Katy nodded, unable to speak.

'Right, I want at least two before this contraction ends.'

7.45 a.m.

'I am telling you, "I'll Be the Other Woman" was a hit in the Seventies for an American band called the Soul

Children. My mother used to play it all the time,' Daniel argued as they approached the reception desk at the labour ward.

'You're making it up, and in any case, "I'll Be the Udder Woman" sounds too disgusting to be in the top five,' replied Katy.

'Too disgusting. Are you serious? Says the woman who has just left a trail of something I do not want to encounter ever again dripping out of her trouser leg all the way down the corridor.'

'For the last time, I'm in labour. It happens. Deal with it,' said Katy, falling heavily into a chair next to the desk.

'You must be Daniel,' said the woman on reception.

'And you must be the ever-charming Audrey who has made my life hell for the last few hours by having a door policy harsher than Heaven.'

'Well, God spots the sinners and I spot the over-hyped birthing partners,' said Audrey.

'God? What has God got to do with it?'

'You said it's easier to get into Heaven.'

'I think she thinks you mean the holy Heaven. Not London nightclub Heaven,' Katy interrupted.

'I see. I forgot there was another Heaven. Look,

Audrey. Get us the best room in the house and we'll call it a truce, shall we?'

'Name,' barked Audrey.

'Daniel Laker.'

'Not yours, hers,' said Audrey without looking up.

'Katy Chapman,' said Katy. 'Is the birthing-pool room free? I'll try anything at this point, and I promise to keep him under control.'

'Follow Nurse Brady here and she'll check for you. Enjoy,' she smiled sweetly at Daniel.

'Birthing pool? What do you mean, birthing pool?' Daniel whispered loudly as they trotted after Nurse Brady.

'It's supposed to be good for pain relief,' replied Katy.

'Looks like you're in luck,' said Nurse Brady after she had peered round a door. 'Come on in.'

Daniel stood in the middle of the large, well-illuminated room and visibly paled.

'What is that? A baby elephant bath? Are we at the zoo?' he exclaimed.

'Daniel, just chill, will you? That is hopefully going to stop me screaming blue murder every five minutes.'

'Why? Is it full of tequila?'

'You settle yourselves in,' said Nurse Brady. 'I'll be

back in five minutes to do an internal and see how we're getting on.'

'Say, why don't I go grab us some Starbucks whilst you get all the weird stuff over and done with,' said Daniel, already starting to feel a little faint. 'A latte will do you the world of good.'

'You really think you're going to get a Starbucks in hospital, Daniel?'

'The sick and dying must be able to get a decent latte, Katy.'

'I'm neither sick nor dying, Daniel, but if you can find me a bacon butty I might let you look away during the gory bits.'

'Promises, promises. Now you keep an eye on that Nurse Brady, she looked a bit fresh to me. No probing for too long, tell her.'

'You really know how to make this whole thing special, you know that, Daniel?'

'Just trying to do my job, girl. I'll be back in ten.'

8.15 a.m.
'Why are you here? Is Katy here? Daniel, wake up, wake up now!' said a faraway voice.

'What the hell. Where am I? What's going on?'

mumbled Daniel, slowly raising his head from the cafeteria table.

'You're at the hospital and it's me, Matthew. What are you doing here?'

'Matthew? Matthew? Oh fucking hell, Matthew. No, it's not you, is it? I'm still asleep and this is some kind of twisted nightmare.'

'No, Daniel. It's me, Matthew.'

'Who called you?'

'No-one.'

'So why are you here?'

'Because Alison started to have some pains in the night. Not labour or anything, but they want to keep her in on bed rest for a few days. They need to be extra vigilant with twins – normally they come sooner.'

'I see. So no-one called you?' Daniel asked again.

'No, why would they? Are you awake yet? You're not making any sense.'

Daniel glanced at his watch.

'Is that the time? Must go,' he said, getting up from his chair.

'No, stop, hold on a minute. You're here with Katy, aren't you? Look, just tell me she's alright, please?'

'She's fine but I've got to go, she's waiting for me.'

'Oh my God, she's in labour, isn't she?' said a shocked Matthew. 'But she's not due for another two weeks. Where is she? I have to see if she's alright. Tell me where she is!'

'No. You just stay right here,' said Daniel, suddenly fully awake.

'You don't understand, I've got to see her. I saw her yesterday and I need to explain. I need to sort things out with her.'

'Oh no you don't. She's going through enough right now without you complicating it yet again. Just drop it, OK, for everyone's sake.'

'I can't just drop it, you idiot. It's Katy and she might be having my baby. How can you tell me to just drop it?'

'Because you're not going to be the one left to pick up the pieces when you screw it all up again. Listen to me. Let it go. It's what's best for everyone, you know that.'

'If you won't tell me where she is then I'll go and find her myself.' Matthew turned and marched towards the door.

'Fuck, fuck, fuck,' said Daniel, hitting his head on the table. He reached inside his pocket for Katy's phone and dialled Braindead's number.

'We're just coming into Leeds now. The relief crew is on its way,' came a too-cheerful voice.

'Look, Braindead, we have a potential hostile takeover emerging. The other father has arrived. When you get to the station get in a cab and tell him to drive very, very fast. Have you got that? I'll be waiting for you at the entrance. You have no time to lose.'

'Right you are. Don't you worry; no-one is taking our main player. Not without a fight.'

'That's the spirit. Now just get here as quick as you can.'

Chapter 22

8.40 a.m.

'Just hold on a minute, we're nearly done,' came Katy's voice from behind a curtain as Matthew entered the room, having already interrupted two other labouring women in his quest to find Katy.

'Looks like you won't have time to go home and get your swimming trunks, I'm eight centimetres already,' she said as the nurse threw back the dividing curtain.

'What the . . . oh God, here it comes again,' she groaned.

'It's OK, love, just breathe easy,' said the nurse, putting the gas mask over her mouth before looking up to see Matthew hovering by the door. She did a double take.

'Who are you? Are you supposed to be here?' she asked, looking between Matthew and Katy.

'Yes,' said Matthew quickly. 'Yes I am. I'm sort of the father.'

'Sort of?' she enquired.

'Long story,' he said before walking over to stand next to the bed. 'Here, hold my hand, Katy. It'll be alright, I promise. I'll stay with her now,' he said to the nurse.

Katy shook her head vigorously from behind the mask and grabbed the nurse's arm.

'She doesn't seem too happy about that,' said the nurse. 'Perhaps you should step outside until she's calmed down a bit?'

'But I need to talk to her,' said Matthew.

Katy let out a heart-wrenching moan.

'What about? Being a sort of father?' asked the nurse with raised eyebrows.

'Where is he? I'll kill him,' gasped Katy, who had evidently finished her contraction. She started to try and get up.

'You're going nowhere, lady. Just sit down,' said the nurse.

'The bastard! I knew I couldn't trust him. He called you, didn't he, just so he could get out of seeing me give birth?'

'If you mean Daniel, no, he didn't call. I just happened to see him in the hospital restaurant.'

'In the restaurant? So you just happened to be in there, did you? Yeah, right. I may be in labour but I'm not stupid, you know.'

'No, Katy, I did. Alison was admitted last night on bed rest. I'd just gone to get a coffee before going to work.'

'Alison?' asked the nurse.

'My wife,' replied Matthew.

'I see. That sort of father,' said the nurse.

'No, I don't think you do see. I'm not that sort of father at all. I'm only a sort of father because, well, because she doesn't know who the father is.'

Katy took a sharp breath and the nurse raised her eyebrows even higher.

'He makes it sound like it's me who's the bad person, but it isn't. His wife is expecting twins any day and that makes him much worse than me,' Katy hit back.

'So it's like that,' said the nurse, gently backing away. 'Tell you what I'm going to do. I'm going to leave you for ten minutes to have a little chat about things, then I'm going to come back in and you tell me whether he's staying. Ten minutes and that's it.'

'We have nothing to say after yesterday,' declared Katy after the door had swung shut behind the nurse. 'And in case you hadn't noticed, I am in labour, so hardly in any fit state to talk to you again.'

'How does it feel?' asked Matthew.

'Oh, yankee doodle dandy. I have Mr Gay UK as my highly inept birthing partner, and I've never known pain like it. How do you think it feels?'

'Well, I actually meant, how does it feel to know that you're about to see your child?'

'Oh, marvellous. Something to really look forward to. As if I'm not on a big enough guilt trip as it is, soon there'll be two little eyes peeping at me wanting to know where its daddy is, and instead it will have Daniel insisting it's cleaned and dressed in designer baby gear before he even touches it.'

'Katy, it's going to be OK, I promise you,' said Matthew.

'Just shut up with that rubbish and give me that gas mask. Another one's coming.'

'Right, right. Here you go, now breathe in, is that better?' asked Matthew, looking around frantically. 'Look, I have this with me. This might help.' He bent over and pulled a book out of his briefcase entitled *Childbirth Without Fear*.

'I believe the recommended chapter is this one. Let me find it. Here we go, "Factors Predisposing to Low Threshold of Pain Interpretation". Shall I read some to you?'

Katy's hand flew in the air, knocking the book clean out of Matthew's shaking grasp. She howled again at him from behind the mask.

'Bit late for that perhaps,' he said. 'What should I do?' he asked her.

She screamed even louder.

'Oh, Katy, it's going to be alright, really,' he said, trying to put his arm around her. His hands were clammy and he felt short of breath as nerves took control of his body. He knew he was panicking. Time to calm down and do what he needed to do, he decided. 'Listen, Katy, I was up all last night thinking. I was so upset to leave you in that state yesterday. And well, you see, I have a plan.' Matthew cleared his throat. 'So we wait a year,' he said, giving Katy a nervous look before continuing. 'I think we have to, because I can't leave Alison now. Everyone says that the first year is the worst, so I think I owe her that at least. But I'll find a way of still seeing you and of course I'll help financially. It'll be tough but . . .'

Matthew was interrupted by Katy letting out an enormous scream.

'Oh, is it coming? Keep breathing, Katy; just keep taking that gas in. So anyway, as I was saying, it'll be tough but I reckon I can start doing some private financial consultancy on the side – you wouldn't believe the demand for it – so that should just about keep our heads above water.'

Katy screamed again. Matthew waited patiently until the noise had abated.

'So this time next year, I figure Alison will be just about able to cope, and my plan is that I'll be earning enough to afford a nanny to help her. And of course I'll need to see the twins as much as possible, so we would need to buy a big house so we can fit everyone in at weekends.'

Another yowl from Katy. By now her eyes were as big as saucers and she was panting heavily.

'So you see, we could do it, Katy,' he said. 'We don't

have to be apart. It won't be nice for a while, admittedly, but it's possible, don't you see? We could be together. You don't have to be alone.'

Katy was starting to quieten down as her contraction eased. However, she held on to the gas mask for grim death, still breathing in heavily and staring at Matthew.

I am getting this so wrong, thought Matthew. In desperation he tried a change of tack.

'Look, Katy, it's you I want. I've spent all night thinking about it. I look at my life with Alison and just see a future of, well, bloody hard work, to be honest. You've seen her. She's turned into some kind of hyper-paranoid control freak. She's not the woman I married and I can't cope with it. I just don't know what to do to make her happy any more. She doesn't need me. She's about to get her kids, and that's all she has ever wanted. And I see you, and I swear, I just want to take you in my arms and take care of you. I know I can make you happy, Katy, really I do. And we'd have so much fun, I know we would. I can give you what you need if you'll just give me the chance.'

Matthew paused to let Katy speak, but she continued to breathe in the gas as though her life depended on it.

'So you see, it could all be for the best, honestly. Alison

gets the kids, which are all she really wants, and we get to be together again, just as we should be. What do you say? Are you able to speak now? Has the pain gone?'

Also at 8.40 a.m.

'Don't you dare not bring him here, Braindead,' Daniel shouted down his phone as he paced up and down outside the main entrance to the hospital. 'I don't care what he's saying, he's come this far and now he has to go and see that baby born. There's no way I'm going back in that room. There's way too much female nudity and intimate interaction going on for my liking.

'No, I will not give you more details or take pictures. Just tell him to get some damn fucking balls, will you, and stop being so pathetic. Look, I'll make it worth your while if you just get him to the hospital door. What do you want? Tell me, anything. Just get him here.

'Yes, I do have friends who are models, very good friends, actually.

'You want a date with a model? I'm not sure I could do that to a friend,' he continued.

'Yes, I know I said anything, but I can't make someone do something they don't want to do, can I?

'OK, OK, I'll see what I can do. But date doesn't mean sex, Braindead, do you understand?

'Yes, I guess on some far-off planet she might fancy you, but I'm just telling you that I am not a pimp. Date means dinner. That's it, OK?

'Yes, of course you'll have to pay for dinner.'

'Right. Enough. If you tell me you have told the taxi driver to come here I'll throw in dinner as well.'

Daniel terminated the call and sank down on a bench. He noticed that a female nurse in her fifties was sitting at the other end, staring at him.

'It's a very long story,' he smiled through clenched teeth. 'I am just the fairy godmother trying to bring two young people together.'

'Oh really,' said the nurse. 'Your methods sound pretty unusual.'

'Well, in these modern times we fairy godmothers have to do what we have to do. Ah, thank the Lord, here is our young Prince Charming arriving now with his idiot sidekick.'

Daniel leapt up and opened the door of the cab before it had even stopped.

'Ben, you are a sight for sore eyes. But you look terrible, which won't do.'

'Get off, will you?' Ben said to Daniel, who was attempting to straighten his crumpled shirt and comb his hair with his fingers.

'Right, are you ready to face the enemy? It's this way,' said Daniel, already pulling at Ben's arm.

'Hang on, hang on. I'm not even sure what I'm going to say yet. Can you just give us a minute?' said Ben, slumping down on the bench where Daniel had been sitting.

'For crying out loud, I thought you were going to talk to him,' said Daniel, losing his patience and turning to Braindead.

'You didn't say anything about that. You just said get him here and I have, haven't I? Have you called your model mates yet?'

'No, I bloody well haven't, and I won't unless you help me get him through that labour ward door.'

'That is so unfair. You said to the hospital door and here he is. Now where's my date?'

Daniel closed his eyes and asked some kind of God for some kind of strength.

He opened his eyes and fell to his knees in front of Ben.

'Ben. The baby is nearly here. She's very close now.

Just go and be with her. Be with her and see the baby born,' he said gently.

'Yeah, listen to him, mate. Don't let that other bastard get his greedy mitts on the kid before you do. You get in there, fight for what's yours,' chipped in Braindead, looking for an approving look from Daniel. When he didn't get one he tried again.

'Look, the other guy sounds like a twat. Just go in there and deck him. That'll get rid of him. Women love a guy who can stand up for himself, you know. Show her who's boss and all that,' said Braindead.

The nurse still sitting at the end of the bench sniggered.

'Hey, we're having a very important private conversation here,' said Braindead, turning to the nurse.

'I'm sorry, but I couldn't help but overhear,' said the nurse. 'May I try? You know, give the woman's perspective.'

'I really don't think you understand. This is man's talk. You have no idea what this poor lad is going through,' said Braindead.

'I've worked in this hospital for twenty-five years and I've seen it all, believe me,' replied the nurse.

'Well, I guarantee you ain't seen a case like this. A right fuckin' mess, it is.'

'Braindead, I don't think that's helping, is it?' said Daniel, nodding towards Ben, who now had his head in his hands.

The nurse edged along the bench, closer to Ben, and laid her hand on his back.

'So, let's see. There's a woman in there who's having a baby that could be yours but also could be someone else's, and at the moment he's the one inside,' said the nurse.

'What the . . .' exclaimed Braindead.

Daniel looked gratefully towards Heaven.

Ben slowly raised his head and nodded at the nurse.

'And it's really complicated, right? The other guy, he's married and they're expecting twins,' the nurse continued.

'Fuckin' spiders, is she real?' said Braindead. Daniel motioned for him to keep quiet.

Ben nodded mutely again.

The nurse also nodded and paused for a long time. The three men held their breath.

'So let's make this simple then, shall we?' she said finally.

All three men nodded simultaneously.

'There's only one really important question that you

need to answer and then you'll know exactly what to do,' said the nurse.

'Oh, yes. Tell us what it is. Please tell us what it is,' begged Daniel before Braindead and Ben told him to be quiet.

'Do you love her?'

'Damn, of course,' said Daniel, jumping up. 'The only question there is. How could I have forgotten that? Stupid, stupid, stupid. You are a genius,' he said, kissing the nurse full on the lips.

'Alright, just calm down, will you? He hasn't answered yet,' said the nurse.

'Of course he does. Now come on, let's go, there's no time to lose,' said Daniel, pulling on Ben's sleeve.

'Just hang on, you,' said Braindead, pulling Daniel's arm away from Ben. 'Let the lad answer it first. Like the lady says, this is important. He has to answer.'

'Thank you,' said the nurse, glaring at Daniel.

'So,' said Braindead. 'Do you love her? You can tell your mate Braindead. I won't laugh or anything, or tell the lads.'

Ben leant back on the bench and raised his hands to cover his face. All three of his audience watched in silence as he took several deep breaths. No-one dared speak. Then gradually he pulled his hands away and almost imperceptibly his head started to move. The direction was unclear to start with until finally it developed into a fully fledged nod and the glimmer of a smile formed on his face.

'Halle-fuckin'-lujah,' said Braindead.

'Praise be the lord,' said Daniel, throwing his arms up to the sky before embracing the nurse again.

'I have no idea where you are from and quite frankly I am not sure I want to know, but you are truly an angel of mercy and God certainly moves in mysterious ways,' he told her.

'Special powers, you know,' she said. 'That and happening to be examining Katy when the other guy arrived. Come on, we're not done yet.' She turned to Ben again and took his hands in hers.

'That's wonderful. You have found a woman you love. Is that right?'

'Yes,' he replied. 'Yes, I have.'

'So now that you've found her, are you going to let her go without a fight? Are you the type of man who just stands and watches while other people decide your fate? While other people make your decisions for you. Is that who you are?'

'No, he fuckin' isn't,' said Braindead. 'Come on, mate, it's time to sort things out, I reckon, don't you?'

Ben stared at Braindead then rose to his feet.

'You and you,' he said, pointing at Daniel and Braindead. 'You stay here until I say otherwise. Got it?'

'Oh yes,' they both said.

'And you,' he said to the nurse. 'Thanks.'

'My pleasure,' she beamed.

He started up the steps into the hospital before turning around. 'One last thing,' he said. 'What do I say?'

'Say what you feel, mate, say what you feel,' said Braindead.

'I was asking her, not you,' Ben said. 'What do you think I should say?' he asked the nurse.

'Say what you feel, like the man says,' she replied.

Ben nodded then disappeared through the hospital doors.

Chapter 23

9.05 a.m.

Ben felt like Forrest Gump. He'd been running forever down endless hospital corridors, searching desperately for Katy. Finally he found someone who could make sense of his exhausted babble and he was shown the door behind which his future lay.

He launched himself into the room, not caring that he looked a shocking mess. He was still fighting a hangover and had not had a shave or a shower for two days. His chin was alive with bright ginger stubble. It was the only part of him that had any vibrancy. His skin was grey, his shirt and jacket rumpled and his trousers saggy. In contrast Matthew looked razor-sharp in a navy single-breasted suit with brilliant white shirt and golf club tie. When Ben entered the room he immediately placed a protective arm around Katy's shoulders. She had still not let go of the gas mask, which was acting as a very effective shield from the reality she was facing.

'Well, look what the cat dragged in,' said Matthew. 'Looks and smells like you've been out all night, drinking. Well, you can go back to your mates and go and get well and truly drunk because we have it all in hand here, don't we, Katy?'

Katy was paralysed, not knowing what to do. She thought Ben looked exhausted and wondered why he was there.

'You see, I'm going to look after her, seeing as you are quite clearly not up to the job. Don't ask me how. That is between me and Katy, but you have no need to feel any responsibility. You are free to go and live your life just like you wanted,' said Matthew. He looked down at Katy and rubbed her shoulders before turning back to Ben. 'Now Katy is very close to giving birth, so I suggest you leave and let her get on with it,' he said firmly.

Ben did not move. He hadn't even looked at Matthew so far, just at Katy. He scrutinised her face, looking for some kind of clue, some kind of encouragement, but could not decipher what was going on behind the mask.

Finally he took a deep breath, reached into his trouser pocket and very slowly pulled something out.

It was a black, rather limp banana.

He held it tentatively towards Katy without moving from his spot just inside the door.

'I got you this. Do you want it? In the class they said it might help,' he said.

Matthew looked at the banana, confused.

Katy stared and blinked a lot before she finally pulled the mask off her face.

'A banana,' exploded Matthew. 'A fucking banana! Are you serious? You bring her a banana now. It's love and stability and security she needs, not a fucking banana. Christ, you really are an absolute idiot. A fucking banana. Unbelievable.' Katy opened her mouth to speak but was brought to an abrupt halt by the onset of another contraction.

'Now look what you've done,' said Matthew, glaring at Ben. 'Easy now, Katy, easy. The book says to just breathe through it.'

'The book says?' said Ben, approaching the bed. 'She

doesn't want to know what some tosspot book says. Go on, let it out, Katy. Have a good scream.'

'No, Katy. Don't listen to him. Screams waste your energy. Just breathe through it. Look, follow this diagram here,' said Matthew as he pushed the book under her nose and pointed frantically at the page.

Katy let out the biggest wail so far.

Ben was stunned, shocked that Katy was capable of such a noise.

Matthew flicked rapidly through his book, looking desperately for some kind of inspiration.

For the second time that morning Katy's hand shot out and knocked the book across the room. With super-human effort and with a contraction in full flight, she raised the hand that wasn't clutching desperately at the mask and slowly and deliberately took the banana out of Ben's hand.

Matthew looked between Ben and Katy in complete bewilderment.

'You can't be serious, Katy? Come on, think about it. You can't rely on him for anything. He'll be gone tomorrow when he realises the extent of the responsibility required, and then where will you be? Come on, Katy. You need to do the right thing here.'

Katy put the banana beside her and reached over to take Ben's hand. Ben raised it to his lips before turning to Matthew.

'Responsibility, you say,' said Ben quietly. 'You're right. It's very important. So let's all just be responsible for a minute, shall we? How about you start by going and finding Alison, your wife, who is about to have twins. That would be responsible, wouldn't it? Then, when you've left the room to be all responsible, I will do the right thing by asking Katy to marry me.' Ben looked down and addressed Katy. 'You can turn me down, obviously, but if you'll have me, I think we should go for it.'

Katy nodded vigorously before letting out another gigantic scream.

'Married? Hello? She hasn't got a clue what she's doing. You cannot marry Katy. I will not allow you to take advantage of her like this.'

Ben looked exhausted as he considered his next move.

'Permission to stick this right up his ass?' he finally asked Katy, picking up the banana.

She let go of the mask and nodded, letting a smile and the tears engulf her before another contraction took over.

'Well, I think that says it all, doesn't it? You'd better

leave unless you want me to carry out the lady's wishes,' said Ben, still brandishing the banana.

Katy screwed up her face in pain and grabbed Ben's hand in a superhuman grip. Matthew was making no move to go anywhere. Ben knew he needed to act quickly.

'I'm really sorry,' he said to Matthew, before pulling back his free hand and giving him a hard-hitting jab across the chin. Matthew reeled backwards and fell heavily to the floor, knocked out cold.

Ben seemed surprised at his success before looking nervously at Katy. 'Forgive me,' he said. 'He left me with no choice. Does it really hurt? Here, grip my leg.' He squeezed on to the bed beside her.

As Katy got to grips with his thigh, Ben leant over to press the emergency call button.

Almost instantly the door flew open and in fell Nurse Brady, Daniel and Braindead, who had been listening from the corridor.

'What's happening, what's happening? Oh my God, I can't bear it,' burst out Daniel. 'Tell me now, is it all over? Please tell me it's all over.'

'Come on, my son. It's a result,' roared Braindead when he saw Matthew out cold on the floor and Ben with his arm around a still contracting Katy.

'Jesus, Katy, I didn't recognise you. You look awful,' Braindead continued.

Katy growled loudly, making Braindead cower in horror.

'No need for that,' he said. 'You just don't seem yourself, that's all.'

'Right,' said Ben, looking dazed but happy. 'Thanks for everything, guys, but I think Katy needs to get on with giving birth now. So if you'll excuse us. Oh, and can you make sure he gets back to Alison,' he said, nodding at Matthew.

Suddenly two men burst in with a bed on wheels.

'Get him out of here, will you?' said Nurse Brady, pointing at Matthew. 'One of you had better stay with him until he comes round so he knows what's happened,' she said to Daniel and Braindead.

'Bugger that,' said Braindead straight away. 'Time for a bacon buttie and a little chat with my new mate Daniel here. We still have some unfinished business, haven't we? A few calls to make, know what I mean?'

'Look, you go and get something to eat and I'll deal with Matthew,' said Daniel.

'What for? You don't owe him anything,' replied Braindead.

'Well, one of us had better make sure he doesn't try and come back. You leave it to me. I'll come and find you later, I promise.'

'Well, if you must. Don't you go forgetting our deal, though, eh? I don't stay up all night for just anyone, you know.'

'I'll be in touch, promise,' shouted Daniel over his shoulder as he raced after Matthew.

'Well, I guess my work is done,' said Braindead, taking one last satisfied glance at Ben, now looking very pale as he tried to console Katy through her contraction.

'No need to thank me, guys. I'll be off unless I can do anything else.'

Katy growled again and Braindead vanished.

Chapter 24

Daniel felt like he had trudged down a million miles of corridor looking for Matthew. The multiple shades of standard hospital grey paint he had experienced were starting to unsettle him. However, he still had a smug smile on his face. He wondered how Katy was ever going to repay him for such heroic, such ingenious and such dedicated efforts to secure her happiness. Maybe that watch he had been coveting would be a suitable reward for such a display of friendship. Perhaps he would invite her shopping and he could drop some subtle hints like, 'Katy. See this watch. You owe me.'

Eventually he found Matthew slumped on a chair in a corridor, crying his eyes out. Daniel sat down and patiently waited for the sobs to subside.

'Fuck off,' were Matthew's first words when he realised that Daniel was sitting next to him. 'Will you just fuck off.'

'I'm only here to make sure you're alright.'

'Why the fuck would I need you to make sure I'm alright? What do you care?' said Matthew.

'What do I care?' said Daniel, now too tired to stay calm. 'I will tell you what I care. I have spent the entire night caring, that's what. No, actually, that's wrong. I have spent most of the last nine months caring, trying to sort you lot out. Listening, talking, trying to make sense of the whole damn mess, and now I am tired and I don't need you telling me to fuck off. Go fuck off yourself and get on with your bloody life.'

Matthew's face crumpled and he turned away from Daniel in embarrassment and started to weep again, his shoulders rising and falling with huge, heavy sobs.

An elderly couple just down the corridor were either too rude or too old to hide their stares. Daniel heard scraping and watched as the elderly woman moved her chair so she could get a better view.

Matthew's sobs were getting louder by the minute, forcing Daniel to take action.

'Showtime's over,' he said to his audience, but they were not to be deterred, staring innocently straight back at him.

Daniel awkwardly attempted to put his arm around Matthew. Matthew shrugged him off but Daniel persisted.

'Come on, lad, you know you'll get over it,' he said quietly. Why he always reverted to talking like his mother when trying to console someone, he had no idea. In fact he realised he had just repeated his mother's exact words after he'd told her he was in love with his male tutor at art college. He was so frustrated at his mother's blinkered stance that he had retorted instantly that he had known he was gay since he was fifteen, when he had been seduced by David Sanderson on a Scout trip.

'David Sanderson?' she had exclaimed in absolute horror.

'Yes,' he had replied.

'You're a liar. You can't say such a thing about poor David,' she had said.

'No, he did, Mum, honest,' he protested.

'How dare you drag a vicar's son into this? I don't know what is worse, pretending to be gay or blaspheming the church.'

His mother's total lack of understanding reminded him that Matthew did deserve some sympathy, even if it was from the man who had been instrumental in plotting his romantic downfall.

Daniel sat patiently patting Matthew's shoulder, waiting for the sobs to subside. Occasionally he heard a shuffle or a cough from the couple, reminding him that there was an expectant audience awaiting a performance.

'Tissues?' Daniel turned to ask them.

'Oh yes,' the woman nodded vigorously, delighted to be promoted to a speaking part as she searched through her handbag.

She pulled out a half-empty pocket-sized packet of Kleenex.

'Sorry it's not a full pack,' she said. 'I had to use some at Connie Waring's wake yesterday. Spilt sherry trifle down me front, I did. And it was one of them funny trifles with jelly in, so bound to stain.'

'I only eat jelly when naked,' said Daniel. 'Now, you two. I need to have what is known as a private

335

conversation with my upset friend here, so we need some alone time.'

'Oh, we won't make a sound,' said the old lady quickly. 'We're very good at being quiet. All the funerals we go to, you see. You just pretend that we're not here. Unless you need any help, of course.'

'Go away or I will report you for harassment,' Daniel shouted, losing his patience.

'OK, OK,' the lady muttered, shuffling away. 'Just trying to be neighbourly. We won't bother next time, will we, Bob?'

Matthew's sobs seemed to have abated. He looked spectacularly sad, his suit crumpled, previously perfect tie all askew.

Daniel looked deep inside for some inner strength. He was tired beyond belief and emotionally wrecked, but he realised his job was not quite complete yet, and he would allow no-one to say that Daniel Laker was a job-half-done kind of guy.

Matthew was now just staring into space, so Daniel decided to plough straight in, in the hope that he could be tucked up in his bed with the strippergram within the hour.

'So, Matthew,' he said. 'Let's see. I guess there's a

lot of stuff going through your head right now.'

Matthew did not move a muscle so Daniel continued.

'Shall we break it down into manageable chunks? I always find that makes it easier, don't you?'

Matthew turned his stare towards him but still said nothing.

'OK, let's get right to it, shall we, and start with you and Katy? This is the way I see it. You are unhappy. You see someone who reminds you of happy times and the world seems a better place. So much so you grab hold of it, wanting some of that happiness back. But it's false happiness, isn't it, Matthew? It's the happiness you remember from a previous time. The happiness of first love, first sex, first everything. The most exciting time in your life. You can't get that back, Matthew. Not even if you get back the person that you shared it with. It just doesn't work like that. Before you know it, you stop talking about your favourite music, why you hate your parents and which lay-by you should make out in, and start arguing over who last cleaned the toilets and why you never have sex any more. You don't love Katy because you don't know her. You know teenager Katy, not nearly forty Katy. Please don't tell her I said she was nearly forty, by the way. She'd kill me.'

337

Daniel heard a sneeze from behind him.

'If I turn around and find you there I am calling matron,' he shouted. There was muttering and the sound of soft soles shuffling across lino.

'Where was I? So you see, you were chasing a false happiness when you should have been sorting out why you were unhappy in the first place. You and Alison are married, Matthew. At some point you loved her so much that you said you would forsake all others to be with her. That's huge. More than huge. You've got to find that place again with Alison. It can't have all gone. You can do it, Matthew, I know you can, and it will be even better this time because you'll have two kids to share it with. Two of your very own kids to love between you. And before you say it, I know that Katy could be having your child, but surely it has to be better that your twins have two parents who love them and that Katy's child has the same, rather than messing it all up and doubtless screwing them up at the same time.'

Daniel sat back in his chair, completely spent. He could say no more.

Matthew looked up at Daniel. Daniel waited for the words of gratitude to come forth as Matthew undoubtedly realised that Daniel was perhaps the most insightful man he had ever come across.

'Daniel,' said Matthew.

'Yes,' said Daniel expectantly.

'Will you now just fuck off?'

Daniel held his hands up finally in defeat.

'I can do no more,' he said.

'Thanks,' muttered Matthew.

Daniel patted his shoulder and disappeared to get lost finding his way out of the hospital.

Matthew sat staring at the crack in the tile in front of his chair for a very long time. Tea trolleys trundled past him, mops flicked around him and a million anonymous pairs of shoes trudged back and forth, all failing to interrupt his thoughts.

After about an hour his phone bleeping finally roused him.

It was a text from Alison asking what he was doing.

He took a deep breath, stood up and walked just around the corner to her room.

She had her back to him and he thought she might be asleep. He tiptoed around to the far side of the bed.

Alison lay there silently crying.

He sat down on the chair beside the bed.

'You're here?' she said.

'Why are you crying?' he asked.

'I'm scared, Matthew,' she said in a very small voice. 'What if I can't do it? What if I let them down?'

'You won't, Alison. You could never let them down. I'm the one most likely to do that.'

'Don't be silly. You'll be there when they need you.'

'I hope so,' he said. He shifted in his seat and felt something dig into his side. He reached into his pocket and pulled out the copy of *Childbirth Without Fear*.

'Want me to read some of this to you?' he asked.

'No. I don't need books now, Matthew. I just need you.'

'Really?'

'Really,' she said.

Chapter 25

'She's awesome,' Ben said for the hundredth time, staring down at the bundle wrapped in a blanket in his arms.

Katy lay back on her pillow in complete and utter exhaustion and complete and utter happiness. The day had ended so differently from how she had feared it would. Best of all had been Ben's face when he had ventured to the weighing machine for a closer look after the baby had been cleaned up. He had turned around and given her the biggest grin ever.

'She's a ginger! She's a ginger!' he had shouted over to her with a big thumbs up.

Ben handed the baby girl over to Katy for a cuddle.

'Thanks,' she said. 'For being here.'

'Well, it was touch and go. Me and Braindead were in Edinburgh.'

'When?'

'Last night.'

'Last night? Why were you there last night?'

'Oh, Katy. After I left you I didn't know what to do with myself. My head was spinning like crazy, so I went down the pub, obviously, and Braindead was in there on his lunch break. Anyway, so Rick calls on my mobile ,wanting to know what time we're leaving on Friday to get to up to Edinburgh for the stag do. I'm in no fit state to make any sense, so Braindead grabs the phone and says to Rick we're leaving now. It seemed like a great idea at the time, so we just walk out of the pub to the station and get on the next train to Edinburgh. No stuff or anything. We fall into the first pub we find when we get there, then all I can remember is at some point Braindead picks up a call on his mobile and starts going on about Daniel.'

'Daniel? Daniel called Braindead? What time was this?'

'No idea. About eleven, I guess.'

'But he was with me.'

'Well, somehow he managed to fit in a right old conflab with Braindead, because he just kept coming out with this stuff. Daniel was trying to get Braindead to convince me to come back. Honestly, if it weren't for the topic of conversation, hearing Braindead talk like Daniel would have been bloody hilarious. He used long words and everything.'

'So what were they saying? What made you come back?' Katy asked tentatively.

He paused for a moment.

'They made me see that I should have been thinking that this could be my baby, not that it might not, and what would I do if he turned out to be the next striker for England and I had to tell the poor lad I hadn't even bothered to turn up for the birth.'

'So football made you come back?' said Katy, feeling her elation wane.

'No, Katy, no. That just kind of tipped it over the edge. But to be perfectly honest, even on the train on the way back down I still wasn't sure. Then Daniel was waiting for me outside the hospital, and he and this nurse asked me the only really important question.'

'What, the do you really love him one?'

'No, the do you really love her one.'

'And?'

'Well, it was yes, of course.'

'Really? Was it?'

'Of course it bloody was. I know I've never said it before, but it's not my thing, you know.' He took her hand and looked her straight in the eye. 'I love you, I always have.'

'I love you too, you know,' she said back.

'You don't have to say that just because I did.'

'No, I do, I really do, and I will marry you, if you meant it, that is.'

'Of course I meant it. But I do have one condition.'

'What's that?' asked Katy, fearing the worst.

'That we never become one of those boring married couples. You know, like the ones who sit in pubs and don't talk to each other and probably never ever have sex.'

'I promise,' said Katy, knowing that life with Ben could never be boring. 'Tell you what. We'll even have sex on a Tuesday.'

Acknowledgements

I'd like to thank everyone I know.

There we are, job done.

Seriously, to everyone I know who sometimes sparks my brain, sending me on a journey that eventually can lead to something like this. A novel! Before you ask, none of the storylines are based on things that have actually happened to anyone I know, but it only takes a turn of phrase or even a look to set me off, so I thank you all for being a constant source of inspiration.

My friends and family make me laugh all the time, and I would particularly like to mention those whose throw-away one-liners have provided some of the funnies in this book. A special mention must go to Steve and Andrea for some top comedy moments. You know what you said.

Also to Tony, who first spotted that no-one ever has sex on a Tuesday, and I thank him from the bottom of my heart for discovering this fact and sharing it with me.

I'd like to thank Araminta Whitley and Peta Nightingale at LAW, as well as Amy Tipper, for being an enormous part of making last year a dream year for me, one I will never forget. Jenny Geras and Selina Walker of Penguin Random House, it means the world to know you believe in me. So excited to be working with you.

Thank you to the team at The One Off, who went above and beyond to inspire the cover for this book and take a picture of me that I actually like. True miracle workers. Richard Walker at Mustard Research who did not baulk when I asked him to find out which day of the week was least popular for sex. Thank you for getting me the right answer. Kate McCann, Diane Moon, Freerange PR, Rachel Abbott and Colin from Prontaprint, who came running when I asked. Thank you.

Finally I'd like to thank my family – mickey-takers of the highest order who taught me that humour is always the answer. Jim, June, Andrew and Helen, you always make me laugh, as well as Tom and Sally, the funniest pair on the planet.

And last but not least, Fanny. Hope you don't mind me taking your name in vain *yet again*.